My feelings f
unexpectedly

He wasn't just son
guy with all those
went back to my a
teenager anymore. I was a grown woman and I didn't truly understand either his feelings or mine.

I recalled his kiss, how hot but sweet it had been. I thought what it would be like to be in his arms right now. I even dared imagine him as my lover, kissing me passionately as he professed his love. If only for a few passing moments, I let Kyle Weston be at the heart of my fantasies, just as I had as a girl of thirteen.

For Carolyn Peery Buchanan

~

JANICE KAISER
is also the author
of these novels in
Temptation

HEARTTHROB
THE MAVERICK
WILDE AT HEART
FLYBOY

Deceptions

JANICE KAISER

MILLS & BOON LIMITED
ETON HOUSE, 18-24 PARADISE ROAD
RICHMOND, SURREY TW9 1SR

All the characters in this book have no existence outside the imagination of the Author, and have no relation whatsoever to anyone bearing the same name or names. They are not even distantly inspired by any individual known or unknown to the Author, and all the incidents are pure invention.

First published in Great Britain in 1994
by Mills & Boon Limited, Eton House, 18-24 Paradise Road, Richmond, Surrey TW9 1SR

ISBN 0 263 78787 7

21 - 9407

Printed in Great Britain by
BPC Paperbacks Ltd
A member of
The British Printing Company Ltd

1

THE CITY MAINTENANCE crew was hanging holiday decorations as I drove down Pearson Avenue for the first time since the previous Christmas. With each passing year my old neighborhood seemed a little more drab, the joyfulness a tad more superficial than it had been when I was a kid, and dreams had still come easily. Of course, I'd long suspected that the change was in me, rather than in Harrisburg, Pennsylvania.

A couple of new fast-food places had sprung up here and there in recent years. They were shiny and seemed especially well lit compared to the surrounding buildings, but I wasn't so sure they were an improvement. I had mixed feelings about my hometown changing, as a lot of people do. Fortunately, the pace was slow and the overall character of the neighborhood remained pretty much the same.

I noted that the city fathers had opted for the big red plastic ribbons this year—they seemed to rotate through three or four different themes—and this was the best, considering the limitations of budget and municipal taste. No sooner had that thought entered my mind than I saw the cynicism and unkindness of it, so I silently apologized to Harrisburg and tried to put myself into a more positive frame of mind.

I'd first left Pennsylvania twelve years earlier to attend college in D.C., which, I suppose, made me an expatriate. Still, I knew I had no reason to look down my nose at the town simply because I'd moved on. No matter what, Harrisburg would always be my home.

I stopped at a traffic light. While I waited for the cross traffic to pass, I watched a man in a cherry picker fastening a red bow to the neck of the lamppost across the street. It was nearly dusk, but from my vantage point I could gaze up the avenue and see festooned streetlights stretching for blocks ahead, before disappearing finally into the falling darkness.

Only one side of the street had been decorated, which made for a strange sight. I was used to seeing Pearson Avenue in all its glory. But it was the day before Thanksgiving, not Christmas week. I guess Harrisburg wasn't any more ready for me than I was for it.

For the first time ever, Mom had asked me to come home for Thanksgiving instead of Christmas. I was not upset about this, though it was a break in a tradition of nearly ten years—one that had become ingrained in me like the migratory instinct in a duck.

Mother had a beau, it turned out—the first gentleman friend she'd had since my father had died nearly twenty-five years ago—and had been invited to his family's Christmas celebration in Pittsburgh. I wasn't about to rain on her parade, so I'd told her Thanksgiving would work just as well for me. That's why I was seeing the old town in November instead of December; seeing it half decorated and swirling in autumn leaves instead of twinkling with Christmas lights and frosted with snow.

Continuing up Pearson Avenue, I checked out the neighborhood. The post office looked the same. The old variety store with the wood floors—Mom called it the five-and-dime—was finally closed, probably a victim of modern merchandizing. The ice-cream and candy store where I'd bought my cavities as a kid had been gone for several years now. In its place was a video store.

I gave my junior high school a nostalgic glance as I went by. In the faint light of late autumn it looked as dreary as I remembered schools to be when closed for a holiday. Continuing along, I followed the sidewalk with my eye, the one I'd trudged up and down hundreds of times on my way to and from school.

When I reached the corner, I turned onto our street, proceeding along the two short blocks to our house. I couldn't see Colton Street without experiencing an emotional wrench and a flood of memories. This was the place where I'd started life, where I'd learned to ride a bike, where I'd kissed my first boy, discovered puppy love and felt my first heartache—all within what was, I now realize, only a few short years.

My mother had been living in the same house for almost thirty-five years. It was as familiar to me as my childhood—filled with the same furniture I'd known from the time of my earliest recollections. Home was laden with memory-filled photos and knickknacks from the past, with smells I never seemed to encounter anywhere else, with objects I'd touched as a toddler, a child, a girl, a teenager, a young woman.

Our little clapboard house got older and older, like me, but it didn't seem to change that much, even if from one Christmas to the next Mom remodeled the bathroom or bought a new chair for the living room. Somehow it always managed to stay what I had known it to be for all of my thirty years—home.

Though my annual pilgrimage to Harrisburg meant a lot to me, I had no desire to visit often. Five or six days around Christmas satisfied my need for family until May, when Mom normally came to Washington to visit me for a few days around my birthday. I had come up once to be with her when she'd had gallbladder surgery, but twice a year was normally all we saw each other. We talked on the phone a couple of times a month, but that was the extent of our contact. We were both independent. We liked our freedom and our space.

Stopping in front of the house I sat for a moment or two, preparing myself. No matter what else had happened in my life, once I was back on Colton Street a part of me became a girl again. It took some adjusting to leave one life and go back to another.

Mostly, Mom and I had a peaceful relationship; but there had been a period of about three years—just after I'd finished college, while I was working to fulfill my lifelong dream to become an FBI agent—when there was a lot of tension between us. Mom had hassled me about my choice of career, and had all but pleaded with me to give it up. Part of it, I recognized, was a genuine concern for my safety. My father had been a cop and was killed in the line of duty—shot through the heart during a busted holdup of a liquor store—and Mom didn't want the same thing happening to me.

Ironically, three years into my law-enforcement career I, too, was shot in the chest—in practically the same spot as my father. I nearly died, and when I finally recovered I left the Bureau for a less stressful career as a private investigator. Mom, relieved, thanked Providence and stopped hassling me, though she didn't hesitate to announce that she'd be even more grateful if I'd get married and have a couple of children. What she didn't say was that it was only partly for me; Mom had had her own agenda.

Besides my father's death, our family had suffered a second tragedy. When I was fourteen, my older sister Cara contracted a heart virus and died within a very short span of time—only two months before she was to graduate from Johns Hopkins and marry Kyle Weston, the guy she'd gone with all through college.

My sister's death was naturally a terrible blow. The loss of a child is never easy, but I think it was especially hard on Mother because she adored Cara so. As I got older I realized Mom had been living her life vicariously through my sister. Cara was beautiful, smart, talented and engaged to a man from a prominent Baltimore family whom my mother considered perfect in every way.

There being eight years' difference in our ages, Cara and I weren't nearly as close as many sisters. Yet, with her passing I realized a heavy burden had fallen on me. I became heir apparent to my sister and the bearer of my mother's dreams.

It was not a role for which I was suited. Both Mom and I eventually outgrew the notion that I should be Cara's surrogate, but in her case the dream died slowly. It wasn't until my near-death experience, when I believe she realized she was lucky to have me at all. Over the past several years things had gotten better, and Mom finally accepted me for who I was—a person very different from my sister.

Darkness had fallen enough that the light glowing from the front windows of the house looked especially inviting. The nostalgia thing had kind of gotten to me, and sitting there on Colton Street I realized that there wasn't another place in the world I'd rather be. Ironically, this was cause for both cheer and sadness. For a woman of thirty, the place of strongest emotional attachment ought to be her own home—not the one she was born in. And it ought to be with someone besides her mother. Yet, here I was, home again and feeling sentimental.

I got out of my car, grabbed my suitcase from the back seat and made my way up the walk. The wind was crisp and autumnlike. I was able to pick up the faintest hint of the smell of burning leaves. Memories, smells and recollections tumbled through my head as I climbed the three steps to the porch and rang the bell.

Mom opened the door, a happy smile on her face. Her light brown hair had only a few wisps of gray. Her pale blue eyes were crystal clear, her skin as smooth and flawless as a child's. But I was struck by a new ebullience.

"There you are, Darcy!" she said cheerfully. "Welcome home, dear!"

She let me step inside and put my suitcase down before we embraced. I inhaled her as I always did and was surprised to find an unexpected scent. "You've changed perfumes," I observed. I didn't exactly feel betrayed, but there might have been a little disappointment in my voice. Some things, it seemed, ought never to change.

"Do you like it?" She had hold of my hand and squeezed it. She looked radiant, her cheeks like she'd been the one coming in from the cold, not me.

"Yes, it's nice."

She beamed.

"My God," I said, gazing at her. "You're in love, Mother!"

She smiled and laughed. "Does it show?"

I was dumbstruck. The last couple of times we'd spoken on the phone she'd talked about Arnold. He was a widower whom she'd met at the hospital where she'd worked for twenty-odd years as a bookkeeper, ever since shortly after my father's death. Arnold had gone by the business office to discuss his bill for bypass surgery, taken one look and invited Mom to coffee. He'd come back the next day to take her to lunch. Dinner had followed on the weekend.

"At the rate you're going, it'll be breakfast following dinner," I'd said on the phone.

"Posh. I'm not that sort of woman, Darcy," she'd replied. "I know that sleeping around is the modern thing, but I married when Harry Truman was president, and I still think the way they did then."

Mom had had her sixty-first birthday in August and still had a few years to go until retirement. I'd never thought of her as old because she'd taken good care of herself and was pretty. But for the past twenty-five years she'd been an inveterate widow, having had no relationships with men of any consequence, so far as I was aware. The advent of Arnold, I was beginning to see, was a pivotal event in her life.

I stepped back to look her over. She was in a new dress and looked really good. "You've lost weight, too," I said.

"A few pounds."

I slipped off my coat and studied her. "Hmm. Christmas with his family in Pittsburgh. This is sounding serious, Mom. Has he popped the question?"

She took my coat. As she opened the hall closet I smelled the familiar smell of mothballs and leather and other distinctive scents I associated with her closet but couldn't name. "Darling, we've only known each other a few months. Talk of marriage is premature."

"It's looking serious to me."

"Well, Arnold's having dinner with us tomorrow. I hope you don't mind. He wants to meet you. And I'll be meeting his children at Christmastime."

I nodded, looking serious. "The getting-family-approval bit."

"It's part of getting to know someone," she said, her voice taking on a plaintive tone.

I gave her another hug. "I'm only teasing, Mom. I couldn't be happier for you. Congratulations."

"Well, it's premature for congratulations, but I have been happier these past few months than since... Oh, I can't remember when."

"Since Daddy, probably."

"Yes, since your father." She took my arm. "Come on in the kitchen, dear. I've got the teakettle on."

Mom and I had a custom of drinking tea together. That had become our ritual upon an arrival—whether it was she at my town house in Georgetown, or me coming home to Harrisburg.

"Let me put my suitcase in the bedroom and go to the bathroom," I said. "I've had to go since York."

"You Hunters," she chided. "Cara and your father were the same way. Traveling with you three was like traveling with the circus or something. It seemed we stopped at every other gas station."

I patted her cheek, took my case and went off to the "children's bedroom" as Mom still called it. There were only two bedrooms in the house and Cara and I had shared the smaller one, much to my sister's consternation. I was the bratty little sister and therefore a pain in the butt, though to me she'd been a goddess—my grown-up sister, whom I mostly adored. Which is not to say we didn't have our sibling jealousies, because we did.

"The children's bedroom," now a combination guest bedroom and shrine, always gave me mixed feelings. Once Cara had gone away to college, it had been converted to my room exclusively. It had remained so until I'd gone to college myself, at which time Mom converted it halfway back to Cara's room, bringing out mementos from my sister's life—her dolls, trophies, awards, diplomas and photos. The display covered the time from when she was a little girl until she died. The other half of the room contained equivalent mementos from my life, though, due to no fault of my mother, they were fewer in number.

It was as though Mom had carefully divided the room—and her love—down the middle, with absolutely no favoritism being shown. I didn't mind because I had loved my sister, too.

During each of my annual visits to Harrisburg I managed to spend a little time taking a mental trip into the past, using the pieces of history my mother kept on perpetual display. I especially enjoyed the photos from Cara's album, which Mom kept on the dresser, side by side with mine.

The picture that fascinated me most, though, was the framed one Mom kept in the living room between Cara's and my high-school graduation photos. It was of Cara and Kyle, taken the Christmas they'd gotten engaged. Mom regarded it as the symbol of the marriage that fate hadn't allowed to take place.

Mom had adored her son-in-law-to-be. Kyle was the perfect young man, "the kind of boy every mother wants her daughter to bring home." I was still treated to that depiction of Kyle Weston from time to time, though Mother had eased up some in recent years. I think she finally realized that bringing home someone like Kyle wasn't part of my life plan.

In fact, I'd never taken anybody home to meet my mother. It wasn't because of a philosophical aversion, or even a matter of principle. The truth was I'd never had that sort of relationship with anyone—not with "the kind of boy every mother wants her daughter to bring home."

The irony of the whole thing was that Kyle Weston had played a bit part in the development of my own romantic life. I'd met him when Cara brought him home that Christmas. I was thirteen at the time and naturally fell in love with him. How could I not?

Kyle had been very nice to me, treating me with more respect than Cara had. She and I were saddled with some of those carryover sibling problems from childhood. But to Kyle I was just a star-struck little girl who happened to be his fiancée's sister.

Seventeen years had passed since then. I have only the haziest recollections of Kyle as a person, but I do recall him whispering to me once that I was going to grow up to be every bit as beautiful as Cara. It was the supreme compliment, notwithstanding the fact that I wasn't too fond of the "when I grew up" part.

Kyle wasn't the only one to have drawn comparisons between my sister and me, though at that time I was an awkward adolescent and hardly compared favorably with my beautiful sister. But as I grew older, I came to resemble Cara more and more. Mother remarked on it constantly until one year, when I was in college and full of myself, I'd asked her to see me for myself and not always in light of Cara. I didn't see the remark to be insensitive at the time, though I suspect it was. But Mom hardly ever drew comparisons between us after that.

I think Mom clung to Cara's memory longer than usual, in part because of Kyle Weston. He didn't disappear from our lives. For several years he would visit us occasionally, perhaps because we were his only living connection to her. He took Cara's death very hard, perhaps never fully recovering from it. And as of the last time Mother had mentioned him, which was a year or two ago, he hadn't married.

Soon after I left for college, Kyle stopped coming to Harrisburg, though he sent Mom Christmas cards and a nice ham each year. In fact, the "Kyle Weston Christmas ham" was a part of our holiday tradition. As I stood at the dresser, paging through Cara's album, I realized it had been over ten years since I'd seen him.

"Darcy," my mother called from the front of the house, "you want something to eat with your tea?"

"No, thanks, Mom," I replied, stepping into the hall. "I stopped for lunch and I'm really not hungry."

"Come and have your tea, then," she said.

"Just a minute."

I went into the bathroom. Although it had been modernized since I'd left home, much was the same. As I'd expected, Mom had put out her expensive guest towels—the ones she'd gotten from Aunt Ellen, my father's sister, as a wedding present.

Over the years Aunt Ellen came occasionally to visit us and Mom always made sure she put the towels out when she came. Aunt Ellen had died five or six years ago, and I found it ironic that now the towels were brought out for me. It said something about my status in Mom's mind. Whether I liked it or not, I was a guest in my mother's house.

Drying my hands on the celebrated towels, I realized how time did indeed move on. I smiled into the mirror and told myself that one of these months not too far down the line, I might well be attending my mother's wedding.

I found Mom in the kitchen, sitting at her table, waiting for the tea to steep. She'd put a few persimmon cookies on a plate, despite the fact I'd declined her offer of food. Like most mothers, she was stuck in a rut when it came to nourishment and her child.

While we had our tea I asked about Arnold, clearly the topic she most wanted to discuss. Dutifully I munched on a cookie or two while I listened. It was evident within a very few minutes that Arnold was no passing fancy. It was a case of true love.

Mother had given me a detailed history of Arnold's marriage and a complete biography of his children when the telephone rang. It was Arnold, so I slipped out of the room to give the lovers a little privacy, pulling the kitchen door closed as I went into the front room.

Resuming my nostalgia trip, I cast my eyes around the living room. I was relieved that Arnold hadn't exorcised the photo of my father from the place of honor on the bookcase, though I did wonder about Daddy's future once Mom remarried. Would I offend her if I asked for the picture? I wondered. I had no idea what the proper social etiquette was in such matters.

I walked over and picked up the "wedding that never was" picture. As I looked at the faces, I made a few calculations. My sister and Kyle had been eight years younger than I was at present. Cara's hair and clothes were dated, but I had to admit she looked like me—or vice versa. I could easily have claimed that smiling girl was me.

Kyle, though looking baby-faced to my spinster eyes, was handsome as hell. How I'd loved him—madly, passionately, as only a thirteen-year-old could. Though I didn't dwell on it, I'd hated Cara as much as I'd loved Kyle. My jealousy had burned so intensely that when my sister died, I'd agonized over whether my jealousy had killed her.

My guilt over Cara's death probably lasted longer than I'd realized, though by the time I, too, was college age, the entire episode had become ancient history. I rarely thought about Kyle, except, of course, when I came to Harrisburg to eat his Christmas ham. Strangely, holding the sixteen-year-old picture in my hand, I felt closer to both of them than I had, say, ten years earlier.

Studying the picture, I wondered about Kyle Weston. It seemed a remarkable testimony to his love for my sister that he'd never married. I knew it was entirely possible that there were other causes, having nothing to do with her, but I liked to think that sort of love existed in the world.

I was not an overt romantic. But I was a secret one. Having reached my thirtieth year, with only a single halfhearted brush with matrimony, I was now frankly skeptical that there ever would be anyone. I myself had become accepting of that fact, though my mother, I was quite sure, hadn't. Now that she had Arnold, I figured I might be spared any further pressures, at least for a while. Mom had her own life to live, and that made me glad.

The kitchen door opened and Mother appeared, glowing even more than before. "Arnold's so worried about tomorrow," she announced. "He really wants you to like him."

"I'm sure I will, Mom. For God's sake, I'm the last person he needs to be concerned about."

"It's nice of you to say that, dear. You'll have to tell him."

I nodded. "I'd be glad to."

Mom walked over to where I was standing and saw that I was holding the picture of Cara and Kyle. "Good heavens," she said, "I completely forgot."

"Forgot what?"

"Do you know who called me this morning, right out of the blue?"

I looked down at the photograph. "Kyle?"

"Yes. Can you believe it?"

"No. It's been a while since you've talked to him, hasn't it?"

"Oh, five years at least. I still get that Christmas ham, as you know, but we haven't spoken in five years and I haven't seen him in seven or eight."

"Did he call to wish you a Happy Thanksgiving?"

"No, Darcy, that's the funny part. He called to ask how to get hold of you."

"Me?"

"Yes, he said he wanted your advice."

"About what?"

"About hiring a private investigator. He thought since you were in the business, your advice would be especially valuable."

"How'd he know I'm a P.I.?"

"Apparently I'd put it in one of those Christmas letters I used to send out. There were a few years there when I felt the need to sing your praises."

I rolled my eyes, but Mom didn't see. She used to work so hard on those letters, trying to strike that tricky balance between worthy news and outright bragging. The only time she asked my opinion of the letters, I told her I thought the whole idea was in poor taste. She made a point of not sending me her Christmas letter after that.

"How strange," I said, as curious about Kyle's call as I was surprised. "Did he give you any idea what his problem was?"

"Not really, though my impression was it has something to do with a woman. His fiancée, I gather."

"So, he's finally getting married."

"That was my impression, though he didn't say it in so many words. Anyway, I gave him your number in Washington, but told him there was no point in calling there today because you were going to be here. I told him he could call you this evening, that I was expecting you for dinner, but he insisted he didn't want to disturb you with business while you were on vacation." Mom smiled and sighed. "Kyle's such a lovely young man. So polite and thoughtful. I still adore him."

I was sure she did. As long as Mom could remember my sister, she would remember Kyle Weston. There was no doubt about that. "So, where was it left?" I asked. "Is he going to call me when I get back to Washington?"

"I told him I'd have you call him from here. I took his number. He said it wasn't urgent, but if you didn't mind, he'd be home this evening and all day tomorrow."

"Well, I guess I should call then, shouldn't I?"

"I would hope so, Darcy." She looked wistful, though her cheeks were still glowing from her conversation with Arnold. "You know, for years I had a secret wish that you and Kyle would get together."

"Kyle and me?"

"Yes. He loved your sister—I'm sure he'd love you. I've often thought that."

"Thanks, Mom, but I don't think that would appeal to either Kyle or me. You like to identify me with Cara, but the rest of the world doesn't. I have no desire to have a relationship with my sister's former boyfriend."

"Darling, that's ridiculous. It's been fifteen years."

"Longer," I said.

"Well?"

I gave her a look. "Now I'm sorry you said I'd call."

"Good heavens, why?"

I fumbled for a way to put it. "I don't like there being expectations."

"By who? Me?" Mother said.

I shrugged.

"Darcy, you're being silly. I'd think you'd be curious what Kyle's like. I certainly am."

"Maybe he doesn't have the same fascination for me, Mom."

My mother appraised me. "You know, dear, there's one thing you could have learned from your sister. Cara was never afraid of her own feelings."

I took umbrage, my brows rising. "What makes you think I am?"

"You *are* afraid of them, Darcy. I know you are. I'm not being critical when I say that. I've been the same way since your father died. Then, when Arnold asked me to have a cup of coffee, I said to myself, 'It's time, Marjorie, to put down your guard.' That's what you've been doing, too, dear. I'm sure of it."

I stared at my mother and she took a long slow breath.

"There, I've said it," she went on. "I won't do it again. You've been old enough to make your own decisions without a critique from your mother. I apologize if I've offended you."

I wasn't quite sure what to say, so I simply said, "Where's Kyle's number?"

2

I STOOD AT THE kitchen counter, listening to the telephone ring on the other end. I was calling rural Maryland—a farm, my mother told me, somewhere near Frederick. It was the first time I'd given any thought to where Kyle Weston lived. In my mind, he'd always been located at a place in time—the distant past.

As I waited for him to answer, I stared out the side window. I could see a couple of girls coming up the sidewalk in the faint light. They were in matching parkas, holding hands, one easily a foot taller than the other. They were probably sisters. I thought of Cara.

The telephone clicked in my ear, but the voice was recorded. I'd gotten an answering machine. Nonetheless, I listened with curious fascination. When the message was over, I waited for the tone, then said, "Hi, Kyle. This is Darcy Hunter returning your call. I'm in Harrisburg. Should be back in Washington Sunday evening, if we don't connect before then. Bye."

I hung up, imagining how my voice would sound when he played back the recording. I'd affected a breezy tone—that of an old friend calling to say hello. I turned to see Mom hovering outside the kitchen door.

"Wasn't he in?" She had a very disappointed look on her face.

I had a sudden realization that my mother had hopes that this chance happening—this call from the past—would lead to something. Only then did I comprehend what a scary thought that was. "For God's sake, Mom," I wanted to say, "Kyle Weston is a ghost." Knowing discretion was the wiser choice, I didn't say a word. Then, on reflection, it occurred to me that Kyle wasn't so much a ghost as Cara. But then, the two of them were inextricably intertwined in my mind.

"I left a message on his machine," I said to my mother. "If it's important enough, he'll call back."

Mom put a roast in the oven and we sat down in the front room to look at photos of Arnold. She wanted me to have a sense of what he looked like before he showed up the next day.

Arnold Belcher was only a few inches taller than Mother. He was on the stout side, but not fat. He had a full head of white hair and a distinguished, almost debonair, air. It only took a few snapshots to decide that Arnold was a total contrast to my father, who'd been a tall rough-hewn man with black hair, a man who looked more comfortable in wool shirts or a police uniform than in a Sunday suit. Arnold was a businessman, the owner of five appliance stores; Dad had been blue-collar, a working man down to his toenails.

I'd already decided Mom's new love was special. He had to be to bring her out of a shell she'd inhabited for a quarter of a century. I'm sure my father had his flaws like every other man, but I knew little about them. I was only five when he died and had very few personal recollections of him. Mother had made him into a saint, and he'd remained one in my mind to this day.

I took great pride in the fact that I looked like my father. Mom always said she had two daughters who were the spitting image of her husband. Cara and I did have Dad's black hair. We were both tall and had his gray eyes, though Cara's picked up a touch of Mom's blue. And she was a bit more fine-boned and, like Mom, was softer in both personality and temperament.

I was a tomboy by comparison—my stint in the FBI was as good a proof of that as any. I had played softball in a coed summer league in Washington that existed for the socializing and beer as much as for sport. That wouldn't have been Cara's style, but it was mine. I dated guys from the league, guys who appreciated a woman who could play with a man.

But there were other guys, too. For some reason I seemed to get romantically involved with lawyers. I don't know why, unless it was because my law-enforcement background created some kind of affinity.

My relationships didn't last long as a rule—most likely because I didn't believe in sex for sex's sake. Wade Armstrong lasted a year, and I came fairly close to marrying him. He was the only man I'd ever slept with for an extended period of time. We finally drifted apart. It ended for good two years ago. I'm not sure why. Maybe the magic was only half-baked.

Wade was the only man in my life that Mother had met—during one of her annual trips to Washington. The three of us had gone out to dinner on my birthday. Afterward, Mom had told me I should marry him. She was willing to settle, I think. I wasn't.

When the roast began to put out a fragrant smell we went in to start the vegetables. I set the table and Mom did the rest. She was a good cook. I'd inherited my skills in that regard from my father who, according to Mom, had trouble fixing cold breakfast cereal.

I sat at the table and Mom gave me the latest office gossip at the hospital. The people there had been her family for years. I knew all there was to know about Jolene, Cathy and Betty. I was intimately aware of Mr. Andersen's faults without ever having met any of these people around whom Mom's days turned. But after all, I was only the daughter who came home each year for the holidays.

We had just started eating dinner when the telephone rang.

"Want me to get it, Mom?" I asked. "It might be Kyle."

"Go ahead," she answered with a sigh.

I went to the counter and took the receiver. "Hunter residence," I said, feeling more like a visiting relative than I'd have liked.

"Darcy?"

The choices were limited. "Kyle?"

"We finally connected," he said affably. "Sorry I missed your call. I was out in the barn."

"So the rumor is true, then. You're a farmer these days." I said it with more familiarity than I was probably entitled to.

He laughed. "I like to think a gentleman farmer . . . or perhaps a hobbyist. That may be more like it."

"Strange to hear your voice after all these years," I told him, knowing I'd soon run out of small talk.

"What's it been? Eight, nine years?"

"Something like that."

"Marjorie said it would be all right to call you in Harrisburg. I hope you don't mind."

I glanced over at Mother, who was listening with the rapt attention due a royal wedding or a flash-flood warning, I'm not sure which. "Not at all," I replied. "What's up?"

"I understand you've become a private investigator since leaving the FBI."

"Yes . . ."

"Maybe you could recommend someone I might hire to help me with a problem."

"What sort of problem?"

"I guess you'd say it's a missing-persons case. Do you know anything about that?"

"I've done some work involving missing children. My specialty is family problems—divorce and custody matters, mostly. But I know some detectives who specialize in finding people. Want a couple of names?"

"Yes, but that's only part of what I need. It's a very delicate situation that I'm not sure how to handle."

"Maybe you could tell me a little about it."

He hesitated. "I'd like to locate a woman who's recently disappeared, dropped out of sight," he stated succinctly.

"Who is she?"

He hesitated again, then said, "Let's just say she's a friend."

"A friend," I repeated.

"That will do for now."

Kyle was being coy and I was curious why. Was he afraid to come out and say girlfriend, lover, fiancée or whatever she was? Was the fact that he had once been engaged to my sister and now felt uncomfortable talking about this new relationship the cause of that?

"What advice are you looking for, Kyle?" I asked.

"I'm not sure how these things work—you know, the ins and outs."

"Frankly, I'm not sure what you mean."

"Look," he said, "I'm having a little trouble discussing this on the phone. Maybe the best thing would be to talk it over in person."

I considered that, realizing that I felt surprisingly uncomfortable with the notion. I was painfully aware that the man I was talking to was the boy in the picture in my mother's front room. He was also the guy I'd had that crush on when I was thirteen, though that hardly counted anymore. Mostly, I guess, it was that he had been Cara's true love, my would-be brother-in-law who, thanks only to the Fates, was not.

"I suppose we could arrange a meeting," I suggested unenthusiastically.

"When Marjorie said you'd be in Harrisburg for Thanksgiving, it occurred to me it might be a good opportunity for us to get together. On your way home you'll be driving within a few miles of my farm, if you come down Highway 15. I thought maybe you could stop by—if it would be convenient, of course."

I saw no point in pussyfooting around. "I guess I could. I'm intending a leisurely drive home Sunday afternoon. But tell me this. Are the police involved?"

"No, not yet. That's partly what I'm concerned about."

I wanted to ask more, but he'd already expressed his desire to speak about it in person, though I wasn't sure how that would make any difference.

"I'm glad to hear you specialize in family matters," Kyle went on. "There's a baby involved. He's here with me. That's partly why this is so sensitive."

Kyle, damn him, was piquing my curiosity, whether he intended to or not. Well, if he could be coy, I could be blunt. "Whose baby is it?" I asked.

"Hers," he replied obliquely.

That, more or less, told me the whole story—or at least a plausible one. Kyle has relationship with a woman. Woman becomes pregnant, has baby and dumps it on Kyle's doorstep. Embarrassed, Kyle doesn't want to involve the police, so he decides to hire a private investigator.

"I take it discretion is the major issue here," I said.

"Yes," he answered, sounding almost grateful that he didn't have to explain.

"But you feel you need advice?"

"If you don't mind, Darcy."

"All right. How do I find your place?"

He gave me directions, which I scratched out on the notepad lying on the counter. After he'd finished, I read them back to him.

"Perfect," he said.

"Guess I'll see you Sunday afternoon, late," I told him.

"I appreciate you taking the time to meet with me. I really do."

We said goodbye and for a moment I stood staring at the notepad, slowly realizing it was an advertising piece distributed by a local real-estate company. A terrible thought struck me. I looked up at my mother, whose rapt attention hadn't flagged.

"Mom," I asked, the horror in my voice barely disguised, "are you thinking of selling the house?"

She lowered her eyes. "I don't know," she replied.

"Does Arnold own a palace, a big castle on a hill somewhere?"

"He has a lovely home just outside of town." The lilt in her voice was unmistakable.

I sighed woefully, but to myself. My past—the life I'd carefully kept in a neat little box so I could take it out and examine it each year when the holidays rolled around—seemed about to blow up in my face. Was nothing sacred?

"So," Mother prompted, as I returned to the table and sat down, "what did Kyle say?"

"I'm going to his farm to talk to him and see his illegitimate baby."

"What?" Mom exclaimed, truly horrified.

I immediately felt guilty for having said something I didn't know to be true, but damn it, she deserved it. This was the house I was conceived in, for crissakes!

"Illegitimate?" Mom echoed, her tone right out of the era of the Truman administration.

For some reason, the face of my angelic sister flashed before my eyes and guilt overwhelmed me. "He didn't use that exact term," I conceded. "That was the conclusion I drew."

"Well, what term *did* he use?" my mother asked, sounding a bit relieved.

I felt like I'd been caught again by the Miss Marple of my teenage years, having falsely claimed I'd slept the whole night with my retainer on, when in fact the damn thing never left the nightstand. "I don't remember, Mom," I said weakly. "But let's eat before this wonderful dinner of yours is cold."

She let me off. I was glad, even if I felt fifteen again.

THE NEXT TWO DAYS were a bit surrealistic. There was a lot of nervous expectation over Arnold Belcher's visit, though not much of the nervousness was on my part. Mom was like a teenager. I did my best to put her at ease, but let's face it, twenty-five years is a long time between holiday meals involving a man.

Arnold turned out to be a nice fellow. I liked him despite secret expectations to the contrary. He was well-spoken and had a bit of a sense of humor. He talked a lot, but he also listened and asked questions, which many men don't know how to do. He was clearly auditioning for the stepfather role and doing a pretty decent job of it.

When Mother and I were able to exchange a few words in private, I told her I liked her beau. That pleased her no end. It's an awesome thing to be able to influence lives. Not that I had any kind of veto. But there's no denying that stepchildren are a factor in marriages and potential marriages, regardless of the age of the children.

While the turkey cooked, we sat talking in the cozy little living room where I once did my homework on the floor in front of the television set. Some of the time I was avidly engaged in the conversation, but some of the time my mind wandered. Often I caught myself looking at Cara and Kyle smiling from their picture frame and from nearly two decades in the past. It made me feel old.

Finally we had our traditional Thanksgiving dinner with all the special side dishes Daddy had loved—wild-rice and mushroom dressing, cranberry salad and Cheddar-cheese bread. I thought about my father as we ate, but Mom obviously didn't. Her mind and heart were elsewhere.

"Do you cook like Marjorie?" Arnold asked me.

"No way," I said. "The only thing I inherited from Mom was her skin and her legs. My sister, Cara, got all her homemaking skills."

"You've never tried to cook," Mother protested, with some justification.

She was only partially right. Once I'd made a serious effort for Wade Armstrong's birthday. I'd invited his best friend and the guy's fiancée. Sirloin steaks and baked potatoes should have been hard to ruin, but I managed. The steaks were well-done and everybody had requested rare. The potatoes were undercooked and the peas mush. The cake I'd bought at the bakery on Wisconsin Avenue was perfect. We ate a lot of dessert. I've often speculated whether that wasn't the beginning of the end of Wade Armstrong.

After Mom and I cleared the dishes and put down the dropleaf table, Arnold said that since he was taking Mom away for Christmas, he wanted to give me a present now. He went out to his car and brought in a CD stereo system. I told him the gift was lovely but much too extravagant. He said it wasn't really, because it came from the stock of one of his stores. I thanked him profusely.

There was another half hour of conversation before Arnold left us with an orgy of hugs and good wishes. Mom and I sat together on the sofa where I cheerfully gave her my blessing. Having thoroughly exhausted the subject of Arnold Belcher, we watched the local news and I went off to bed to gaze wistfully at the ceiling of my room, just as I had through four hormonally charged years of high school. The more things change, the more they remain the same. The phrase took on more profound meaning.

The next day was more like old times. Mom and I braved the crowds and went shopping. I ran into a friend from high school, and admired her baby. When we said goodbye to my friend, Mom had tears in her eyes. I knew why. I was childless, manless and without a good excuse—except perhaps that I couldn't cook a steak. I dared not say that other things had taken precedent in my life.

That evening we went to bed early. The next day I tackled my annual project on the house. What I lacked as a cook, I more than made up for as a handyman—I never quibbled over sexist language. The Christmas before, I had painted the kitchen. This year I caulked the bathtub, fixed the leaky kitchen faucet and painted the kitchen table and chairs.

After I'd finished the painting, I sat back on my haunches and blew my bangs up off my forehead. Mother had been standing at the counter, watching me.

"You know, dear," she said, "you'd make some man a wonderful wife."

"Husband, don't you mean?"

"What I mean is, you're so industrious and conscientious. Not many girls are like you anymore."

"Mom, it's easy when it's only for a couple of days, once a year. I wouldn't want to do this day in and day out."

"What *do* you want to do, Darcy?"

"Just what I'm doing. I like my life, Mom. I really do."

She didn't like my answer, but that was all right because I didn't like the question. We were getting close to the end of my visit. Both of us could tell. Things always got a touch more prickly the last day or so.

After lunch the next day I kissed Mom goodbye, carried my case to the car and headed for Frederick, where I was to meet up with the first man I'd had a crush on, Kyle Weston. Actually, our conversation had been kicking around in the back of my mind the past few days. I was very curious to know what was going on. But I was also eager to see him. What did he look like after all these years? And what was he like as a person?

It was a cold, blustery day with lots of gray clouds. I encountered a few raindrops on the drive, but that was it in the way of weather. The route that took me to Frederick wasn't the most direct, but it was not far out of my way, either.

After crossing the Maryland line I looked for a place to make a pit stop. I finally settled on a café a few miles outside of town. Two state police cars were parked out front—always a good sign. It meant, as a minimum, that the coffee wasn't bad.

After visiting the ladies' room, I sat at the counter, a few seats down from the troopers, who were chatting. I eavesdropped. The conversation seemed to be about hunting and vacation leave. I had a leisurely cup of coffee, resisting the temptation of a piece of pie. Like most people, I had a tendency to put on a few pounds over the holidays. The bathroom scale wasn't as good a measure as the fit of my jeans.

I wasn't in jeans at the moment, having opted for a decent pair of wool pants and a sweater. I wouldn't have put on heels for Kyle, but I had a desire to look good for him, rationalizing that I had a family standard to maintain.

Having finished my coffee, I tossed a couple of quarters on the counter and went to the cash register to pay my bill. As I put my wallet back in my purse, I felt a tap on my shoulder. I turned and looked into the grim face of one of the troopers. He was staring at me through his sunglasses.

"You have a permit to carry that, miss?" he asked, gesturing toward my handbag.

I knew he wasn't referring to my purse. I kept a silver-plated HKP7 9-mm semiautomatic with me at all times, and he'd seen it when I opened my bag. "Yes, officer, I do."

He gave me an officious grin. "Mind if I see it?"

I shrugged. "It's in my wallet." I was aware he wouldn't take kindly to me reaching for it precipitously. For all he knew, I was out robbing convenience stores and service stations.

"Take it out slowly."

I carefully removed my wallet, noticing the cashier's rounded eyes as she stood frozen. "My name's Darcy Hunter," I said to the cop. "I'm a P.I. out of the District." I showed him my license.

He looked it over and handed it back, nodding. "Sorry, but I was standing here and saw that semiautomatic in your purse. It's not common that a lady carries a concealed weapon out here, understand? You can't be too careful."

"I know. I'd have done the same thing in your shoes."

"Were you law enforcement once upon a time?"

"Yeah, FBI."

"Oh?" He glanced at my hand, to see if I was wearing a ring. I wasn't interested in shop talk or flirting, though obviously the trooper was curious about me. I saluted him. "See you around."

"Have a good day," he said, looking a little disappointed.

I headed for the door as the other cop sauntered up.

"And happy hunting," the first one called after me.

I backed through the door, smiling at him. "Haven't had to use it yet."

"Wish I could say the same." I left the café and the troopers, returning to my car. I took a minute to look over the directions Kyle had given me. Then I started the engine and drove out of the parking lot.

The distance to the farm wasn't great, but there were a number of twists and turns along the way. Though women, they say, aren't born with the same instinct for direction as men, mine was pretty well-developed. Perhaps it was my training at the academy, or perhaps my second X chromosome had the extra odd gene on it.

My generation in law enforcement was not the pioneering one for women. By the time I got there we were accepted, though the older men in particular still harbored some prejudices. But I never got mixed up in that stuff. I just did my job and did it well, until getting stopped one bright shiny day by a bullet from a 9-mm semiautomatic.

The sun was just sinking below the horizon by the time I was close enough to start looking for Kyle's mailbox. The scattered clouds in the western sky were aglow with oranges and yellows, the rolling hills autumn mellow in the twilight. When I finally came to Kyle's turnoff, I found myself peering at a large farmhouse at the end of a long tree-lined drive. It was lit up and seemed inviting, sort of like a big jack-o'-lantern on the hill. I was struck by the cheerfulness of the scene.

Going slowly up the drive I was surprised at how nervous I felt. My heart was beating nicely by the time I pulled into the parking area near the house. I turned off the engine and got out of the car, my mind tumbling with a strange anticipation. I'd done some calculating. Kyle was thirty-eight or -nine by now—practically old enough to be the father of the young man he'd been the last time I'd seen him.

I took my jacket out of the back seat and slipped it on. Then I grabbed my purse. As I stood there, staring at the house, gusts of wind kept blowing strands of hair into my eyes. I kept my hair jaw-length because it was easy to manage and flattering, but it was long enough for the wind to wreak havoc with it.

I started walking toward the house and saw the front door open. Kyle—or more specifically, an older version of the man I'd once known as Kyle—appeared.

The wind was making my eyes tear so he was a little blurry at first. I saw him wave, though, and I waved back. As I got closer, I could see he was in a brown sweater and slacks. His hand casually in his pocket, Kyle was watching me intently as I walked toward him. The closer I came, the more familiar he looked. His brownish-blond hair was shorter than in that picture at Mom's. Gone was the boyish freshness. In its place were manly good looks.

He descended the steps to greet me. Up close I could see tiny lines at the corners of his eyes and a look about him that said he'd lived. The wind tossed his hair. He smiled. There was both delight and awe on his face. He extended his hands.

"My God, Darcy, you look just like your sister."

The pleasure reflected on his face made me smile. His words had clearly been meant as a compliment, and I took them as such. Yet I couldn't help wincing a little. I'd been defined in terms of my sister so many time before, but in spite of that, I'd never truly grown comfortable with it.

I brushed back my bangs and put my hand in his. Kyle looked back and forth between my eyes. Suddenly I felt tongue-tied and awkward. I don't know why this new Kyle was affecting me the way the old one had, but I was like a thirteen-year-old again. Maybe it was some trick of memory that wouldn't let me remember that I was a grown-up now.

"Good to see you," I said, giving his fingers an extra squeeze before I pulled my hand from his.

"You know," he said, "I had a hunch this was the way you'd turn out."

He laughed, then took me into his arms for a big hug. The gesture was warm and familial, but I knew it wasn't me he was reacting to so much as it was his memories of Cara. Oddly enough, I felt sorry for him.

Kyle pulled back from the embrace to gaze into my eyes. "You look great."

"So do you, Kyle."

He stood shaking his head, clearly still amazed.

I was beginning to feel embarrassed. "Tell me, how have you been?" I asked.

"I've got some problems at the moment, but otherwise, I'm okay." He kept his arm around my shoulders as he guided me toward the house. "Let's get in out of the cold."

We went up the steps. "So, how's your mother?" he asked.

"Great. She's got a boyfriend. She's in love. It's like having a mother in her second adolescence."

Kyle laughed. "I've been intending to drive up to Harrisburg and see Marjorie for some time, but I just haven't gotten around to it," he said, as we stepped inside the door. "She was always real sweet to me."

"She thought the world of you, Kyle. Still does, as a matter of fact." With the door closed, I was able to straighten my wind-tangled hair, combing it with my fingers.

Kyle watched me, and I could tell by his expression that it was as if he were seeing my sister coming to life again. My heart went out to him, yet I was aware that I, too, was dealing with memories of tremulous young love. The difference was I was comparing Kyle to himself, whereas he was comparing me to someone else.

"Let me have your coat," he said.

I let him help me slip it off. He hung it in the coat closet, then stepped past me to turn the dead bolt on the door. It struck me as a bit odd—the sort of thing a person did in the inner city, not on an isolated farm.

"I've gotten more security-conscious lately," he explained. "We had an attempted burglary last week, so I'm gun-shy."

"A burglary out here, in the country?"

"Attempted. They didn't get in. The alarm went off. My housekeeper, Mrs. Mitchell, was here alone with the baby at the time. I was away on business."

I glanced around, noticing the pleasant aroma of food overlaying the woodsy, spicy smell of the fine old house. A grandfather clock indicated it was nearly five-thirty.

Kyle again put a hand on my shoulder and guided me toward the front room. I could feel the warmth of his fingers right through my sweater. His house was tastefully decorated, but with an informal country charm. There was an inviting fire crackling in the large stone fireplace. We stopped in the middle of the room. He gave my shoulder a light squeeze before he removed his hand.

"How about a drink?" Kyle suggested. "Something to warm you up."

The offer sounded appealing. Kyle was being hospitable and a drink seemed like a relaxing touch. "If you are."

"I have a nice dry sherry," he said amiably. "Sound good?"

I nodded. "Fine."

"Make yourself at home. I'll only be a minute."

I picked out a big chintz-covered easy chair near the fireplace and snuggled into it. The house had a warm cozy feel. The sofas and chairs were big, soft and informal, with lots of cushions. There were a couple of nice antique mahogany pieces, and old prints of landscapes hung on the walls. I sensed the work of a decorator.

I watched the fire, very aware of its warmth and cheer. Ironically the place bespoke wholesomeness. I was again caught by the thought that this could well have been my sister's home. I could have driven out from the District to have Sunday dinner with them—played a game of Scrabble and drunk some hot chocolate with the kids, said goodbye, then headed for home, having dutifully played the role of auntie.

The reality was very different, though—one that confounded me. The business of a woman not his wife, and a baby, didn't fit well. It was at odds with my notion of Kyle Weston.

In the back of the house I heard a telephone ring, followed by a woman's voice.

"Would you answer it this time, Mr. Weston," she said. "I'm afraid to pick up the receiver anymore."

I could only barely make out the woman's words, but there was a discernible note of distress in her voice. It struck me as odd. Then I heard Kyle saying hello, his voice growing louder as he repeated himself.

"Hello? Hello? Who is this?" I heard him say. "What do you want?"

Next I heard him speaking to the woman in a quieter tone, though I couldn't make out his words. Without understanding what was going on, I had a feeling the little vignette I'd overheard was part of the reason I was there.

A minute or so later Kyle reappeared, a glass of sherry in each hand. He didn't look quite as merry as before, though he did smile. I took one of the glasses from him. He sat in the chair across from me.

With the shadows from the fire dancing across his face, his manly ruggedness and good looks were accentuated. I tried—and partially succeeded—to relate to him not as Cara's fiancé, but simply as an attractive man, an old family friend. Kyle's craggy smile replaced sober reflection and he lifted his glass slightly in salute.

"Here's to seeing you, Darcy, after such a very long time."

"It has been a long time, hasn't it?"

"Unfortunately long," he said.

We each sipped our sherry. I looked into the fire, wondering whether my strong reaction to Kyle was because of our past, or if I would have been attracted to him if he'd been a complete stranger. The irony was, I'd never know. Either way, the simple fact was I'd come in friendship—to offer my help and advice. I knew there was no use letting my feelings complicate that. I turned to him.

"You indicated you were having problems," I began. "What sort of problems? What's going on?"

He contemplated me for a moment, then he said, "I'll tell you all about it later, but I'd rather talk about something more pleasant first. Tell me about yourself, Darcy."

I gave him a self-conscious smile, searching for an honest response. Strangely—perhaps because of the few days I'd spent with my mother—the four words that popped into my mind were *No man, no children.* But what I said was, "I'm doing work I really enjoy. I like my life a lot."

Kyle rubbed his chin and nodded. "Tell me about your work. Tell me what you've been doing the last several years." A faraway look came over his face. "I'm really interested to know."

3

I GAVE THE THREE-MINUTE summary of my career, mentioning some of my more interesting cases. Though I didn't talk about my personal life, I did tell Kyle that my flat in Georgetown doubled as my office. He asked how I got my cases and I explained that I was well established with several law firms and got quite a few referrals. Happily I was in a position to pick and choose the cases I wanted to take.

"Why did you leave the FBI?" he asked.

"I'm surprised the story didn't make it into one of Mom's Christmas letters."

"I don't recall if it did."

"I got shot," I told him. "During a bank-robbery investigation. After that, I lost my taste for playing games with criminals." I smiled. "Though to be frank, irate spouses can be pretty scary at times, too."

Kyle had been looking at me intently as I talked. His eyes didn't exactly get glossy, but I knew his mind was flirting with the past. He steepled his fingers. "How old are you now, Darcy?" he asked.

"Thirty."

"Thirty," he repeated, sounding amazed. "And never married?"

"Nope."

He slowly nodded, seeming to let it sink in.

"You haven't been married either, I take it." I sipped my sherry.

He shook his head, but didn't comment. He did continue looking wistful. I was sure he was seeing Cara.

I started feeling uncomfortable. I glanced around. "You've got a nice place here, Kyle. Had it long?"

"About five years. I sold my house in Baltimore—actually it had been my parents' place—and moved out here."

"Horses?"

"A few."

"What do you do with your time?" I asked.

"I guess you could say I manage my portfolio. I'm active in a couple of charities. Serve on the boards, that sort of thing."

"You sound like you're retired."

"I am, in a manner of speaking."

"What did you do before?"

"Investment banking. I built my company up to where it was worth quite a bit of money, and then sold it. A boy millionaire at twenty-eight. Retired to the farm at thirty-three."

I observed him, watching the shadows dance on his face. Kyle had an easy, natural way about him and he seemed to lack all pretense. In spite of the fact that he'd accomplished quite a bit at a young age, he didn't seem overly impressed with himself. He'd simply been stating facts.

As a teenager, I'd assumed that because his family was rich, Kyle would be a snob. I think the fact that he'd been down-to-earth and had a charming personality had sent my heart soaring as much as his college-boy good looks. Interestingly, I found those qualities every bit as engaging now as I had then.

"Are you happy, Kyle?" I asked him.

"Yeah," he said, neither sounding passionate about it nor disingenuous. "How about you?"

"Yeah, I'm happy, too."

He gave me that slow nod again. After a long moment passed between us he said, "You know, I have a vivid recollection of you that Christmas Cara took me with her up to Harrisburg. You must have been what—twelve or thirteen?"

"Thirteen."

"Do you remember it?"

I smiled. "I remember it very well. I had a terrible crush on you."

"Really?"

"You and Cara getting engaged was the most fabulously romantic thing I could imagine. I was mesmerized by the whole thing. And heartbroken."

Kyle seemed fascinated by the admission. "I remember you as a sweet little girl."

"I wasn't sweet at all. Cara was furious with me because I was always hanging around."

He smiled. "I do sort of remember that, now that you mention it. But as I recall, you and I got along."

"You were very nice to me. I was totally unaccustomed to being treated respectfully. I guess I figured anyone that nice to me deserved my love."

He seemed amused by the comment. His eyes twinkled as he studied me and, for an instant, I actually had the feeling he might be seeing me and not my sister.

Kyle sipped his sherry, and I found myself staring at his mouth, recalling how I'd once so fervently fantasized about him kissing me.

There were footsteps in the hall. We both turned toward the door where a woman in late middle-age appeared. She was tall and full-bodied. She had on an apron. "Excuse me Mr. Weston," she said. "Would dinner in half an hour be all right?"

"Yes, I think so." He turned to me. "Darcy, will you stay for dinner?"

"Oh, no, thank you. I'm sorry I arrived a bit later than I'd intended. Here I am cutting into your dinner hour." I scooted to the edge of my seat, looking at my watch.

"Oh, stay," he coaxed. "I'm dining alone. In fact, I asked Mrs. Mitchell to cook for a guest, as well, in case you could be persuaded."

"I shouldn't," I replied, my initial resolve weakening.

"You'll have to eat. You don't have other plans, do you?"

"Just to get home."

"It's an early dinner. You'll still make it back to Georgetown at a decent hour." He gave me his craggy smile. "I'd enjoy the company."

"Well, all right, if you really wouldn't mind."

"I'd prefer it." He turned to the housekeeper. "Dinner for two. Miss Hunter is staying."

"Fine, sir," the woman said. She started to turn away.

"Oh, Mrs. Mitchell," Kyle called after her, "how's Andrew doing?"

She turned toward the stairs. "Haven't heard a peep in quite a while. I was thinking I'd go up and check on him. He should have awakened long before now."

"Why don't I do it? You're busy with dinner."

"That would be nice, Mr. Weston."

Kyle got up as the woman headed off for the kitchen. He looked down at me. "Would you like to see the baby?"

I shrugged and put down my sherry glass. "Sure."

As we went to the entry hall, he again touched my back, guiding me toward the stairs. His hand lingered there only for the briefest moment, but I sensed he'd done it more to connect with me than for any other reason. We started up the stairs.

"You said your work involves children," Kyle said. "Are you especially fond of kids?"

"I don't really work with them directly. Except in a professional capacity, if you know what I mean."

"In other words, you hunt down missing children, you don't change diapers," he said with a laugh.

"Something like that."

We came to the top of the stairs and went down the hall. "Would you like to have children of your own?" he asked.

"At the right time, maybe."

He stopped at the doorway to a dark room. Pausing, he looked into my eyes and I felt a connection with him that had nothing whatsoever to do with our conversation.

"After marriage, in other words," he stated.

"Pardon?" I'd completely lost the flow of the discussion.

"You were hinting that the right time to have kids is after marriage."

I laughed to cover myself. "Yeah, I'm terribly traditional that way."

Kyle smiled at me, then stepped into the nursery and flipped a switch that turned on a dim lamp across the room. There was a large crib where a bed would normally have been. Kyle went to it; I followed.

In the crib was a sweet little baby who looked to be about six months old—I wasn't very experienced in such matters. He wore blue sleepers and was sound asleep, looking perfectly angelic.

"This is Andrew," Kyle said softly, peering down at him rather proudly.

"He's adorable," I whispered. "How old is he?"

"Seven months next week." He brushed the baby's cheek with the back of his finger, smiling.

The gesture was gentle and loving, but in no way diminished Kyle's manliness. To the contrary, I found it rather appealing that he wasn't afraid to show his love for the child.

"Compelling little devil, isn't he?" Kyle remarked.

"He belongs to your lady friend," I guessed. "The one who's missing?"

"Yep." He continued looking at the baby.

"You want to find her because you're unhappy she dumped the baby and took off?" I ventured.

"To the contrary, I want to find her because Andrew's in limbo. Frankly, my intent is to adopt him, and I can't without Camille's permission."

"You mean he's not yours?" I was astonished.

Kyle looked up at me, a bit dumbfounded. "No. Did you think he was?"

"Well . . . I wasn't sure. You haven't told me much."

"No, that's true. Well, he's not mine, though I wish he were. It would make things much easier."

I would have liked an explanation for that comment, but I didn't ask. Instead, I watched as Kyle took the baby's hand

and cooed. "Andy, my man," he said, "do you plan on sleeping all evening? Time to get up, kiddo." He reached down and lifted the baby into his arms, holding him to his chest.

Andrew blinked awake and looked at me uncertainly. He didn't appear unhappy to be in Kyle's arms, but he wasn't too sure what he thought of me. I reached over and took his little hand. He squeezed my finger without looking particularly pleased to be making my acquaintance.

"It takes a while to warm up, doesn't it, son?" Kyle said.

Andrew screwed up his face and cried, turning his head away.

"I have a sneaking suspicion a change of diapers might improve your disposition," Kyle murmured to the baby. "What do you think, Andy?" He looked at me. "Do you mind putting off formal introductions until we've had time to make some sartorial adjustments?"

"Sure," I answered with a laugh.

Kyle carried the baby to the changing table. Then he pointed to a nearby rocker. "Make yourself comfortable, Darcy. This'll take a few minutes. I'm thorough, but not terribly efficient."

I sat in the rocking chair and watched him removing Andrew's sleeper. This was not a context in which I was accustomed to observing a man—or a woman either, for that matter. I recalled hearing that men found something inherently sexy about a woman with a baby, but it occurred to me that the opposite was equally true. Whether it was sex appeal or not, I was utterly fascinated.

"You seem pretty proficient," I said. "How long have you had him?"

Kyle thought for a second. "It's been almost six weeks."

"How long has—what was her name?—the mother—"

"Camille."

"Yes, Camille. How long has she been gone?"

"Two weeks."

"Did she indicate her intentions?" I asked.

"You mean with regard to Andrew?"

I shrugged. "Yeah."

"She told me to take good care of him, said she'd be in touch if she could, then packed a suitcase and left without saying where she was headed." Kyle had Andrew's diaper off and was cleaning him with a baby wipe.

"She was living here, then?"

"Yeah."

"Care to explain?"

He gave me a look. "It's a rather complicated story. The bottom line is, I'd like to locate Camille and get her to sign off on Andrew so that he's mine."

It was an evasive answer. I could only conclude this was something he didn't want to talk about, and it wasn't my role to press him. "You seem kind of determined on that point."

Kyle nodded. "I guess I am."

"And you want a recommendation from me who might best help you find Camille."

"Right."

"I'll give you a couple of names. Two guys in D.C. come to mind. And maybe somebody in Baltimore."

"How about you, Darcy? Is this the sort of case you might handle?"

I thought for a moment. "Well, it's not beyond the realm of possibility, but to be frank, I'm not sure it would be a very good idea."

"Why not?"

"Because I'd be asking a lot of questions, Kyle. A whole lot of questions. And if you don't mind me saying so, you don't seem to want to be very forthcoming."

"You mean about Camille."

"For starters."

Kyle, who'd diligently powdered the baby, was putting a fresh diaper on him. I watched as he put Andrew into a clean sleeper. "Would every detective have the same attitude?" he asked.

"I'm afraid so," I said. "Anybody who works for you would want to know what's going on. I gather there's nothing illicit, but for anybody to do their job, to find Camille, they'd have to know who she is and what she was doing giving you her baby, to cite just two examples."

"Would the police have to be brought into it?"

"That depends. If there's a crime involved, no legitimate investigator would or should ignore it. Compounding a felony is a crime itself."

Kyle picked the baby up and kissed his head. Andrew looked a lot happier. "I don't want to give you the impression there's some horrible deed I'm trying to cover up, because there isn't. There are a number of things I don't understand myself, and others that are...well, sticky. I guess the point is, I want this handled discreetly."

"Discretion's not a problem. But forthrightness would be a necessity. At least for me, Kyle. I think this is something you should take to someone else."

"If it's going to be the same with everybody I talk to, then I might as well deal with you. At least we know each other."

I grinned. "Yeah, I had a crush on you seventeen years ago and have been eating your Christmas hams ever since."

"Don't knock it. How many P.I.'s can say that?"

The telephone rang again somewhere in the house, and a stricken look crossed Kyle's face.

"Uh-oh," he said. "I'd better get that. Would you mind holding the baby?" Without waiting for my reply, he thrust Andrew into my arms and left the room. "I'll get it, Mrs. Mitchell," I heard him call out as he hurried down the hall.

I could hear the phone ring a few more times, then it stopped. The house was in silence. I couldn't hear a thing but the cooing of the baby. He had that nice clean baby smell. I gave him a little squeeze to test the feel of his body. He felt solid, yet soft and warm.

I wasn't used to domesticity. Babies and 9-mm semiautomatics didn't normally go together, at least in my mind. And Kyle's acting so mysterious didn't quite ring true, either. He had always seemed straightforward; but then perhaps that was the impression I'd garnered from my mother. Lord knows, I hadn't spent all that much time with him myself.

Still, I was perplexed by Kyle's reticence about Camille. Clearly something was going on that concerned him. The question was if it should concern me.

Andrew grabbed my hair playfully and pulled his head back to get a look at my face. I sat him up on my knee and we peered at each other. For a while I stared at his little face. He didn't seem as distressed as I might have expected. He was all trusting. I wasn't sure he was fully justified.

I couldn't even recall the last time I'd held a baby in my arms. In an odd way, I liked it. The realization gave me pause. Were maternal instincts suddenly rumbling around inside me? I wondered. The thought made me shudder. Motherhood shouldn't be something a woman embraced instantly, at the sight of a cute baby.

I was glad, though, that my mother wasn't there. She'd have freaked at the sight of a baby boy on my knee.

Andrew seemed content with our mutual regard. I brazenly tried baby talk, despite having read somewhere that mothers were encouraged to speak in normal language to children. But what the heck, I was an amateur.

I heard Kyle coming back. He appeared at the door, looking distracted, though he did take a moment to savor the sight of me holding Andrew. Mother and child. The term wasn't even in my lexicon.

"Everything all right?" I asked.

It took him a moment to realize I was referring to the telephone. "Oh, yeah. False alarm."

"Have you been having trouble?"

"Yes. It started this afternoon," he explained, coming over to the rocker. "The phone rings, but nobody's there. Mrs. Mitchell has gotten fairly upset by it. The poor thing has been jumpy ever since the burglary attempt."

"The calls started today?" I asked.

"Yes, it's happened four or five times."

"And she answered each time?"

"Yeah, that's right. Until earlier, when I took the call. This last one was just an ordinary wrong number. The person apologized."

"What about the earlier call?"

"There was nobody on the line. No heavy breathing. No nothing."

"Do you think it could have been Camille?"

"Funny, the possibility occurred to me, too. But I can't imagine why she would do it. It's not like I threw her out. And my voice certainly holds no magic for her."

I found the comment instructive. I can't say there was bitterness in Kyle's tone, or even cynicism. It was more an admission than anything else. "How long did the caller stay on the line?" I asked.

"Several seconds. Ten or fifteen at the most. I said hello. When I got no response I said, 'Who's this?' Nothing happened. Whoever it was just hung up. Mrs. Mitchell's experience was the same."

"It could be innocent," I said. "Maybe kids fooling around."

Kyle nodded vacantly, pondering.

"Tell me about the attempted burglary."

"It was at night. I was gone at the time. Mrs. Mitchell was here with Andrew. The burglar tried to come in a downstairs window in back. The alarm went off and he took off."

"Did she see anyone?"

"No. Apparently the burglar had driven partway up the drive. In any case, she saw the taillights of the vehicle about the time it neared the road. The police came, but there wasn't much for them to go on. Rural crime seems to be on the rise. It wasn't very reassuring, especially to Mrs. Mitchell. Thank goodness for the alarm."

He was standing there with his hands on his hips, looking down at us. I scrutinized him. Kyle was gradually becoming a real person to me, instead of the icon I'd carried in my head for so many years. That was just as well, because I knew that there was no sense dwelling in the past.

Still, there was a tiny part of me that was taken aback that he was now relating to me as an adult woman. I wasn't sure how I felt about that, or about the attraction I felt for him. It was as if we were playing an old game by new rules.

"Well," he said, "shall we go downstairs? Dinner will be ready in a few minutes."

I grasped Andrew firmly under the arms and stood. The baby hung from my hands.

"Want me to take him?" Kyle asked.

"Yes, my maternal technique is a little rusty."

"It comes quickly," he reassured with a smile.

"Your maternal instincts seem to have blossomed fully," I teased.

"Maybe I've found my true calling."

I followed him out of the room, turning out the light as I left. We went downstairs. The cooking smells that greeted us sparked my appetite. I'd fully intended to make amends for Thanksgiving over the coming week, but saw the diet might have to be delayed a day.

We found Mrs. Mitchell in the dining room. "You can be seated, Mr. Weston," she said. "Dinner's ready to be served. I'll take the baby as soon as I have everything on the table, if that's all right."

"Sure," he replied.

"I've already opened the wine." The woman gestured toward the sideboard.

"Fine."

Mrs. Mitchell left. Still holding Andrew, Kyle seated me at one end of the long dinner table. A silver candlestick sat at either end of the table. There was a dimmed chandelier overhead. I watched as Kyle fetched the bottle of wine—a cabernet, as it turned out—and poured a splash in his glass, then came to fill mine. Andrew, who looked perfectly content, observed it all.

"You seem well suited for the father role," I noted. "How is it you haven't married and had a family?"

"I don't know," he answered, filling his glass and putting the wine back on the sideboard.

"Really?"

"Really," he said, taking his place at the other end of the table. He settled the baby on his lap.

Mrs. Mitchell wheeled in a cart and served us dinner. The meal consisted of roast beef—a filet by appearances—new potatoes, creamed carrots, Parker House rolls and a tossed salad. She put the serving dishes on the sideboard after she'd finished, wheeled the cart out, then came back for Andrew.

"Come, Master Andrew," she said, lifting him into her arms. "Now it's time for our dinner."

When they were gone Kyle and I looked at each other. He had a surprisingly contented expression on his face. He raised his wineglass, obviously preparing to make a toast. I took mine.

"Welcome to my home, Darcy. And *bon appétit.*"

"Thank you for your hospitality," I replied.

We sipped our wine.

"But to get back to your sister . . ." he said.

I arched a brow. "Were we talking about Cara?"

"You were thinking about her and have been all evening. And so, frankly, have I. So we may as well talk about it instead of pretending we don't have to."

I found it an insightful comment. I waited.

"I was affected by her loss for a long time, as you probably know," he went on. "But I can't honestly say her death condemned me to eternal bachelorhood, at least consciously. I think that was what you were wondering, wasn't it?"

"Maybe it was," I admitted.

"The problem I've had may be that nobody I've met since Cara has compared. I'm stubborn and a romantic," he declared. "That's a dangerous combination."

I appreciated the forthright manner in which Kyle spoke. It indicated a man in tune with his inner self—if one who in some way still suffered, even years after his loss. And there was a poignancy about him that appealed to my soul. I smiled to myself, realizing that a part of me was still in awe of him. Taking a sip of wine, I realized Kyle was indeed a special man—certainly different from those I'd known. But I cautioned myself not to get caught up in the romance of the situation. There was no reason to get swept away by what he was saying, even if he was utterly sincere.

"If you've been looking to replace Cara, that's probably a mistake," I told him.

"I'm smart enough to know I was a different person then and that my needs and desires are different now. I don't think it's Cara that I long for so much as the feeling I had for her. I've never felt that kind of love since."

"That's very insightful."

"I've had a lot of time to think about it."

We ate for a while.

"Hasn't there been anyone at all?" I asked, my curiosity about Kyle growing acute.

"I've had relationships, of course, but none of them was right for marriage. Some guys are inveterate bachelors. I may be one."

The wind had kicked up, and whistled around the eaves. I shivered involuntarily, even though the temperature inside was quite cozy.

"What's your excuse?" Kyle asked.

"For being single?"

"Yes."

"I guess I'm an inveterate spinster."

He smiled. "Haven't even had a close call?"

"One semiclose call." I told him about Wade Armstrong.

Kyle listened to me talk, a pensive expression on his face. He occasionally took a bite of food, but mostly his eyes were riveted on me. His awareness of me was growing in intensity. I was no longer completely sure it was Cara who was in his thoughts. And I found the shift in perception unsettling.

After I'd stopped talking, Kyle continued to ponder me without saying a word. I couldn't decide if it was sadness I saw in him—whether it was poignancy, regret or what.

"What are you thinking?" I finally asked.

"That it's a strange time for us to run into each other again."

"Because of your troubles with Camille?"

"It's not just that. My brother, Dale—I don't know if you ever heard me speak of him—was tragically killed in a boating accident on the Chesapeake about two months ago."

"Oh, I'm sorry, Kyle. You have been hit with one thing after another, haven't you?"

"It's been a rough year. But I don't mean to moan."

"Don't be silly. Sometimes a person has to discuss their troubles. Men don't do that enough, I think."

"You may be right, but I don't want to cry on your shoulder."

I saw an opportunity to be helpful and tried to take advantage of it. "Were you and your brother close?"

"Not as close as we might have been. And maybe that's what troubles me most about the loss. Our parents have been gone now for several years, so it was just Dale and I. He had a family, though. A wife and two daughters. I feel worse for them and have tried to do what I could, but Sally has lots of family and has been getting her support from them."

"That is one of the hardest things a woman has to face—losing a husband and having children to raise alone. I saw what my mother went through."

"There's no question this was a blow. Dale and Sally had had some problems and they'd decided to put their marriage back together. He took some time off from his job—he was a lawyer in the criminal division of the office of the attorney general—and as soon as the girls were out of school, the whole family went to Europe for a couple of months. They'd only been home a few weeks when he was killed."

"I'm really sorry."

"It made me do some soul-searching," Kyle said. "A thing like that will make you take stock of your life. It's one reason I feel so strongly about Andrew, have the need I feel to...take him in."

I could see that Kyle was speaking from the heart. He was a sensitive person and very self-aware. But I had an uncomfortable feeling about his relationship with the baby. I don't know if it was because of his reticence on that particular subject, or something I detected in his behavior. His unwillingness to talk about Camille also was troubling, though he certainly had no obligation to confide in me. Everything seemed to be getting more complicated by the moment. And most disquieting of all was the way I felt myself being drawn in. In spite of my conviction that I shouldn't get involved with his problems, I found myself caring.

"Time is the great healer," I reminded, trying to find something constructive to say.

Kyle gave me another long, pensive look—one that made me feel self-conscious and uncertain. Then he said, "Darcy, I'd really like you to take this case. I'll tell you whatever you need to know."

I was a bit taken aback by his earnestness, not to mention the timing of his announcement. It was as though he'd overheard my thoughts about caring about his problems. But reason told me to be cautious. "You really think it would be a good idea?"

"I feel good about you, about confiding in you."

"I'm flattered. Thank you," I replied, at a loss.

I'd pretty well cleaned my plate and Kyle asked if he could serve me more. I thanked him, but said no. There was a dessert, berry pie, but I declined that, as well. He suggested we go into the front room where we could be more comfortable while we talked.

The fire had burned down and Kyle added some more wood. I watched him, tormented once more by the nagging realization that by all rights he ought to be my brother-in-law. We had talked openly about Cara, and that had helped, but I knew the subject wasn't going to fade easily from my mind.

After Kyle had the fire going nicely, he asked if I'd like coffee. "Can't beat a fresh-brewed cup and a crackling fire," he said, making it sound especially appealing.

"Sure, why not?"

Kyle went to the kitchen. For a while I looked at the fire, then I got up and wandered to the window. It was pitch-black out. In the distance I could see the lights of a neighboring farmhouse. I could hear the wind whistling. I rubbed my arms, wondering about the disconcerting, almost-ominous feeling I had.

Then I noticed the lights of a couple of vehicles coming down the road. They were half a mile away when they stopped, approximately at the entrance to the farm. I didn't think much of it—people did pull over when traveling along a highway, turned around in driveways or stopped to chat with a friend. But it was my nature to notice things. My work depended on it. At one time, so had my life.

I was watching the two cars when I heard Kyle returning. He was carrying a tray with cups and saucers, and a china coffeepot, sugar bowl and creamer.

"Everything all right?" he asked. It was an odd question that played strangely into my progressively unsettled mood.

I glanced at the distant headlights that still hadn't moved. "I was just watching some cars down at the road," I told him.

"Oh?" Kyle put down the tray and came over to the window.

He put his arm around my shoulder as we stared out at the distant headlights. It was a friendly gesture—not intimate, but his proximity heightened my awareness of him. Involuntarily I took in his scent. I was aware of the weight of his hand and its warmth. I felt myself tense.

"Believe it or not, Andrew had his dinner and showed signs of wanting to go to bed. Mrs. Mitchell put him back down and has retired for the evening."

"You won't be keeping him company in the small hours after all," I told him.

"No, but I have a hunch he'll be wanting to play around five or six in the morning."

"The perils of fatherhood," I observed.

Kyle squeezed my shoulder, sending a little tremor through me.

Down at the road one of the vehicles started moving. It was coming up the drive toward the house.

"Looks like you've got a visitor," I said. I glanced at Kyle. He didn't look pleased at the prospect.

"Apparently so."

It took a while for the car to make it up the hill. As it rounded the crest and turned, the headlights swept across the face of the house and into our eyes. When the vehicle came to a stop outside I saw that it was a state police car.

The first thing that went through my mind was where I'd left my purse. Kyle dropped his hand from my shoulder.

"The police," he said. "What do you suppose they want?"

"I think you're about to find out."

4

KYLE WENT TO THE ENTRY hall and I stayed at the window, watching. A trooper got out of the cruiser and mounted the steps to the porch. I heard the front door open, then Kyle's voice.

"Good evening, officer. What can I do for you?"

"We've a manhunt in progress, sir," came the reply. "An escaped killer. We've tracked him to the neighborhood and are checking with people. Have you seen any suspicious persons around this afternoon or evening?"

"No, officer, I haven't."

Hearing what was being said, I got up and wandered toward the entry hall.

"Is that Escort sedan parked out there yours, sir?" the policeman asked.

"No," Kyle replied. "It belongs to a guest."

"I have to tell you, sir, the vehicle is similar to the one hijacked by the escapee."

"Well, I assure you my guest arrived in it an hour or so ago," Kyle declared. "It's not the one you're looking for."

I stood at the entrance to the foyer. From my vantage point, I was able to see the stocky officer standing just outside the front door, under the porch light. Kyle was in the doorway.

"The car out there is mine," I said, walking across the entry hall.

The officer squinted, peering into the light at me. "Evening, ma'am. Sorry to trouble you, but we're checking as carefully as possible. You haven't seen any suspicious persons around, have you, ma'am?"

"No, I'm afraid not." I stood next to Kyle.

The man rubbed his chin, looking back and forth between us. "May I ask, sir, how many people live here?"

"Apart from myself, there's my housekeeper and . . . my baby."

"Are they be home now?"

"Yes, they're both here."

"Could I speak to your housekeeper, sir?"

"Is it really necessary? She's retired for the evening."

"Can you say for sure she didn't notice anyone hanging around?"

"If she had, I'm sure she'd have mentioned it to me."

"All the same, I'd like to speak to her myself, if you don't mind."

Kyle looked at me, sighing with exasperation. "All right, I'll go get her. You might as well come on in."

The officer, a large man in his forties, stepped inside. After Kyle closed the door, he went off to get Mrs. Mitchell. The policeman and I exchanged long looks. Something about him bothered me. He was perspiring profusely and seemed unnaturally nervous—the opposite of the cool character I'd run into at the café that afternoon.

The trooper I'd seen earlier was all spit and polish. This guy was disheveled by comparison. He needed a haircut. The sloppiness could be explained if it was the end of his shift, if it was possibly an overtime situation, but not the haircut.

"Sorry to interrupt your evening," he said, noticing my scrutiny, "but we're being as thorough as we can be."

"How long has your manhunt been going on?" I asked.

"All day. We've been combing the countryside. Had to call in units from the outside."

I thought again about the troopers in the coffee shop. They certainly hadn't seemed part of a massive manhunt. To the contrary, they'd appeared fairly laid-back, leisurely drinking their coffee and chatting like it was a routine day.

"The baby upstairs?" the cop asked inexplicably.

"Yes."

The officer nodded.

Outside I heard another vehicle. Headlights again raked across the house. It was then I noticed the trooper's shoes—brown wingtips. They weren't uniform shoes. My suspicions became acute. But then I heard footsteps behind me. I turned as Kyle and Mrs. Mitchell came into the entry hall. The housekeeper was wearing a heavy robe and slippers. She had a disconcerted look on her face. Kyle, too, appeared unhappy.

Mrs. Mitchell and Kyle suddenly stopped. Horror registered on their faces as they looked past me at the policeman. When I turned back to him I saw he'd drawn his service revolver and it was pointed at the three of us.

"You folks stay nice and calm and nothing's going to happen to you," he said. "If one of you so much as moves, though, you'll all get it. Understand?"

I heard Mrs. Mitchell gasp. I looked at my purse, lying on the chair behind the officer, who I now realized was no cop at all. He backed toward the door, keeping his gun leveled on us.

"What in the hell is going on?" Kyle demanded.

"Shut up, Weston!" the man spat angrily.

I now understood the reason for his nervousness. But I still had no idea what he was up to.

He opened the door a crack and, without taking his eyes off us, shouted to someone outside. "All clear! I've got 'em. Come on in!"

My mind was spinning. I glanced again at my purse, wondering if I could get to my gun without arousing suspicion. There was a sound of footsteps on the outside stairs.

"Okay, folks," the bogus cop said, "turn around slowly. I want you to walk into the living room, nice and easy. Remember, one false move and I start shootin'. Now let's get movin'."

Kyle and Mrs. Mitchell were only a few steps away from me. The housekeeper had her hands clutched to her breast and she was moaning with fright. Kyle put his arm around her shoulders and the three of us went into the front room.

"Sit on the couch," the man commanded.

I could hear the sound of feet in the entry hall behind us.

"Where's the kid?" a man's voice asked.

"Upstairs," the phony cop replied.

Kyle spun around.

"Sit down!" the man shouted.

We sat. Kyle was in the middle. The sweating man in the police uniform stood across from us, the gun pointed casually in our direction.

"I demand to know what this is about," Kyle said.

"It's about you shutting up before I shoot you to make sure I don't have to say it again. Now be quiet before you piss me off."

Mrs. Mitchell whimpered. I could hear Kyle's breathing. My heart was pounding. I knew now that they were after Andrew. I kept thinking about how I could get to my gun.

The baby's plaintive cry came from upstairs.

"Oh, my God," Kyle said under his breath.

Andrew's cry carried through the house.

"If you want money..." Kyle began.

Without a word, our captor lifted the service revolver and, grasping it with both hands, aimed it directly at Kyle's head. Mrs. Mitchell began to weep into her hands. After a tense moment, he lowered the gun and gave a half smile.

Andrew's crying became louder and there were footsteps on the stairs. Two men in dark clothing and ski masks appeared. One was carrying Andrew, who had been hastily wrapped in a blanket. I could see the baby's arm flailing futilely. We had only a glimpse of them as they passed the entrance to the front room, but I observed what I could of the abductors.

Kyle was cursing under his breath, his clenched fist trembling on the sofa between us. Judging by Andrew's fading cries, he'd been taken outside. The second man came into the room, carrying a cloth sack. I frantically looked him over for identifying characteristics. All I could get was size. He'd concealed his identity well. Strangely, he wore only one glove. It was on his left hand.

"Cuff 'em," he commanded, tossing the sack on the floor. Then he took a semiautomatic from his belt and aimed it at us.

The kidnapper in the trooper's uniform picked up the sack and dumped the contents onto the floor. There were half a dozen pairs of handcuffs and some rope. He took a pair of cuffs.

"All right, lady," he said, pointing to Mrs. Mitchell, "get your butt over here."

She rose hesitantly from the sofa. "Don't hurt me," she begged. "Please don't hurt me."

"I won't if you get moving. Hurry it up."

He cuffed her hands behind her back. Next he did the same with me. Last, he handcuffed Kyle. Then he brought three straight chairs from the dining room. Backing the chairs to each other, he made us sit. With a short length of rope he tied our feet together, then used a long piece to wrap around our torsos.

"Rip out the phones," the masked gunman told him.

The bogus cop left the room to tour the house in search of telephone extensions. The other man moved about the room, first peering out the front window, then into the entry hall and up the stairs, where his accomplice had gone. He came back into the room.

"That baby needs proper care," Kyle said to him. "Don't neglect him. Feed him properly."

"Button it," the man commanded.

"What is it you want?" Kyle persisted. "How much money?"

The kidnapper gave a derisive laugh, but didn't bother to answer. He went to the foyer again and called for his accomplice to hurry. Returning to the front room, he walked around us to make sure we were securely bound.

"Why didn't Camille get Andrew herself?" I asked, hoping to bait him.

He gave me a quizzical look, then turned away, going once more to the window. We heard the man in uniform hustle down the stairs, breathlessly.

"Think I got them all," he said.

"You'd better hope so," his friend replied, going to the door.

The phony trooper saluted us mockingly from the doorway and said, "You folks make yourselves at home now." He hurried out, thoughtfully shutting the front door behind him.

"Bastards!" Kyle shouted at the top of his lungs.

Mrs. Mitchell broke down and sobbed.

"We've got to get loose," I said to Kyle over the housekeeper's weeping. "If we can notify the police in time, they might be able to throw up roadblocks." I began twisting my body, but the kidnapper had bound us tightly. Each movement caused the ropes to bind. Mrs. Mitchell cried out in pain. I felt the cord cutting into my flesh, as well.

Kyle said, "Even if we manage to free ourselves, the phones are out and it's over a mile to the closest neighbor."

"I've got a car phone," I told him. "But we have to get loose first."

"Maybe if we can shift the positions of the chairs we can get a little slack from the ropes," he suggested.

"It's worth a try," I said.

I looked over my shoulder. The backs of the three chairs were wedged together tightly, but by sliding a corner of one of them just half an inch one way or the other, it seemed we'd be able to change the angle enough to get some slack.

We began moving and shaking as best we could, trying to ignore the pain caused by the ropes. It didn't work.

"Let's all try exhaling at the same time," I suggested, "and see if that gives us slack."

We tried once. Nothing happened. We tried a second time. I felt a little give.

"Once more," I said.

Kyle pushed and twisted so hard that he partially lifted his chair from the floor. Mrs. Mitchell cried out, but the corner of my chair gave a little and there was some slack in the rope.

I squirmed as hard as I could and managed to slip down some. That produced more slack. The chair shifted a little more and pretty soon I was able to writhe free of the ropes. The problem was I was on the floor with my feet tied and the handcuffs binding my hands behind me.

By bending my knees and pulling my feet up toward my buttocks I was able to reach the rope around my ankles. While I was working on that, Kyle got out of his chair and was on the floor. Mrs. Mitchell didn't bother. She stayed put.

Finally I got my feet untied and crawled over on my knees to Kyle. I untied his ankles. We were both able to stand.

"Now what?" he asked.

"My keys are in my purse. I guess I'll try to reach the police on my car phone."

"I'll come with you."

"We've got to hurry," I said. "Time is critical."

"You rest, Mrs. Mitchell," Kyle said as we left the front room. "We'll be back in a few minutes."

Even with my hands secured behind me, walking unrestricted was a joyous feeling. In the foyer I dug through my purse. It was terribly awkward having to do everything with my hands behind my back, but I got my keys. Kyle had opened the front door and we hurried down the steps into the dark, cold night.

"What do you think they're intent is, Darcy?" Kyle asked as we moved across the parking area toward my car. "Do you think Camille's somehow involved, or is this for ransom?"

"I made that remark about Camille to see what kind of reaction I'd get. He was cool, but I don't think her name was unfamiliar."

"So what do you make of it?"

"I don't know."

"For the first time in my life I feel capable of killing with my bare hands," Kyle said. "If those people harm Andrew, they'd damn well better fear for their lives."

"Our best chance is the police." I fumbled with the key, trying to get it into the lock. I dropped the key ring and groaned. I had to get down on the ground to pick it up. I got to my feet and tried the lock again. "This is harder than it looks," I said.

"I should have thought to bring a flashlight."

Finally I got the door open. The interior light was welcome, but now I had to figure out how to get hold of the phone.

"You are within the mobile net here, aren't you?" I asked, the issue of radio range suddenly occurring to me.

"I believe we're on the fringe of it," Kyle replied.

By scooting across the driver's seat, I managed to get to the phone. But dialing, I realized, would be tricky. I was barely able to get the receiver far enough around my back to see the keypad. It took several attempts, but eventually I was able to raise an operator. By laying the receiver on the seat and pressing my face close to it, I could to speak with her. She put me through to the police.

Lying across the seat, my hands secured behind me, my derriere hanging out the door of the car, I was not in the most ladylike position. But I figured Kyle was too preoccupied to take notice. When I did look back at him, though, I wasn't so sure.

Once help was on the way, I wormed back out of the car. Kyle and I stood facing each other in the cool wind, our faces illuminated by the dome light from my car. It was a strangely awkward situation—both of us with our hands cuffed, unable to do anything but look at each other.

"Thank you, Darcy." His voice was thick with emotion. "If we get the baby back quickly, it'll be because of you."

"I'm sorry I couldn't do anything to stop them," I said. "I know you must be hurting terribly, but I couldn't think of a way to get to my gun."

"You have a gun?"

"I carry a semiautomatic. It's in my purse."

"It's just as well. A shoot-out might have been disastrous."

"I don't imagine they'll harm Andrew," I told him. "In most cases, a kidnapper won't."

He lowered his head, his eyes turning liquid. I could see he was terribly upset. My heart went out to him.

The wind gusted. It was bitingly cold. We were both shivering. I inched nearer. I couldn't put my arms around him, though I would have liked to. Kyle had the same awareness as I. He leaned closer to me. Our bodies touched. I lifted my face and looked into his eyes. The wind blew wisps of hair across my face.

We pressed even closer. He kissed the top of my head. Then, when I lifted my face, he kissed my forehead and my cheek. It was more than simple affection. More than gratitude. We were bound, but the intimacy we managed to share was no less sweet, the arousal as intense and poignant as it could be.

My wrists strained at their bonds. Kyle's mouth moved slowly toward mine. My lower lip sagged open and he covered my mouth with his. For a long moment we kissed, sharing our anguish at one level, but most of all giving in to the attraction we had felt from the moment I'd arrived.

My heart pounded hard. I ached for more, but feared it, too. What was I doing? This was Kyle Weston, the guy in the picture in my mother's living room, the guy who was going to marry my sister all those long years ago. Why had I let this happen? Why *did* it happen?

I pulled my mouth free. Kyle looked hard into my eyes. He didn't smile. Maybe what had happened disconcerted him as much as it had me.

"Maybe we should get inside," I said. "Mrs. Mitchell will be upset."

"Yes," he agreed. "You're probably right."

5

IT TOOK FIFTEEN MINUTES for a patrol car to make it to the farm. Kyle led the officers inside. I'd given what little information I could over the car phone, but the kidnappers had at least half an hour's head start. That was more than sufficient for them to make a clean getaway, but I didn't tell Kyle that.

The officers immediately cut the chains of our handcuffs, but the steel bracelets couldn't be removed until the technicians arrived sometime later. Two FBI agents showed up just after we'd gotten them off. They wanted us to go over the story of the kidnapping again.

Kyle, though anxious and impatient, held together fairly well. He supplemented my account, but I did most of the talking. Mrs. Mitchell was too emotional to be of much help. Soon after the FBI arrived, she went to her room to lie down.

The agents, Len Barnes and Tom Edleson, looked very much alike physically. Edleson was a bit fairer and younger than Barnes, but they seemed almost like clones. They worked well together. Their questioning was direct and thorough, workmanlike.

"All right," Barnes said, "let me get the situation straight with the victim. The baby lives here with you and a housekeeper. Is that right?"

"Yes."

"What about your wife, the mother?"

Kyle had a pained expression on his face. "She's not my wife."

"Then you're not married?"

"No."

"But the kid is yours."

"Well, no, not technically. That is, I'm not his natural father. But I'd hoped to adopt Andrew. Camille agreed to it."

Barnes scratched his chin. "All right, tell me about the mother. What's her full name?"

Kyle gave me a slightly distressed look. It was easy to understand why. He hadn't told me a thing about the woman and now I was going to get the whole story right along with the FBI. Recalling his desire for discretion, I felt sorry for him, yet at the same time I was damned curious what he was going to say.

"Her name is Camille Parker," Kyle began. "Or more accurately, that's the name she goes by. Her real name is Camilla Panelli. Parker is a stage name."

"She's an actress?"

"A lounge singer."

"I see. Where is Miss Parker now?"

"I don't know. She's disappeared. Dropped out of sight. I haven't seen her for over two weeks."

"How is it you've had the baby?"

"Camille moved in with me six weeks ago. The purpose was to discuss arrangements for Andrew's adoption."

"She wanted to give up her kid?" Edleson said with surprise.

"She was willing to give me custody, let me raise him, though she wanted to retain her own parental rights. At least, that's where things stood when she left."

"What was your relationship with Miss Parker?" Barnes asked. "I don't mean to get personal, but we've got to be clear about the situation here."

"I understand," Kyle replied. He drew a breath, glancing at me. "Camille and I were friends."

"Friends," Barnes repeated.

"Yes."

"So, you're saying that your friend, Miss Parker, and her baby were living with you. You wanted to adopt the child, and she had agreed. Then two weeks ago she disappeared."

"That's right."

"Without telling you why or where she was headed."

"Correct."

Barnes looked unhappy with Kyle's answers. I found the story exceedingly strange myself. "Who's the father of the baby?" the agent asked.

Kyle hesitated, then gave an uncertain shrug.

"She never told you who the father was?"

"Does it matter?" Kyle asked, clearly not liking the question. "A baby was kidnapped by two masked men and a guy dressed like a state policeman. The object of this exercise is to get Andrew back, not establish paternity. Or am I mistaken?"

Kyle had gotten a little hot under the collar. Barnes and Edleson exchanged glances.

"Listen," Barnes said, "I know this has been an emotional night for you, Mr. Weston, but we're just trying to understand who's who in this situation. Some supposed kidnappings aren't kidnappings at all. Now I grant you, crimes apparently were committed here this evening—based on what you and Miss Hunter have told us, anyway—but according to what you've said, you don't even have legal custody of the child."

"It's still kidnapping. You aren't suggesting those men have a right to come in here and carry off, at gunpoint, a baby left in my care."

"No, of course not, Mr. Weston. But if we're to solve this case and find Andrew, it'll help a lot if we know the players, know what's going on. It's natural that we'd want to speak to the baby's mother."

"Believe me, I'd like to speak to Camille, too," Kyle replied. "If you find her, please let me know."

Barnes turned to me. "Miss Hunter, you said you're an old family friend and that Mr. Weston invited you here this evening for advice. Is it relevant to what we're discussing here?"

"Kyle was interested in finding Camille and wanted help doing so."

"Did he retain you for that purpose?"

I glanced at Kyle, who remained bewildered. "He asked if I'd take the case, but I was also giving him referrals for other private investigators. Basically, we were discussing his various options when the kidnapping occurred."

"I see." Barnes scratched his chin, then looked at Kyle. "We'll try and find Miss Parker. She may have information that would be helpful to the investigation. But I'm afraid the same would be true of the father. You see my dilemma, Mr. Weston." He paused, staring at Kyle.

Kyle stared back at him. "Would you feel any better if I told you the father is not a factor in this at all?"

"I'd feel better if I knew *why* he wasn't a factor."

"We don't like taking things on faith," Edleson added. "The facts are much more reliable."

Kyle took another deep breath. "Can I count on your discretion?"

"We don't run our investigations past the media, if that's what you mean."

"People, innocent people, could be badly hurt if this becomes public."

Barnes contemplated him. "We have no control over what information might come out in a public trial, Mr. Weston, but as regards what you tell us, it will be kept in confidence. I've got to warn you, we may feel it necessary to talk to the father, but we won't be publicizing names."

"You won't be talking to him," Kyle stated glumly. "He's dead."

"Oh?"

Kyle looked at me. "If I've been evasive, Darcy, it's because this whole business is very sensitive." He turned to the agents. "Andrew's father was my brother, Dale Weston. Dale was killed in a boating accident a couple of months ago. Last year he had an affair with Camille and got her pregnant. She wanted him to divorce and marry her, but he wouldn't do it. The whole thing got nasty, but Dale managed to keep it from Sally."

"His wife?"

"Yes, that's correct. Their marriage had been troubled for some time, but Dale came to the realization he either had to save it or let it go. When he decided he wanted to stay with Sally, he told Camille it was over. Needless to say, she was unhappy. Then when Dale was killed, she was really left holding the bag. For Sally's sake, and the children's, I didn't want Camille going after Dale's estate. So I stepped in. For the past couple of months I've been dealing with Camille and shielding my sister-in-law and her children from the truth."

Barnes nodded. "I understand your reluctance to talk about it, Mr. Weston."

Kyle looked at me, seeming very sad. My heart went out to him, because I understood his predicament. In fact, everything, including his reluctance to discuss Camille, suddenly made sense. Kyle was being noble in trying to protect his brother's family.

"We can't control what other people might say," Tom Edleson said to Kyle. "But there's no reason this information will be disseminated by us. We appreciate your candor."

Kyle ran his fingers through his dark blond hair. "The important thing is that you find Andrew."

For the first time, I understood Kyle's passion over a child not his. The baby was his nephew. It made sense that he'd want to look out for him, give him a home. Compassion for Kyle welled inside me.

"I'd like to ask you a few more questions about Camille Parker," Len Barnes continued. "You said you were dealing with her on your brother's behalf. Who initiated the process? Did you go to her, or did she come to you?"

"She came to me. Dale had brought her out here once to discuss finances, so she knew where I lived. But I'd known for several months before then that Dale had been having an affair with a lounge singer, and that he'd gotten her pregnant. But he hadn't decided whether he was going to leave Sally or not. He asked me to help him make financial arrangements for the baby.

"Camille was six months pregnant when I first met her. I wasn't pleased about being a part of a cover-up, but I didn't see it as my place to sit in judgment, either. Privately I told Dale he couldn't procrastinate, that he'd have to make up his mind what he was going to do."

"When did your brother tell Camille he was staying with his wife?" Edleson asked.

"Right after Andrew was born. I think early in June. He gave Camille fifty thousand dollars and promised to set up a trust for the baby as soon as he got back from Europe. He asked me to make the arrangements for everything while he was gone. I spoke to Camille once on the phone during the summer to reassure her that everything would be taken care of. She'd been very upset ever since Dale gave her the news that he was staying with his wife. I couldn't blame her, but I tried hard to convince her to be satisfied with the financial arrangements Dale was making."

"How was he managing that without his wife finding out?" Barnes asked.

"I helped him get the funds from a family trust our parents had established. That avoided the need for using joint assets and thus involving Sally."

"What happened when your brother got back from Europe?"

"His marriage was back together and he was more determined than ever to take care of Camille and the baby as quietly as possible. So far as I know, he didn't see her again. He and I met a couple of times about the trust that he was setting up for Andrew, but he was killed before the paperwork was completed. As soon as Camille heard about his death, she came to me."

"What was her attitude?"

"She was upset. She'd been bitter when Dale dumped her, but frankly I think she really loved him. Her immediate concern was that Andrew wouldn't lose out because Dale had died. She made sounds about going to a lawyer, but I assured her I'd make good on my brother's obligations."

"How is it she came to live here?"

"I offered to let her move in while arrangements were being completed. I had an ulterior motive. Andrew. I was worried about his future, the life he'd have. Camille always seemed less than the ideal mother type. Her intentions were good, it seemed, but it was evident a baby didn't fit in well with her life-style."

"Why do you say that?"

"She said she was eager to resume her career. I had a good idea what that would mean for a child. Frankly, I didn't want my nephew to live that way."

"So you offered to adopt him?"

"I didn't know what I wanted to do at first. I thought the best way to feel out the situation was to have them both here for a while. It wasn't a week before I decided I wanted to raise the baby myself, if I could get Camille to agree."

"What was her reaction?"

"When I first broached the subject she said she wouldn't ever give Andrew up, but when I made it clear she could retain parental rights and simply leave the responsibility to me, she decided she liked the idea, after all."

"Do you think she's changed her mind?"

"If so, she didn't tell me," Kyle replied. "All she said was to take care of Andrew and that she'd be in touch. It seems to me that if she wanted to raise Andrew herself, she'd have taken him with her."

"I suppose you're right about that," Barnes replied. He scratched his chin again. "All right, so it looks like we don't have anybody with a motive to kidnap, except for ransom. Does that sound right, or is there somebody or something we haven't discussed?"

Kyle shrugged helplessly. "I can't think of anything. It's got to be for money."

Barnes turned to me. "But you felt the kidnapper with the mask and glove reacted to Miss Parker's name when you mentioned it."

"I can't be sure," I said. "With the ski mask on, it was difficult to read his reaction, but he was blinking and moved his head in a way that suggested the name meant something to him."

Barnes turned to Kyle. "Did Miss Parker mention anyone who might have cause to give her grief? Any enemies, any problems?"

"No," Kyle answered. "She didn't say anything. We didn't have a close personal relationship."

Judging by the look he gave me, Kyle wanted me to understand that every bit as much as Barnes and Edleson. I was flattered that with all his problems, he even cared what I thought.

Edleson interrupted our mutual regard by saying, "It would be helpful if we had a picture of the baby. Do you have any around?"

"Yes, as a matter of fact, I took a roll of film about three weeks ago," Kyle said. "Would you like me to get the prints?"

"Please."

Kyle went off and Barnes gave me a weary smile, shaking his head. "The lives some people live never cease to amaze me."

I nodded, but said nothing. Both agents were aware of my background with the Bureau. I'd mentioned it first thing to the police. It had expedited the questioning considerably. Also, the critical information got to the field right away, saving even more time. It was obvious to me, though, that the kidnappers were pros, and I'd said so.

"What's your sense of this thing, Ms. Hunter?" Barnes asked. "Are we dealing with a kidnapping for ransom, or is there some kind of custody or financial dispute at play?"

"I believe Kyle," I said.

"Is that a professional opinion or the opinion of a family friend?"

"Today is the first time I've seen him in ten years or more, so I think I can be objective. I can't see any reason why he'd be less than honest. It's clear the kidnapping has him upset and he wants that baby back."

Edleson kind of twisted his mouth and frowned. "Do you think he might have played down his relationship with the Parker woman?"

"What do you mean?" I asked.

"Just a thought. I've got nothing in particular to go on. But maybe they had a relationship of some sort that he didn't wish to talk about."

"Camille wouldn't have to kidnap her own child, if that's what you're suggesting," I said. "Unless she was in complicity with someone in a kidnapping for ransom."

"You mean to extort money out of Weston?"

I shrugged. "It's possible."

"She would be aware of both his wealth and his feelings toward the kid," Barnes agreed. "We'll have to keep that in mind." He studied me. "Did you bring that up because of the reaction of the guy during the kidnapping when you mentioned her name?"

"It went through my mind."

"Am I getting a sense from you that there's more to this than meets the eye?"

I agonized. "I don't want to prejudice anybody's thinking, but I've got a funny feeling about Camille's disappearance. Maybe it's washing over into the kidnapping."

"Intuition's fine," Barnes said, "but I like solid evidence better."

"So do I," I agreed. "But you work with what you've got."

Kyle returned and the agents selected photos of Andrew that they would get to units on the street as quickly as possible. The snapshots were spread out on the coffee table. Among them were pictures of an attractive dark-haired woman holding the baby.

"Is this Camille?" I asked, picking up the picture.

Kyle nodded. "Yeah."

Without being too conspicuous, I studied the photo. Camille had nice eyes, but was a bit too heavily made up for my taste. By anyone's standards, though, she was a pretty woman. There was an air of vulnerability about her, even under all that makeup. I wondered about her. Was she another woman who'd had an affair with a married man and then was left holding the bag, or was she a hardhearted schemer? Either way, I felt sorry for her—sorry that life had given her few choices, and all of them bad.

When I looked up from the picture, Kyle was watching me. I casually put the photo down. "She's pretty," I said, deciding to meet the challenge head-on.

"Yes, she is," he replied.

Barnes had listened to the exchange, I'm sure taking in every nuance. He was not a stupid man. He then engaged Edleson in conversation about the picture. Kyle moved to sit next to me on the sofa. I was surprised when he reached over and took my hand.

At first I passed it off as a simple attempt to connect—affection between old friends after a harrowing experience. Then I remembered our handcuffed kiss out at my car. The significance of that hadn't fully registered before because of the continuing excitement, but now I couldn't look at Kyle without thinking about it.

Barnes, who took note of Kyle's hand on mine, gave Edleson the photos and sat back in his chair reflectively as his partner went off. He let the silence hang. I slipped my hand from Kyle's.

I was aware of voices in the other room. Technicians were setting up the phones for receiving a ransom call. In addition to the FBI, the state police were well represented.

While we sat, each in his own thoughts, a policeman came in to inform us that the stolen state police car had been found five miles east of the farm. People from the crime lab were at work on it. The news aroused considerable interest. Nothing in the way of physical evidence had been left at the crime scene except the ropes and handcuffs. The patrol car could provide important clues.

The bogus cop was our best lead since we had a detailed description of him. They hoped to get some prints and wanted us to go through mug books to try to identify him. With Kyle having to stay close to the house to take any ransom calls and Mrs. Mitchell in a frazzled state, it was agreed I'd go to FBI headquarters in the morning and try to identify the guy. My own theory was that he was a small-time thug—maybe someone who'd been imported to do the job.

As I told Barnes and Edleson, the operation seemed well planned with definite professional overtones. That suggested a financial motive, though kidnapping for ransom was not a crime of choice for true professionals.

"Could anybody besides me use a cup of coffee?" Kyle suggested after a while.

There were several favorable responses and he asked me if I wanted to help him make some for the crew.

"Sure," I said. "Coffee and tea are the only things I can make without raising the ire of the health department."

"You aren't a cook like your sister was?" Kyle asked, as we made our way to the kitchen.

It was the first mention of Cara since our conversation about her. I knew, though, that she'd been on his mind. "No," I said. "I got my father's policeman gene instead."

I helped Kyle make coffee. After carrying it out to the others, Kyle and I sat at the kitchen table with cups of our own. The tension had taken its toll. He looked beat. I wasn't in the best shape myself. It was nearly midnight of a day that had begun with my mother in Harrisburg. Thanksgiving seemed like two weeks ago.

Kyle sat hunched over the table. He ran his fingers through his hair, sighing. He'd been through a lot. We both had, though the emotional strain wasn't as severe for me. I'd held the baby for a few minutes, but Kyle had had six weeks to get attached to him. Plus, Andrew was Kyle's own flesh and blood.

"I wish there was something I could do," I said.

Kyle reached out and took both my hands. He rubbed the backs of them with his thumbs, looking me in the eye. "I wouldn't wish this experience on anyone, but I'm glad you were with me, Darcy."

I knew he meant it as a compliment, but just how, I wasn't sure. My eyes drifted to his mouth. I remembered our kiss. Maybe I even blushed a little.

He shook his head. "I still can't believe Andrew's gone, that he's not upstairs in his bed."

A sudden emotion welled up in me and I bit my lip. "Don't worry. We'll get him back."

"You think so, or are you just trying to make me feel better?"

"Statistically, most kidnap victims are returned unharmed."

"The hell with statistics," he said. "I want to know what you feel inside."

I couldn't tell him about my uneasy feeling—my undefined suspicions—because I didn't understand them myself. So I tried to focus on the object of our concern. Andrew. Who couldn't feel compassion for a baby snatched from his bed? "I believe we'll get him back," I said earnestly, though maybe more from hope than conviction.

Kyle pulled my hands to his cheeks. "God, I hope you're right."

The prickle of his beard on my skin sent a tingling sensation up and down my spine. I didn't know what to make of his continuing show of affection. He gave my fingers a squeeze before letting them go.

A state police officer came in for more coffee and I got him some. When I returned to the table, Kyle was leaning back in his chair. I'd caught a glimpse of him watching me move about the kitchen.

"How long do you think they'll be staying here?" Kyle asked.

"I suspect they're wrapping things up now. The next step is preparing for a ransom demand. You'll be briefed on that, then I expect them to go."

"Why don't you spend the night?" he offered. "We've got a nice guest room. It would be cruel to make you drive all the way to the District at this time of night."

I was sure the invitation was innocent, but it set off an alarm bell in my mind anyway. That bothered me. True, Kyle had been friendly—and he hadn't been afraid to show it—but the *real* reason I worried was because I'd found him so attractive. "Don't worry about me," I said, trying to hide my true feelings. "I'm resilient and I function well even when I'm fatigued."

"I'd like you to stay, Darcy. In the morning we can go in together to do whatever it is they need."

I studied him, looking at the situation from his point of view, trying to understand his motive in pressing the invitation. We went way back, it was true. Still, I couldn't pretend to know him, not the Kyle Weston he'd become, even if what I'd seen today was consistent with the man I'd known as Cara's fiancé.

And no matter how hard I tried to forget it, that emotional angst-filled kiss we'd shared bothered me. I didn't understand it—I didn't understand what had driven us to reach out to each other the way we had.

"Thank you," I replied. "You're being considerate, but I don't think it would be a good idea. I like sleeping in my own bed."

Kyle gave me a half smile. "Thank you for not challenging my motives. I wouldn't want you to get the wrong idea."

"I know you're an honorable man," I assured him.

"Thank you for that, too."

I looked at my watch. "Well, unless they need me for anything further, maybe I will head home."

Kyle reached out and took my hand, stopping me before I could get up. "What happens now?"

"What do you mean?"

"I guess I don't have a question so much as a request. Getting Andrew back is the first order of business. Can I hire you to work on that instead of finding Camille?"

"Kidnappings are not my thing, Kyle. There's not a lot more that I can do in addition to what the police and the Bureau will be doing. But I'll help in any way I can. I feel partly responsible—being here when it happened and not stopping it."

"Don't feel that way," he said. "I feel very fortunate to have you as a friend." His mouth lifted at the corners. "You *are* my friend, aren't you?"

"Of course." I got to my feet and so did he. I hesitated and he came around the table. He extended his arms and I melted into them almost naturally. We hugged as friends would. But he didn't release me immediately. I heard him inhaling my scent, and acquainting himself with my body by moving his hands around my waist to the small of my back.

At one level his embrace made me very uneasy, but at another I had an almost perverse desire for more. I was unable to decide whether what was happening was wrong or right.

His embrace tightened and I looked up into his eyes. I was frozen with uncertainty. Taking advantage of my indecision, Kyle kissed me lightly on the lips.

I accepted the affection passively, but with an acute awareness. Afterward, I stood very still for a moment, feeling the beat of my own tripping heart. This had meant something, I was sure about that; but right then I didn't have the nerve to find out what. My sole desire was to escape. Easing from his arms, I left the room.

6

I LEFT THE FARM IN a state of emotional confusion. My feelings for Kyle were unexpectedly intense, and strange to a point of surreal. He wasn't just some man I'd met. He was the guy with all those associations—memories that went back to my adolescence, decade's-old photographs. He was Cara's true love. Most recently, Kyle had been Mother's Christmas-ham benefactor, her concept of an ideal young man—and yes, the son she'd never had.

And as for me, I'd been the bridesmaid to the aborted fairy tale, the one Mom kept alive on the shelf of our family home in Harrisburg. I'd been witness to it all, living it vicariously at first, not thinking or worrying much about Kyle the past ten years—not until his Thanksgiving call.

And tonight Kyle might have kissed Cara's little sister, but I wasn't a thirteen-year-old anymore. I was a grown woman and I didn't truly understand either his feelings or mine. I knew from experience, though, that crises did funny things to people. Heightened emotion, adrenaline, fear—they could do things to one's inhibitions, not unlike booze. They could even alter perceptions and make the unreal, real.

I guess I knew not to make too much of what had happened. But the ease with which I'd fallen into it confounded me. Maybe I was needier than I realized.

Driving along the near-deserted highway in the small hours of a Monday morning, I made a decision. To the extent that when I saw Kyle again, I would have to be the one to take responsibility for keeping things in perspective. Circumstances had made him emotionally vulnerable. I didn't have that excuse.

It was after two when I got to Georgetown. The residential streets were quiet. Even Wisconsin Avenue was almost completely devoid of activity. Still, favorable as traffic conditions were during the graveyard shift, parking conditions were not. My only chance of finding a legal space after midnight came by courtesy of a late departing guest. More than one married gentleman had a mistress in Georgetown, which, if nothing else, kept a certain number of spaces rotating. That night I was less lucky than usual and had to settle for a semi-legal space at the far end of R Street, on the same side as the park.

I thought of the stereo in my trunk, Arnold Belcher's gift, and decided to leave it there until morning. Unseen, it should be safe, unless my car was stolen, which was unlikely, considering it was cheap transportation. But I did grab my suitcase from the back seat.

When it came to walking alone at night, I had more confidence than most, thanks to the HKP7 in my purse. Even so, I felt jumpy. Part of it was the fog that had spread up from the river, giving an eerie feel to the night, but it was also the day I'd had.

I crossed the street, preferring the danger that might be lurking between the town houses to the gloom and shadow of the park. Each pool of light under the streetlamps created a small haven of security, and I found myself walking quickly from one to the next. When I climbed the steps to my flat, I finally began to relax.

I unlocked the door and stepped inside, sighing with relief as I bolted it behind me. The automatic timer had switched off, so the room was dark. Days of my absence had left the air chilly and a bit dank, but it had the accustomed scent of home. I turned on a light and glanced around, steeping myself in the familiarity.

Half of my front room was for living, the rest was office. The easy chairs in the bay window were my seating area, but the large desk and the credenza behind it, both of which I'd purchased at a used-furniture store, dominated the space.

There was a computer stand, a computer, printer and modem, filing cabinets and a couple of visitor's chairs. I'd scattered some plants around to make the room look a little homey.

I don't know if it was the hour or my mood, but the flat had a peculiar feel, despite its familiarity. I was reminded of going with my mother to open house at school when I was a kid. At an odd hour of the evening my classroom wasn't the same place in which I'd toiled all day, all the visual evidence to the contrary notwithstanding.

Maybe there was something about two in the morning that brought out a person's philosophical proclivities, because as I gathered the mail lying under the slot in my door, I found myself wondering why this place I called home was what I'd chosen for myself. I'd heard it said that people end up in life with what they settle for and perhaps deserve. Could that really be true?

Seeing nothing in the mail of an earthshaking nature, I tossed it on my desk to be opened the next day. I looked at my answering machine and saw that a couple of messages had been left. My first instinct was to put them off until morning, but I changed my mind and listened.

The first was from a lawyer I'd worked with on a recent case with a question on the final report I'd written up. It must have come soon after I'd left for Harrisburg. The next was from Dave Hirsch, the last guy I'd dated. We hadn't been out in three weeks. I didn't see him as much, now that softball season was over. He played catcher on a rival team.

"Hunter," he'd said into my machine, "it's Dave. You dead or out of town? If the latter, give me a call. If the former, forget it."

I smiled. Dave was a nice guy. I enjoyed watching a game on TV and having a beer with him. We always bet on the outcome because "money doubled the sex appeal" of any sporting event. I usually managed to lose. Dave claimed that with a betting partner like me, he had enough beer money for the next three seasons.

It was an unusual relationship. We were "companionable," as he liked to call it, but it wasn't going anywhere special and we both knew it. I often asked myself why it was that my feeling for a guy would only go so far, then stop. The best I could come up with was that my soul simply wasn't into the relationship. It made me wonder sometimes about my soul.

There was one other message on the machine. I listened, surprised to hear Kyle's voice. "You're on your way home, I know," he said, "but I wanted to call and thank you for all you did." That was all. Just a simple thanks. I was touched.

I carried my suitcase back to the bedroom, but didn't bother to unpack anything other than my makeup bag. Mom had asked if I wanted to throw my laundry in with a load she'd run early Sunday morning, saying I might as well take clean clothes home with me. So I had.

There was a picture of my mother on my dresser. Thinking of her made me glance at it, a symbolic way to connect. She would be wondering how things had gone with Kyle. I made a mental note to call her in the morning. Chances were the kidnapping would be big in the news. It was only decent that she hear it from me first.

The bathroom felt like an ice-skating rink. I'd have liked a shower, but it was late and too damned cold. I brushed my teeth, though, and undressed in front of the mirror. It was my face I saw, but as I stared at the pale white skin framed with black hair, the wide-set gray eyes and slightly pointed nose, I was searching for Cara. I knew well it was my sister Kyle had seen.

Stripped to my underwear and shivering, I removed my bra. I stared for a moment at the silvery scar, marking the place just above my left breast where I'd been shot. I touched it with my fingertip, as I sometimes did when communing with my mortality. It also made me feel close to my father, knowing I'd lived and he'd died only because of advances in medical science between the two shootings.

Grabbing my flannel nightgown from the hook on the back of the door, I slipped it on and went to my bed. I jumped in and turned off the lamp on the nightstand. The sheets were cold as ice and for a couple of minutes I lay shivering until my body heat finally wore off the chill.

Fatigued, but awake in my cold, dark bedroom, I thought of Kyle's cheery house as I had first seen it, lit-up on the hill. I remembered its cozy, homey feel—the crackling fire, the glass of sherry and Kyle's intense gaze. Images from the kidnapping were in my mind, as well, but I tried to repress them and concentrate on the warm things I'd experienced that evening.

Tears came to my eyes when I thought of Andrew's plump little body and how cuddly he'd felt in my arms. I hoped that wherever he was, he was comfortable and cared for. It seemed senseless and cruel that anyone could make an innocent baby suffer. Kyle, if he was awake, must have been having the same thoughts.

Inevitably I recalled his kiss, how sweet it had been. I thought what it would be like to be in his arms right then. I even dared imagine him as my lover, kissing me passionately as he professed his love. If for only a few passing moments, I let Kyle Weston be at the heart of my fantasies, just as I had as a girl of thirteen.

THE NEXT MORNING I was awakened by the telephone ringing. I looked at the clock. It was seven forty-five. Normally I'd have been up by then, but considering I'd only been in bed five hours, it wasn't surprising I'd been sound asleep.

I tried calculating the consequences of not answering, which meant taking inventory of the current happenings in my life. The telephone had rung three times before I remembered Kyle and the kidnapping. I was crawling on my stomach toward the phone when the answering machine took the call in the front room. I cocked my ear to listen to the caller's voice. It was a woman, but I couldn't make out what she was saying. I decided it didn't matter, that I'd find out in due course. I let my body sink right where it was, down onto the cool sheets of no-man's-land, as I fondly called the other side of the bed.

"Lord," I said to myself as I mulled over the night before, "all that really happened, didn't it?" If I hadn't been fully awake before, I was now. I was supposed to be at the Bureau first thing to look at mug shots, whatever "first thing" was. Arbitrarily I decided it was nine o'clock, which meant I was already late.

The bathroom was still an ice rink but I turned on the shower, threw off my nightgown and was into the steaming hot water before I could utter the words *National Hockey League*. It was no time for the feint of heart.

Since I was an early riser, my engine was revving nicely by the time I'd finished my shower and dried myself off. I toweled my hair, then combed out the tangles. Being a practical person, I kept my hair jaw-length and God had made it straight, which meant I was always within three minutes of perfect hair. That is, perfect by my standards, which probably fell somewhere just below the national average.

After dressing more businesslike than the day before, in a brown suit and brown pumps, I headed for the kitchen and one of my patented two-minute breakfasts. Passing my desk, I remembered the call that had awakened me. I listened to the recording. It was a reporter from the *Post* wanting to interview me about the Andrew Panelli kidnapping. She left a number and asked me to call.

What was the etiquette in this kind of situation? I had no desire whatsoever to talk to the press, and no experience with it, either. Was a person expected to call back and say they had no comment, like declining a regrets-only invitation? Or was it all right to ignore the call?

I hadn't yet decided what to do, though I had managed to get about half a cup of coffee down before the phone rang again. I decided to take it and went to my desk.

"Hello?"

"Miss Hunter?" It was a woman's voice.

"Yes."

"Kate Kellman of the *Post*. Can I get a statement from you about the Andrew Panelli kidnapping?"

"Who gave you my number?" I asked the question with more curiosity than chagrin.

"You're the only P.I. named Hunter in the book."

"Oh."

"Would you describe for me what happened yesterday at the Weston farm?"

"Look, I'd really like to help you, but I'm on my way out the door. I'm supposed to meet with the FBI agents handling the investigation."

"How about afterward? I can meet you at the FBI building."

"Maybe another time. Sorry, but I've got to run."

"Can I call tonight?"

"Yeah, sure."

I hung up, thinking I probably ought to contact Kyle and see if he wanted me to cooperate with the media or not. I was sure Barnes and Edleson had mapped out a strategy for using the media for their purposes, as well. I decided to lay low, though, for the time being.

I realized that it was a case with a lot of media appeal. In the past I'd been in on cases involving prominent people, but never in a visible capacity. And never before had I been both witness and victim of a crime, as I had been last night.

The call did remind me of my intention to give my mother a jingle. I didn't really have the time, but later would be too late. I quickly dialed her number.

"Darcy," she said breathlessly, "I just heard on the radio. Kyle's baby was kidnapped? It's the same Kyle Weston?"

"Yes, Mom."

"Oh, good heavens." She gave a little gasp. "And you were the private detective who was there at the time. They didn't give a name, but I was sure it was you."

"It was." I was not mortified, but certainly embarrassed—more so than I'd been the evening before. The story, even on my mother's lips, made me look like a dolt, an incompetent. It was like being a night watchman who'd slept through a burglary.

"Were you hurt? They didn't molest you or anything, did they? I know they don't always put the truth on the air or in the newspaper."

"We were tied up. That's all."

"They didn't hurt you? I mean . . . Well, you know."

"No, Mom. I don't even have rope burns."

"Where are you now?"

"At home. I'm about to go in to look at mug shots."

"Was it dreadful?" she asked.

"Right now it's more embarrassing than anything. But to answer your question, no, it wasn't particularly pleasant. We were all scared." I'd found from experience my mother always responded best to the truth. She saw right through a soft soap job.

"How's Kyle, the poor dear?"

"I'm sure he's upset. He was last night when I left."

"I'll have to send him a card or a little note or something," she said. "How did he look?"

Now Mom was getting to the part she really cared about. I didn't want to cut her off, but glancing at my watch, I saw that I might have to, soon. "He looked fine. Like I remember, only older."

"Well, we're all older, aren't we?"

"Yeah, we certainly are."

"Did you have a chance to talk to him at all?" Mother asked hopefully.

I knew what she was getting at and decided to give it to her all at once. "Yes, we talked quite a bit, had dinner, caught up on old times. The kidnapping came toward the end of my visit. I was about to go home."

"What terrible luck. For the poor little angel foremost, of course. Did you get the story on the baby, by the way? Is it Kyle's child?"

"No, Mom, a friend's. But he was intending to adopt Andrew. A sweet little baby, by the way. I feel dreadful about it."

"Thank the good Lord you and Kyle weren't hurt. I will write to him, or do you think I should call?"

"I'd write, I think. But listen, I really have to run. I'll phone if and when there's news. Meanwhile, give my best to Arnold. I hope you told him how much I liked him."

"First thing."

"Great. Well, got to go. Talk to you soon."

I hung up, blowing my bangs off my brow. What was it about mothers? You loved them to death, it seemed, but at the same time found them terribly frustrating to deal with sometimes. Or was it just mine? Or just me?

It was a crisp, sunny day, but I grabbed my trench coat from the closet anyway, checked my purse to make sure the HK was on the top, and took off. As luck would have it, my car was already ticketed. It was the second I'd gotten that month.

The worst of rush hour was over. I got to the J. Edgar Hoover Building at 10th and Pennsylvania in good time. I spent a few minutes in a reception area waiting for Tom Edleson, who was on his way down to escort me upstairs. I picked up the morning paper. Not surprisingly, there was nothing in it about the kidnapping. It had happened too late at night to make the first edition.

Tom, who couldn't have gotten to bed any earlier than I, looked surprisingly alert—bright-eyed and bushy-tailed, as my mother used to say. "I appreciate you coming in early," he said.

"I bet you do." I laughed.

"It's a figure of speech."

Tom, I could see, was quite literal-minded.

"Anything developed in the case?" I asked. "Ransom demands? Positive IDs? Anything at all?"

"Nothing major that I'm aware of. There's a team out at the house with Weston. The technicians did lift some prints off the state car and we're running them now."

"Maybe I'll find a familiar face in your books," I said, hopefully.

"Let's go see."

Edleson led the way to the archives. I hadn't spent much time in headquarters during my days with the Bureau. He hadn't, either, he told me. Normally he worked out of the field office in Baltimore. I thanked him for coming down to the District to meet with me.

"I had a couple of other errands to do down here," he said, as we sat down at a big worktable piled high with mug books.

"Connected with the case?"

"Sort of."

"Care to elaborate?" I asked.

"Len wanted me to check you out."

"Oh, he did? Why's that?"

"Just to know who we're dealing with. He figured you could be real helpful, because of your relationship with Weston."

I felt like asking what sort of relationship he thought we had, but on second thought I felt it wouldn't sound professional. I let him have his assumptions. At least for now. "So tell me," I said, "what impression does my file give?"

"A-number one," he replied. "I wouldn't have brought it up if it was otherwise. Based on your performance ratings, you never should have left the Bureau."

"I developed an allergic reaction to lead."

"Yeah, I saw that."

"So what's the bottom line, Tom? Can I be trusted?"

"That really wasn't the issue. Len just wanted to make sure you weren't a flake. I did have a question, though. We weren't real clear on your official status in the case."

"You mean with Kyle."

"Yes."

"I don't have one. For the moment, let's just say I'm an interested friend of the family."

Tom Edleson brushed back his short blond hair. "Can I assume you're willing to talk frankly?"

I gave him a quizzical look, not sure what he was getting at. "You have anything in particular in mind?"

"Well, Len liked your theory that the woman, Camille Parker, might be involved in an extortion plot."

"It's not so much a theory as a possibility I raised."

"Well, maybe you're psychic then, Darcy, because I did some checking on Ms. Parker. The result is a little surprising."

"I take it you aren't going to leave me hanging."

He grinned. "First thing this morning I ran her through the computer. What I found was that the lady is not much of a lady. To be more precise, she has a pretty shady background, including a criminal record. Nothing heavy-duty or recent—mostly nickel-and-dime stuff. Solicitation, possession, that kind of thing. She's never done any real time apart from a few days in the county jail here and there, but she's definitely not the type of woman you'd expect to be involved with a family like the Westons."

"With Dale Weston," I corrected.

Edleson shrugged. "She and her baby were living at Kyle's place."

"But you know why, Tom. What Kyle did, he did for his brother and his brother's family."

"Regardless, you've got to ask yourself why."

"You clearly have," I said. "What are your conclusions?"

"Don't have any," he replied. "We're just talking here, kicking ideas around. I'm interested in your opinions."

"So ask me a question."

"How long have you known Dale Weston was the father of the baby?" he asked.

"I found out when you did—last night."

"You think it's a straight story?"

"You mean, do I think Kyle's lying about it?"

"Or was misled."

"By who?" I asked. "Dale or Camille?"

"Either, both. I don't know."

"I assumed it was true, but now that you mention it, proof positive might require some DNA testing. If it's important, it probably could be arranged, couldn't it? Dale's only been dead a couple of months."

"I'm just talking off the top of my head," he said.

"So where's this leading?"

Edleson thought for a moment or two. "With the natural father dead, there's one less person with a motive to abduct. Suppose, though, Dale Weston wasn't the father, for whatever reason."

"Then we'd have a different ball game, Tom. A dead man won't do much kidnapping." I studied him. "You aren't suggesting any intentional deception, are you?"

He scratched his short-cropped hair. "No, no. We just don't want to leave any stones unturned."

I nodded.

"Maybe, if you spend time with Weston, you can be alert for evidence pointing to any of these possibilities," he said.

"Sure, Tom. Once a feebee, always a feebee, is that it?"

The agent smiled. "It's nice to have a friend of the Bureau on such good terms with a principal in the case," he said.

I had the feeling I was the one being vetted. I could hardly blame them, though. It was an unusual case that was looking more and more peculiar all the time.

"Well," I said, glancing at the mug books, "I've got hours of work ahead of me and other things to do. What say we get started?"

Tom Edleson left me alone and I went to work. Every once in a while he came to check on me, bringing coffee. Around eleven he brought more coffee and a doughnut, which I ate, only because I'd always had trouble turning down free food. I asked if there'd been any developments out at the farm. He told me that there hadn't been any ransom calls.

"What do we have?" I asked. "Timid kidnappers, or kidnappers with motives other than money?"

"Your guess is as good as mine, Darcy," he replied.

On his next visit I was informed that the computer couldn't do a make on the prints they'd gotten off the state police car and that there still had been no ransom call.

"I'm getting a funny feeling, Tom," I told him. "Those boys were pros. Maybe they had something in mind besides Kyle's money."

"If you're right, the woman, Camille, is off the hook, too," he said.

Edleson left and I sat wondering where things were headed. If extortion wasn't the motive, and if Camille was clean, who had reason to kidnap that baby? Could Len Barnes be right that maybe Dale Weston wasn't the father, after all?

The mug books turned out to be a bust. The heavy, sweating, bogus cop had either gained fifty pounds and twenty years, had had a sex-change operation, or simply wasn't in Uncle Sam's photo albums. Eventually, I gave up.

"We can have the housekeeper and Weston look through them, too," Edleson said. "They might pick up on somebody you missed."

"Maybe," I agreed.

"Well, you're free to go."

I thought for a moment. "You got another line out to the farm?"

"Yeah, we got a com line so that the regular phone line is free. Why?"

"Mind if I have a chat with Kyle on it? It'd save a trip out there to talk with him."

"No problem. Come with me."

He took me to an adjoining office with a desk, a phone and a couple of chairs. He took the receiver and made the connection, asking the agent out at the farm to put on Kyle. Then he handed the phone to me and left the room. I waited until Kyle came on the line.

"How are you holding up?" I asked.

"Darcy." He sounding pleased to hear my voice. "Glad you called. Where are you?"

"At headquarters in the District. I take it you haven't heard from the kidnappers."

"No, unfortunately."

"It's hard to know what to hope for," I said. "But the best way to track them down is if there's communication."

"Yes, that's what I've been told. The waiting's not easy, though."

"I wanted to thank you for the message on my machine last night, Kyle," I said. "That was very sweet of you."

"I meant it."

A silence hung on the line.

"No news to report from here," I told him. "I had the impression last night we were dealing with professionals, and the investigation thus far is bearing it out."

"What does that mean?" he asked.

"It means a pro is less likely to harm the victim. They might be harder to catch, but they're less likely to make stupid mistakes."

"I guess that's good."

"I think it's important to stay optimistic." I remembered the call I'd had from the reporter. "By the way, how do you want to handle the press? Somebody's already contacted me." I told him what had happened.

"God, they're swarming out here, especially the last couple of hours. The state police are turning them back at the gate," he said. "As far as I'm concerned, say whatever you want, except the part about Dale, of course. The FBI is handling all questions about the investigation."

"My instinct is not to grant an interview," I said. "Hopefully the woman who called is the only one I'll hear from."

"Don't count on it. They're persistent."

The circumstances weren't easy ones in which to have a conversation. I could tell Kyle was as aware of that as I. But talking to him was somehow reassuring. I found myself wanting to linger on the line.

"You know, Darcy, I feel we haven't really finished our conversation. If you happen to be out this way, feel free to drop in."

I laughed. "I can't think of any business I've got in your neighborhood, but I'll be thinking of you."

"How about coming out for dinner one evening? I've sent Mrs. Mitchell to her sister's for several days' rest, but I'm not a half-bad cook. You could do worse, believe me."

"It's an enticing offer, but I think you've got a lot on your plate as it is."

He laughed. "Well, if I can't charm you into coming, how about a business proposition?"

"What sort of business proposition?"

"I want to hire you to help find Andrew and Camille. We never came to a bottom line on the subject."

"I'm flattered, but to be honest there's nothing I can do that the FBI and the police aren't already doing."

"Are you saying my money's no good?"

"I'm saying there's no point in wasting it. But I do plan on staying in touch with Barnes and Edleson. If I get any ideas or suggestions, I'll pass them on. And if you feel you need a sounding board, give me a call. Whether I work for you in a formal capacity or not, you're still a friend of the family, Kyle."

I heard him sigh. "I appreciate that. And I will call you, if only to keep you posted."

"Thanks," I said. "Keep your spirits up."

I hung up the phone, knowing I'd done the right thing, but feeling a bit sad, just the same. My thoughts and prayers would be with Kyle, but for my sake, if not his, I knew I had to go on with my life.

7

KATE KELLMAN, THE CUB reporter, was waiting at my door when I got back to Georgetown. I gleaned that I was one of her first assignments, so, taking compassion on her, I consented to a brief interview. We talked for about fifteen minutes. Essentially she wanted an eyewitness account, so I walked her through the crime, giving as much detail as I could remember.

"What were you doing at Mr. Weston's farm?" she asked. "Had he hired you for something?"

"No," I told her. "It was just a coincidence. He's an old family friend."

Kate made a note. I worried how the "old family friend" epithet would read. But if I'd said Kyle was consulting me on a professional matter, she'd have wanted to know *what* professional matter. Even more questions would have been raised.

"Did you know the baby's mother, Camille Parker?" she asked.

"No."

"But if you're a family friend, you must know about her relationship with Mr. Weston."

I could see where this was headed. "Look, I'm not going to discuss Kyle's personal life. If you have questions about that, you'll have to talk to him."

Kellman was not pleased with my stonewalling. She had a few more questions. Some I answered, some I didn't. Then I politely ended the interview and ushered her out the door.

There were more messages on my machine. One was from an assistant producer for the news department of one of the local TV stations. I didn't return the call. The next was from one of my lawyer clients, and the last from Dave Hirsch.

"The neighbors report no noxious odors coming from your place. That means you're probably still alive and haven't been cooking recently. How about inviting me over for Monday Night Football?"

I had to laugh. Dave knew me too well. The prospect of kicking back with a beer and watching a football game was certainly appealing. And Dave, with his good sense of humor, would be a welcome distraction. I called his office. He was the sales manager for a software firm in Arlington.

"Come on over," I invited. "But you provide the beer."

"What will you provide? Or is it ungentlemanly to ask?"

"Get your mind out of the gutter, Hirsch," I said. "I'm providing the popcorn."

"Okay, but maybe you'd better let me make it."

"It's microwave popcorn, Dave. I can handle that, for cripes' sake."

"Well, I suppose I can trust you with the microwave."

"Shut up or I'm withdrawing my invitation. Think what you are doing to my self-confidence."

"Honey, with legs like yours, you don't need to cook."

"I'll take the Forty-Niners and you can have the points," I retorted, deliberately changing the subject.

"Ten bucks?"

"Twenty," I said. "I've got some making up to do."

"Darcy, you lose much more and you'll have to start paying me in kind. And you're definitely the kind I like."

"See you tonight, Dave."

Next I called my lawyer client, but he wasn't in. I left a message that I'd returned his call.

I had two cases currently in progress, but in terms of fieldwork, both were on the back burner. So I decided to catch up on some bookkeeping. Between that and some paperwork, I managed to while away the afternoon.

Around seven I fixed a TV dinner. At eight-thirty Dave showed up with a six-pack of beer and a bag of potato chips.

"What are the chips for?" I asked. "I've got popcorn."

"The chips are backup."

I gave him a whack in the stomach. Dave used the excuse to give me a bear hug. He was a big guy with dark curly hair and hams for arms. He had a lot of body hair, which made him even more like a teddy bear.

"I don't like being a teddy bear," he'd groused when I first told him that.

"Why not?"

"They don't have much of a sex life."

"No, but girls love them," I said.

"Yeah, and eunuchs have the run of the harem. Big deal."

We laughed over that. Dave and I had long since agreed to disagree about sex. But he was fun and I enjoyed his company.

I managed to make two bags of microwave popcorn without trauma, and we were ready to munch by the time the game came on. The TV was on a cart in the bedroom. When I headed back to get it, Dave said he wouldn't mind watching the game in bed.

"With innocent intention, I'm sure," I said over my shoulder.

"I've never spilled food on anybody's sheets yet," he called after me.

"And there's one sure way to make sure you never do," I replied with a laugh.

By the second quarter we'd each had two beers and Dave had wiped out all the popcorn. Even though the Niners were making my twenty bucks look fairly good, I found myself thinking of Kyle, alone out at his farm, waiting for a phone call that probably would never come. I also thought of the kiss he'd given me.

It was halftime, and Dave had gone off to use the bathroom, when there was a knock on my door. I looked through the peephole and was surprised to see Kyle Weston. I was wearing jeans and an old sweatshirt, but there wasn't a lot I could do about that. I opened the door.

"Kyle," I said. "What a surprise."

"I'm sorry to drop in on you like this, Darcy, but I wanted to talk to you. Do you have a few minutes?"

"Sure. Why not?" I moved back, opening the door wider. "Come on in."

Kyle stepped in. He was wearing a suit and tie, but had a trench coat on, hanging open. He'd been dressed casually the day before, but Kyle was appealing—dressed up or down.

He glanced at the TV, then at Dave's size-twelve athletic shoes on the floor next to mine. He did a quick calculation and turned to me, a slightly stricken look on his face.

"Hey, I'm interrupting," he said. "This isn't a good time."

"No, don't worry about it. A friend and I are just watching a football game. Come on and join us. Do you like football?"

Before Kyle could answer, Dave sauntered down the hall. He looked right at home in his stocking feet and sporting his teddy-bear demeanor. I made the introductions.

Dave shook Kyle's hand vigorously, not overly perturbed by the intrusion. He was a good-natured guy.

"Hey, have a beer with us," he said. "You and I can drink the last two. Darce loses complete control of her libido if she has three. I usually stop her at two—as a humanitarian gesture."

"Shut up, Hirsch," I chided. "You don't know a thing about my libido." I winked at Kyle. "Forgive him. Dave's knowledge of women is broad, but not deep."

"You can say that again," he said, dropping into a chair. He turned his attention to the TV. "Come on, Saints!"

"Look," Kyle interjected, "why don't I give you a call tomorrow? I was driving down Wisconsin and stopped by on an impulse."

"It's no problem, really, Kyle. If you want to talk, let's go into the kitchen."

He glanced at Dave, then at me. "Sure you don't mind?"

"Not at all. Here, give me your coat."

He slipped it off, but kept it on his arm. "I'll only be staying a few minutes."

"Keep her for the half," Dave said affably. "The Niners are no good without her and I need a touchdown pretty bad right now. Next month's rent is riding on it."

Kyle grinned. I led him back to the kitchen and gestured for him to sit at the table. In the front room the second half was getting under way. I went to the refrigerator. "What would you like? Besides the beer, I've got juice. Or I can make you some of my patented instant coffee."

"Not a thing, really."

Kyle had his hands folded on the table. His expression was sober and I knew I had to change gears to a more serious frame of mind. He had real-life problems that couldn't be washed away with a few beers and some laughs.

I sat down, trying to bring myself to a fully sober state. "Have you heard from the kidnappers?" I asked.

He shook his head. "Not a word. The consensus is building that it's not a kidnapping for ransom. The FBI wants another day or so to be sure, but that's the way it looks now."

"Any other news?" I inquired, uncertain of the cause of his pensive, worried look.

"Something else came up. I drove to Washington to deal with it. Then I started having second thoughts, and decided to get your advice."

"What is it, Kyle?"

"Sally, my sister-in-law, came to the farm this afternoon, all upset. She was in tears, actually."

"Why?"

"She had an anonymous call from a woman suggesting that Dale's death may not have been accidental, that there may have been foul play."

"What?"

"That's right. I was shocked. And in light of Andrew's kidnapping, worried."

"You mean, you feel there may be a connection?"

"No, not necessarily. But this could expose Sally and the girls to what is going on with Camille, and I want to avoid that. If I mention it to the FBI they might get heavy-handed, even if this call amounts to nothing. In fact, my first thought was it was an insensitive prank. I decided to check it out myself—that's why I came to town this evening. Then, the more I thought about it, the more I felt I should turn it over to a professional. That's when I thought of you."

Listening to Kyle, my heart rate went up, though it was hard to say how much of that could be attributed to his words and how much to his presence. "Maybe you should start at the beginning," I advised.

"Sally said the caller was very emotional and apologetic. The woman had heard about the kidnapping and understood that our family had been through a lot of tragedy recently. She had information that might bear on Dale's death and had been wrestling with her conscience for weeks over it. The kidnapping finally tipped the scales." Kyle shook his head. "This is really bizarre, Darcy, but the woman caller told Sally she'd been having an affair with a married man who owned a boat in the Annapolis Marina, where Dale kept his boat. She claimed that she and her lover trysted there regularly. She was with him the night before Dale's death."

"She said that—the night before Dale's death?"

"Yes. According to Sally, those were her words. The caller said Mr. *X*—she wouldn't say his name—and she had just made love and he went up on the deck to smoke. While he was up there, he saw two men dressed in black sneak onto Dale's boat. They had flashlights and went below. About ten minutes later they left. At first he thought they were burglars, but changed his mind when they didn't carry anything off with them. Then, when they saw in the papers that Dale's boat had exploded, they wondered if there could be a connection."

"Dale's boat exploded?"

"Yes. It was a Saturday and he'd gone down to take the boat out. Sally wasn't a sailor, so she never went with him. Their oldest girl likes to sail, but she had a dance class that day. So Dale was alone. The boat had just cleared the marina when it blew up.

"The investigators speculated that the gas tank for the outboard engine had leaked, spilling gas into the bilge pump. They theorized that the spark suppressors failed after Dale started the engine and an explosion resulted. It took a combination of unlikely events, but we were told that freak accidents of that nature do happen from time to time. Sally's caller hypothesized that the accident may have had some help from the mystery visitors the night before."

"Why didn't they notify the police?" I asked.

"Apparently they didn't want any publicity. Mr. *X* didn't want have to be a witness at a trial, or explain things to his wife. His girlfriend felt guilty all along and, when she heard about Andrew, called Sally. But she begged her not to go to the police, suggesting she find another way to use the information. Sally came to me. I thought I'd talk to Mr. *X* and see if the story was legitimate."

"Do you know who he is?"

"Sally thinks she knows. It has to be somebody with a boat close to where Dale's was berthed. By a process of elimination, she figured it was probably Ed Harmon. He's a gynecologist here in Washington."

"So we're talking Dr. *X*."

"Yes," Kyle said. "I was headed for his home when I started having second thoughts."

We heard a loud whoop from the front room. "Saints just scored, babe!" Dave shouted. "You may lose your chastity yet!"

I rolled my eyes. Kyle chuckled.

"Your friend seems fond of you," he said.

"It's platonic."

"Does he think so?"

"Well, I do, and that's all that really counts."

Kyle gave me an endearing smile—so endearing that I wanted to leap across the table and plant a kiss right on his mouth. He was presenting my libido with a problem. Then Kyle's look turned brooding and sexual. I wondered if he'd been thinking about our kiss, too. A part of me was sorry that Dave was there.

I struggled to get back to the topic at hand. "You were saying you had second thoughts about seeing the doctor."

"Yes, I was afraid I might not have the requisite finesse. Sally doesn't want to cause problems, but we both want to know if this should be pursued. I thought some discreet checking might be in order before the police are involved."

"I understand."

"Then you'll do it?" Kyle asked hopefully. "I'll pay your normal fee—double your normal fee."

"It sounds like just a few hours of work. I'll bill you for whatever time I spend."

"Add on the time you spent out at the house," he said.

"You already fed me dinner for that."

Kyle looked at my mouth. I felt such a strong attraction, I could hardly stand it. We sat for a long moment, just staring at each other.

"Getting tied up and interrogated has to be worth at least two dinners," he finally said, his voice sensuously rich and deep. His eyes shone intensely.

"I think we're square," I told him softly, my voice dropping to a whisper.

"Shouldn't we vote or something?" he asked. The corner of his mouth lifted.

"It would have to be unanimous."

"Surely you can be persuaded."

My heart was pounding so hard I almost said, "I am persuaded, I am!" Then better judgment prevailed. "I'll talk to the doctor for you," I said. "That's enough, for starters."

"Uh-oh," Dave called from the front room. "San Francisco just scored. You're looking good again, Darce."

"I think you look good whether they score or not," Kyle murmured under his breath.

My cheeks colored.

"When will you talk to the doctor?" Kyle asked.

"Tomorrow, if I can arrange it."

"When can I expect a report?"

"How quickly do you want it?"

"As quickly as possible."

I knew we were talking about a job, but judging by the electricity going back and forth between us, the subtext was about something entirely different—us. I swallowed hard, unable to suppress the lump in my throat.

"I'll call you with the result," I said.

"Couldn't we meet?"

I hesitated. "Let's say if I turn up something hot, I'll report in person."

He drummed his fingers on the table, giving me a wry look. "Do well tomorrow."

"I'll do my best."

Kyle looked at his watch. "I'll let you get back to your game."

His voice was level, businesslike. The mood was broken. Yet I found I didn't want the repartee, the connection, to end. I wanted more of Kyle Weston. A lot more. "Stay and watch the end, if you wish. Dave doesn't mind, I'm sure."

"He was invited and I wasn't. Anyway, my game's baseball. The Orioles."

"They're my favorite team, too!" I exclaimed, realizing too late that I sounded overly enthusiastic.

Kyle grinned. "I've got season tickets. Perhaps you'd like to go with me, come spring."

I got control of myself. "Well, who knows. That's a long time away. Thanks for asking."

"It's an open invitation," he said, getting to his feet. "Keep it in mind."

We went to the front room. Dave had his feet propped up on the other chair and was deep into the sack of potato chips. I glanced at the TV and saw the Saints were threatening to score.

"This could be your demise," Dave warned.

"She's pretty good at landing on her feet," Kyle told him.

Dave nodded without taking his eyes off the set. "You discovered that, too, eh?"

Kyle smiled. He reached over, gave my hand a brief squeeze and went to the door. "I hope to have a report tomorrow," he said to me. Then to Dave he said, "It was nice meeting you. Sorry to interrupt your evening with business."

"No problem," Dave replied, saluting him. "I've got a good team and points. What more can a man ask for?"

"I envy your good fortune," Kyle said, with a wink at me.

Dave pointed to the set. "My good fortune is riding on the Saints' place kicker."

Kyle opened the door. "May the best man or woman win."

I smiled. "She will."

He pointed a finger at me and left, pulling the door silently closed behind him.

THOUGH THE 49ERS WON, they only beat the spread by one point. Still, they did win, making me richer by twenty dollars. I think Dave was glad to pay up. He gave me a boozy kiss goodbye, which I allowed, though the affection I treasured from the evening was the little squeeze Kyle had given my fingers before he went out the door.

After Dave left, I puttered aimlessly, trying to sort out my feelings. It was clear I'd become infatuated with Kyle Weston. Again. The proof of how silly—adolescent, even—my feelings were was the flutter that went through me when he'd said he was an Orioles fan. Would anybody but a fifteen-year-old see predestination written all over a guy who was both devastatingly attractive *and* the owner of season tickets to my favorite team? Granted, it was a step up from basing true love on a common passion for butter-brickle ice cream, but it was a small step, and I felt shame. The problem was, I didn't feel a lot of shame.

The biggest danger sign was that I kept trying to justify in my mind getting wholeheartedly involved in Kyle's case. It would mean seeing a lot of him, and therein lay the dilemma. It was a pity that things bad for you were so often what you desired most. Certain foods and certain men had that trait in common.

I went to bed that night and had erotic dreams about Kyle—another danger sign. I awoke with a somewhat more sober outlook. What was it about sunlight that chased the specters from one's soul?

I was not pleased about the prospect of questioning Dr. Harmon on a subject that could only have come to my attention via his mistress—and even less enthusiastic about having to report to Kyle about the results. Not that he'd lost his appeal. The sobering effects of the daylight simply had brought me back to earth. I probably would be better off to delay things and see if, after a passage of time, there were still sparks. But no sooner had I gone through my rationalization than I recalled Mom's comment about me fearing my feelings. Was she right?

I decided to let fate and Dr. Harmon decide. If the interview turned up something important, I'd go to Kyle and report it, as he'd requested. If nothing came of it, I'd call, tell him, and that would be the end of that. A new case—preferably one that took me out of town—would undoubtedly be the best thing for both of us. It seemed like a reasonable compromise, even if my mother wouldn't have agreed.

After a cup of coffee and a bowl of cereal, I dressed in grown-up clothes, took my purse and headed for the gynecologist. Dr. Ed Harmon's office was downtown, only seven blocks from the White House. To my consternation, his waiting room was already occupied by six women, three of whom were conspicuously pregnant.

The nurse-receptionist, a severe woman who looked over her half-frame reading glasses like she was looking down the sight of a hunting rifle, asked dubiously if I had an appointment.

"No," I said. "But I'd like to talk to Dr. Harmon about a private matter."

"I'm afraid Doctor has no free time today," she replied. "He's got patients waiting, and is expecting to have to run over to the hospital momentarily."

"This is very important," I assured her. "To him more than me."

She gave me a strange look. "What is it regarding?"

"I'm afraid it's personal."

"Then I'm sorry, I can't help you," she said, closing the sliding-glass window and cutting me off.

I was annoyed, but maintained my cool. I rapped on the window. She opened it with exasperation.

"There's really no point in taking my time," she declared sternly. "I can't help you. Period."

"Let me put it this way," I said, lowering my voice and leaning toward her. "If Doctor knew what I had to say, and he found out you'd kept me from telling him, you probably would be unemployed before he peeled himself off the ceiling. Period."

She did not look pleased, but I had gotten her attention. "What's your name?" she asked.

"Hunter. Darcy Hunter. But my name won't mean anything to him." I thought for a second. "Do you have a piece of paper?"

She handed me a sheet from a pad advertising birth-control pills. I took a pen from the counter and wrote, "Boat. Night. Boom!" Then I folded it twice and gave it to the nurse. "Give him this."

I sat down between two very uncomfortable-looking matrons. Childbirth was never one of my favorite fantasies. One look at my neighbors told me why.

I picked up that morning's *Post*. The lead story in the metro section was about a storm due to hit our area that night. In the lower right corner of the front page was an update on the kidnapping. I read it and turned to a back page, where the story continued. Then I spotted a companion story entitled, "Eyewitness Account of Kidnapping."

There, to my surprise, I found my name in print, together with the story I'd recounted to Kate Kellman. "Darcy Hunter, Washington private investigator," was the way I was identified. I looked around the waiting room, feeling as though everybody would be looking at me. My sisters appeared to have other things on their minds, however.

A moment later the door to the examining rooms opened and a man in a lab coat with a stethoscope around his neck peered at me reproachfully. He was a nice-looking guy, whose age I'd put at forty-five. He was bespectacled, slightly balding, and had a solid, respectable, good-husband-and-father look about him.

"Miss Hunter?"

"Yes."

"Come in, please."

I followed him to a book-lined office with a handsome antique desk and leather chairs. He closed the door, told me to sit down, and went around the desk, sitting in the big chair.

He folded his hands, leaned over the desk and gave me a scolding look. "What's this about?"

"I want to know everything you can tell me about the men who boarded Dale Weston's boat the night before he was killed."

He sat in silence, assessing me. Finally he spoke. "Who sent you?"

"The point, Doctor, is that they sent *me*, not the police. It's a courtesy to you. You don't want publicity and I'm happy to accommodate you, provided I get the information I want. Tell me everything and I'll go away quietly."

He acted skeptical. "What makes you think I know what you're talking about, that I can be of help?"

"I know what I know. The point is, I want to know what you know. Just tell me what you saw that night."

He swallowed hard. "You want money? Is that what this is about? You're trying to blackmail me, right?"

"Doctor, you don't look old enough to need a hearing aid. If I wanted money, I'd tell you. I don't care about what you were doing that night. I don't even care who you were with. I only care about what you saw."

He cleared his throat. "I hardly saw a thing," he said, his voice trembling slightly. "There were two men. They came up the dock, boarded Dale's boat. They were carrying flashlights. They were below for maybe ten minutes, then they left."

"That's it?"

"Yes, that's all I saw. They didn't see me. At first I thought it was Dale, but when they came out, I knew they were both strangers. I'd never seen them before."

"What did they look like?"

"It was dark. I couldn't see them very well."

"Give me a description."

He pondered the question. "My impression was they weren't real young. I'd say thirties or forties. Both were Caucasian. One was taller. They were both fairly thin. Both were dressed in dark clothes. They wore hats."

"Anything else?"

"One of them was carrying a small bag, a sort of gym bag. He had it with him when he arrived and when he left."

"Is it possible something was taken out or put in the bag while they were below? I mean, did you notice a change in size?"

"No, I really didn't notice."

I thought for a moment. So far I had little or nothing. "There must have been something distinctive about them. Voice, accent, mannerisms, something."

"If they said anything, it was in a low voice and I couldn't hear it. But now that you mention it, there was one thing."

"What's that?"

"One of them, the taller one, was wearing a single glove. On just one hand."

My heart lurched. "Are you sure?"

"Yes, it struck me as unusual."

"Do you know which hand?" I asked.

He thought. "I think maybe it was the left, but I can't be positive."

I sat contemplating him, my mind racing but going nowhere except back to the man with one glove. I'd seen a guy like that myself—in a ski mask. He had carried off Andrew.

"Anything else, Doctor?" I muttered.

He shook his head.

I rose. "You've been very helpful. I appreciate it."

He got up, too. "That's it?"

"Yes. I probably won't bother you again, but in fairness I should tell you that it's possible that what you witnessed could be evidence of a crime."

"Oh, God."

"Nobody will intrude on your life unnecessarily, I'm sure, but I figure I owe you the truth."

He looked pale.

I gave him a faint smile. "At least you have time to think up a reason you were there."

He nodded.

I went to the door and stopped, looking back at him. Like a lot of women, I'd put an awful lot of faith in male doctors over the years. I guess when you're trusting someone with your body, you expect them to be a cut above mortal men—as a minimum, at least in control of their lives. But good old Dr. Harmon had destroyed that illusion for all time. Going to the gynecologist would never quite be the same again. "Well," I said, "see you around. Thanks again."

I left the good doctor's office, turning my thoughts to the thrill of the hunt. I also had a new concern. I'd promised to let Kyle know if I'd turned up something hot. A smile touched my lips. That would teach me to make pacts with the devil!

8

IT WAS TEN-THIRTY BY the time I got to Frederick. The sun had given way to a gray overcast, as predicted. There was one private security guard at the gate to Kyle's farm, hired to keep the press at bay. Upon hearing my name, he waved me through.

Up at the house, I saw at once that the police presence had been reduced to a minimum. Having been with the Bureau, I knew their vehicles. It looked like there was a single team in residence to deal with any late-arriving ransom call.

I got out of my car and slipped my trench coat on over my navy blazer and slim gray skirt. As I walked toward Kyle's front door I glanced at the slate sky. There was moisture in the air, all right—rain or maybe snow, as the paper had said.

Kyle answered my knock, his eyes rounding with delight at the sight of me. "Darcy! Come in, come in."

I stepped inside, feeling like a shy schoolgirl. Kyle always looked good to me, and yet, at the sight of him, I had a sudden desire to shrink away. Deep inside, I guess I was afraid. Maybe my mother was right. Maybe I feared my own feelings.

"So tell me," he said. "Did you win or lose last night?"

"I won. The 49ers helped me out."

"It's a shame he had to lose, but he seemed fully capable of dealing with defeat."

The way Kyle said it, I would have thought he was referring to Dave losing me, not the bet. Maybe that was what was on his mind. I looked into his earnest eyes, trying to get myself into the sober frame of mind befitting the situation at hand.

"I promised to report personally if I discovered anything hot," I said.

His delight instantly dissipated. "Good news or bad?" he asked huskily.

"It's hard to say." I glanced around, knowing there were at least two FBI agents in the house. "Can we talk in private?"

"Let's go outside. I could use some air anyway. Just let me tell them I'm going for a walk." Kyle went off and returned a minute later. "Were you into pinochle when you were with the FBI?" he asked, getting his sheepskin jacket from the closet.

"Are the guys card players?"

"Lord, they even had me playing for a while."

We went outside and down the steps. "I take it there haven't been any ransom calls," I said.

"No."

There was a road that ran off from the house between two white-fenced paddocks. At the end of it was a barn. We headed in that direction. Kyle had his hands thrust into the pockets of his sheepskin coat. I smoothed the lapels of my trench coat.

"I talked to the doctor first thing this morning," I began. "He confirmed the story your sister-in-law got."

"Then it wasn't a prank."

"No, the details were the same. But there was one additional point that puts a new light on everything, Kyle."

Hearing the gravity in my voice, he turned toward me. I told him about the man with the single glove.

"He was one of the kidnappers!" Kyle exclaimed, his mouth dropping.

"Either that or it's a hell of a coincidence. Dr. Harmon didn't see them clearly, but the general description fits the guy who was here that night."

"Lord," he said solemnly.

"It not only means there's a probable connection between the kidnapping and your brother's death, it also suggests the boating accident might not have been an accident at all."

"You're saying Dale was murdered?"

"It's a possibility."

Kyle was silent for a long time. The news had to be disconcerting. "This changes everything, doesn't it?" he said.

"We're going to have to do some serious rethinking," I told him. "This still doesn't tell us who the kidnappers are, but it definitely raises new questions."

"The implication being that whoever wanted the baby also had it in for Dale."

"Perhaps."

He stared at the ground as we strolled. "What now, Darcy?"

"I think we've got to tell Barnes and Edleson."

"That means the whole sordid business with Camille is going to come out. Sally will find out."

"Not necessarily. But it's certainly important we find out who wanted Dale dead. That could lead us to the kidnappers, and the baby."

"I wanted to protect Sally, but I guess there are limits."

"Let me talk to Len Barnes," I said. "Maybe he and I can work something out to shelter her as much as possible."

"Okay," Kyle agreed. "Do what you think is right."

We stopped at the fence and looked out across the paddock where three thoroughbreds were grazing in the increasingly dank air. There wasn't much wind, but the clouds to the west looked dark.

I inhaled the smell of earth and vegetation and wood smoke. Winter was around the corner, autumn almost gone, the fragrance of baking apples and burning leaves with it. Christmas—the smell of pine boughs, cinnamon and mince pie—was only weeks away. Psychologically, I wasn't ready for it. Not even remotely. I was stuck in the emotional abyss between the two holidays.

"I can't fathom what's going on," Kyle said. "It makes no sense."

"Did Dale ever express fear for his life?"

"Not to me."

"Maybe we should talk to Sally," I suggested.

"I can arrange it, if that's what you want."

I watched the horses for a minute, then said, "Let's go in and I'll call Len first."

We returned to the house. Kyle introduced me to the two agents on duty. I asked them to get hold of Len Barnes for me. It took about fifteen minutes, but they tracked him down in the field and patched the call through the com line.

"Len," I began, "I've stumbled across something I think you need to know about." I told him about the anonymous phone call and my meeting with Dr. Harmon. I explained Kyle's concern about Sally.

"This is quite a development. We'll find out what sort of investigation was conducted of the boating accident. Foul play may never have occurred to them. I'll get somebody on that right away. Since you have rapport with the family, would you like to talk to Weston's sister-in-law first? You've done well by us thus far. Tom and I can follow up as necessary."

"Sure," I said. "I'd be glad to."

We agreed to touch base that evening. Barnes gave me his home number. I went to the front room, where Kyle was waiting by the fire.

"It's all taken care of. Barnes asked me to talk to Sally. I didn't even have to suggest it."

"Good," Kyle said. "I'll give her a call now. Shall I see if we can go right over?"

"The sooner the better."

Kyle went off and I took his place by the fire. It was the time of year when the chill went through to the bones.

Thinking about Kyle, I knew he was more than simply taken aback by the news I'd brought. His world, troubled as it already was, had been set further askew. I assumed he was having second thoughts about Camille. I know I was. Her disappearance had been bizarre, and given her shady background, complicity in an extortion plot wouldn't have been all that surprising. But even without a ransom demand,

Camille was the only common link between Dale's death and the kidnapping. It wasn't a stretch to come to the conclusion she might somehow be involved.

Kyle came back promptly. "I got hold of Sally. We can go right over. Their place is near Randallstown. We can be there in half an hour."

"Tell me what she knows about you and Camille and the baby," I requested, "so I don't put my foot in my mouth."

"Sally's been preoccupied with her own problems, but I did tell her I was planning on adopting a baby, that the mother was bringing it to live here until the necessary legal arrangements could be made. Naturally, she knows about the kidnapping. She hasn't said anything to the girls, since they've had so much to deal with because of Dale's passing."

"Okay, I've got it."

Kyle wanted me to ride with him, but I knew my best defense was to keep things businesslike. I told him that I had to get back to Georgetown, and that driving both cars made the most sense. With the case heating up, I hoped to get our minds off us. It wasn't going to be easy.

Following his Mercedes sedan along Interstate 70, I found myself thinking about Kyle Weston. Why, out of all the men in the world, was the first one I felt a dizzying attraction for none other than Cara's old fiancé? It was a nasty trick of fate.

Under other circumstances it might not have been so bad, but over the past few days Kyle had been under a lot of stress. And in a strange way, so had I. The more certain I was that I needed to keep some distance between us, the more I got sucked in, whether by circumstances or choice.

We left the interstate and snaked through the hills of the suburbs of Baltimore. Sally's home was in a gated subdivision called Deerfield Woods. Its curving lanes meandered past two-, three- and four-acre wooded lots with streams and scattered ponds. The houses were large. Colonial seemed the motif of preference. A few homes were already decorated for Christmas, which I found depressing, since I was the type who got my tree up, if at all, a couple of days before heading for Harrisburg.

The Mercedes pulled into the drive of a brick Colonial with white trim. Deerfield Woods was definitely for the country-club set. It was an environment that, as a blue-collar girl from Harrisburg, Pennsylvania, I didn't often frequent.

Kyle had money, too, of course—probably a lot more than Sally and her neighbors—but a country gentleman seemed somehow more a part of the natural order of things than neat enclaves of Yuppies. Or had I simply romanticized Kyle because he'd been an occupant of my mother's living room for so many years?

Kyle got out of the Mercedes and I got out of my car. We met at the foot of the steps and he took my arm as we went up. He'd prepared Sally for me, so there wouldn't be any explaining to do. As for preparing me, he'd simply said his brother's wife took herself fairly seriously, which—rightly or wrongly—I took as a euphemism for arrogance and conceit.

Sally opened the door herself, greeting us with a slightly demure, slightly sad, slightly martyred, slightly aloof smile. She was exactly what I'd expected—blond, but not too blond; pretty, but not too pretty; dressed, but not too dressed. She was Junior League right down to her toes.

Kyle made the introductions and Sally shook my hand. Though she was about my height, she managed to look down on me, checking out my clothes, obviously assessing that they—and I—were not designer. Her mouth tightened just the tiniest bit before she turned to Kyle with a smile. "I'm so sorry to have dragged you into this. I probably should have called the police. It's not as though you don't have enough problems of your own."

"Nonsense, that's what family is for," he said predictably. Kyle, I could see, was a good soldier.

"Still no word from the kidnappers?"

Kyle shook his head as he helped me off with my coat and hung it in the hall closet.

"And you, Miss Hunter," she said, as if suddenly recalling her duty as a hostess, "my apologies for bringing you out here."

"It's what I'm paid for," I replied matter-of-factly.

Sally's smile faded only slightly. "Well, come on in," she said, sounding resigned to an ordeal. "I've made some tea."

We started back through the marble foyer, but were instantly intercepted by a girl of eight or nine, who came running down the hall, a brown-and-white cocker spaniel in pursuit.

"Uncle Kyle," she cried, throwing her arms around him with theatrical excess.

The girl, Deirdre, as it turned out, was blond like her mother, her curly hair pulled off her face with a black velvet ribbon. She wore white tights and a velvet jumper with lace trim, patent-leather shoes and a tiny gold watch. She looked like she was ready for Easter Sunday, not an afternoon at home.

"Have you come to take us to a movie or out for a sundae?" she enthused.

"Deirdre, don't assault your uncle," Sally admonished. "He's here on business."

"But we can go somewhere, can't we? After business? Can't we, Uncle Kyle?"

"Not this time, honey," he said, stroking her head. "Maybe this weekend. Right now Miss Hunter and I have to talk to your mother."

Deirdre regarded me for the first time, a frankly disapproving expression on her face—as though I was the cause of her problem. I kept myself from laughing, but the truth was she reminded me so much of her mother that her petulance amused me. But before I could so much as crack a smile, Sally deftly separated her daughter from Kyle. "You've got an hour of piano yet, dear. Why don't you get it over with while we talk?"

Deirdre tromped off, decidedly unhappy. The dog obediently followed.

"Teachers' conferences this afternoon and a dental appointment this morning," Sally said, looking after the girl, "so I kept her home all day."

"Where's Julia?" Kyle asked.

"In school, thank God." She looked back and forth between us with teary eyes. "They've had school to keep them going. I envy them that."

I suddenly felt uncharitable. Sally Weston had been widowed for only a little over two months. Maybe what I'd interpreted as disdain was fear or anxiety. I saw her turn away quickly, before the crack in her composure broke. She led the way to the salon.

The room was large and formal, with high ceilings and huge oil paintings in heavy gilt frames. The chairs and divans were upholstered in Williamsburg green. We went to the main seating group, facing the marble fireplace. A gas fire added a cheery touch. Tea was already laid out on the table.

Sally deftly poured and I watched with begrudging admiration, certain she'd had classes during her formative years. This, I told myself, was the kind of woman that Kyle's family had undoubtedly expected him to marry into. And yet, I recalled that Cara had met Kyle's mother, and had been warmly received. Maybe I was being overly defensive, feeling insecure because of my own, more modest, background. Reverse snobbishness was every bit as loathsome as the more usual kind.

Sally asked what I took with my tea and I replied nothing. She and Kyle both took a splash of milk. Armed with our teacups, we apprised one another briefly. The silence ended when Sally took a sip of tea and said, "So, Miss Hunter, Kyle tells me you talked to our neighbor at the marina, Dr. Harmon."

"Yes," I said. "He confirmed what the caller told you."

Sally nodded meaningfully and sipped more tea. Somewhere in the back of the house came the sound of Deirdre practicing scales. "I don't know Ed well, but I feel sorry for him," she said. "It has to be a terrible embarrassment. I could hardly ignore what happened, though, could I?"

"This may mean your husband's death was not accidental," I told her.

"Yes, I know," Sally said, looking me straight in the eye. "I fully understand the implications."

"I realize this isn't an easy thing for you, Mrs. Weston, but do you have any idea at all who might have wanted to kill your husband?"

"No," she answered, almost too quickly. "Dale was a prosecutor, as I'm sure Kyle's told you, so I suppose there was no shortage of criminals who might have wanted revenge. But I'm not aware of any specific threats."

"Dale didn't seem worried prior to his death? You didn't notice anything unusual in his behavior?"

The pianist stopped. Before I could appreciate the blessed silence, Deirdre started in on a different set of scales. I don't know if Sally was immune or if I was hypersensitive, but I found the noise grating, particularly when a note was misplayed.

Sally had given my question due consideration. "No, I can't say I detected anything wrong. To the contrary, Dale was very happy and at peace." Her eyes got glossy again. "The four of us had been on a wonderful trip to Europe. We'd only been back a few weeks when this happened." She bit her lip. "The last three months were the happiest we'd had in years."

Her emotion was understandable, yet I sensed it was being acted out according to the book. Was I being cynical again? Or overly critical? I thought about it and decided I wasn't. Something told me that appearances were uppermost in Sally Weston's mind. I did not matter, but Kyle was family, and she was probably all too aware of the standards she had to maintain vis-à-vis him.

Playing a hunch, I said, "Kyle, would you mind going in and supervising your niece's piano practice?"

"What?" He looked at me with surprise.

"It might be a good idea if Sally and I talked in private, woman to woman."

He sort of hunched his shoulders, put his teacup and saucer down and got up. "Sure." He gave us a smile and left.

With Kyle gone, there was no longer any need for pretense. I spoke in a frank, no-nonsense tone. "I'm aware you and your husband had ironed out your troubles, but I have a hunch that jealousy or revenge or unrequited love might have played a part in his death."

Sally gave me a stony, but not-altogether-hostile look. She didn't seem quite as much on her guard. "You're asking me about Dale's affair."

"Yes."

"I don't know who she was," Sally said, elevating her chin slightly, "but I'm satisfied that Dale had put an end to it. The reason we went to Europe was to heal ourselves." She sniffled. "Dale loved me in the end. He loved me alone."

"I understand that, but—"

"I know, you're asking about what went on before. Could *she* have wanted revenge? Or was there a jealous husband? I don't know the answer to that. I truly don't."

"If you don't know who the woman was, do you have any idea where your husband met her, what the connection was?"

"Oh, he met her at work, I'm almost positive. Chances are it was some young attorney on the staff. There was a time last year when Dale was completely wrapped up in some case. He didn't get home until late. I suspect she was working with him. They found themselves alone a lot. And it happened."

I pondered her answer. I couldn't tell if her seeming certainty was an attempt to sound sure of herself, or if she had a basis for her conclusions. "Is it possible he was using work as the excuse, and he was really going somewhere else to be with her?" I asked.

"It occurred to me. But I often called him at the office late and usually I found him there. Other times he'd be gone, it's true, but I don't suppose they always . . . you know . . . did it there in the office."

"Did Dale go out much on his own?"

"What do you mean?"

"You know, go to bars, night clubs, out with the boys, that sort of thing."

She looked horrified. "Heavens, no. Dale detested anything tawdry. I'm not saying he was above taking a mistress, but my husband had his standards."

I hid my smile. "So there wasn't a history of . . . cocktail waitresses, airline hostesses, whatever?"

"No, certainly not. I believe his first dalliance was with a friend of mine, which at least showed a modicum of taste. It was many years ago and long forgotten, but Dale was discerning. If you want to track down this last one—the one that caused all the trouble—you don't have to go any farther than Dale's office. Trust me."

"You certainly knew the man better than anyone. I'll have to take your word for it." My tea had cooled and I took a long drink. "Well, maybe I should gather Kyle and get out of your hair," I said. "I've got a lot to do."

"If I'm not mistaken you came in separate cars, didn't you?" Sally observed. She paused to get my full attention, wanting to take control of the situation now that the questioning was concluded. "I don't want to impose on Kyle—for goodness' sake, the man can decide for himself—but I was hoping he'd stay for a while. My girls love him so and he's especially important in their lives since they lost their father."

Listening to Sally, I picked up on something that should have been obvious, but it had sailed over my head until that moment. She had a thing for Kyle! That had to account for at least a fair amount of her distrust and disdain.

"I can understand how they feel," I said. "Maybe I'll just tell him goodbye and be on my way."

"Let me get him for you," she offered, rising. She hesitated for a moment. "You were the detective who was at the farm when the kidnapping occurred, weren't you?"

"Yes."

"Kyle told me you were a longtime acquaintance, so I assume you know him well."

"No, actually I don't. The day of the kidnapping was the first time I'd seen him in years."

"Oh." She seemed interested in hearing more.

"Why do you ask?"

"It's nothing. I was simply trying to understand what Kyle has been trying to do. I can't imagine why he'd want to adopt a child when he could have one of his own. I don't understand at all." But then she smiled. "I suppose he's too goodhearted for his own good. He's always done things his own way. Nobody can accuse Kyle Weston of not being his own person." The last she said with noticeable admiration. Then she sighed. "Well, excuse me. I'll tell him you're leaving."

She went off and Kyle returned alone a few moments later. He sat on the sofa across from me.

"How did it go?"

"She thinks your brother was having an affair with somebody at the office—sounded convinced of it."

"Sally's proud," he said softly. "She couldn't accept the fact that Dale might have been involved with a lounge singer."

"No, she may be entirely wrong in her conclusions, but I don't doubt her conviction."

Kyle shrugged. "Then she's mistaken."

I thought for a moment. "Do you know how Dale met Camille? Did either of them ever tell you?"

"No," he replied. "But I assumed it was at the club where Camille worked. She once commented that Dale loved her voice."

That didn't jibe with what Sally had said, but Kyle was probably right—the wife's pride was blinding her. "Well, I'd still like to find out what was going on at the office. Dale's murder might be a simple matter of a convict exacting revenge. Probably no one has considered that because the possibility of murder has just come to light."

"But how do you explain the guy with the single glove being in on the kidnapping?"

"Maybe we're making more of that than we should," I said. "It could be that the Michael Jackson thing is big in criminal circles. They may not have heard it's passé."

Kyle laughed. He reached out and touched my cheek. It was a natural, spontaneous gesture, but I felt the consequences deep in my gut. Hard as I'd tried to be a true professional and focus on the work at hand, my vulnerabilities never seemed far from the surface. A look, a gesture, a touch from Kyle would be my undoing.

"Well—" I cleared my throat "—I've got to get going. I understand you're wanted here for some surrogate fathering."

"Yes, I'll stay until Julia comes home, which won't be long. What are you going to do?"

"Figure out how to tap into the gossip circuit in the attorney general's office."

"Listen, why don't we meet for a late lunch? Do you know Haussner's on Eastern Avenue in Baltimore?"

"No. I've heard of it, but never eaten there."

"Well, my dear, you're in for a treat. It's been my favorite restaurant my whole life."

"Quite a recommendation."

"Meet me there at two." He looked at his watch. "That gives you a couple of hours to solve this case."

I got to my feet. "Wonder Woman, I'm not."

Kyle took my chin in his hand. "Everything is relative. If your ego can stand it, Darcy, I think you're pretty wonderful."

I guess my mouth sagged open when he said that—not that the words were so shocking, but I wasn't quite prepared for the underlying sentiment. Where was this leading? And did I want to go there?

"What's the matter?" he asked, I suppose reacting to the expression on my face.

"Nothing," I replied, shaking it off. "I...just don't want to get sidetracked from the business at hand."

"Is appreciating you getting sidetracked?" he asked.

"Uncle Kyle! Uncle Kyle!" Deirdre cried, running into the room and saving me from having to answer the question. "Mommy said you're staying for lunch!"

"I'm staying to play a few games of Chutes and Ladders with you, angel, until Julia comes home."

She threw her arms around him. Relieved, I gave him a smile and took the opportunity to get out of there. "See you latter, Uncle Kyle." I headed for the door.

"Two o'clock. Haussner's," he called after me. "We'll talk."

9

I HEADED TOWARD Baltimore, trying to decide the best way to find out what had been going on during the last year or so of Dale Weston's professional life. I had a circle of acquaintances in the legal profession. Chances were the friend of a friend of a friend would know someone in the criminal division of the Maryland attorney general's office. But even if that got me a few minutes of somebody's time, it wouldn't necessarily get me candor. That was more a function of the person I hooked up with and how we hit it off.

As I thought about it, I decided this was one of those rare situations where hardheaded honesty would get me as far or farther than tricks and guile and subterfuge. I would try a frontal assault.

It was nearly one by the time I got downtown, where the criminal division was located. There had been a few sprinkles on my windshield during the drive in. As I walked from the parking garage to the office building, a light rain began falling. I had retrieved my collapsible umbrella from the back seat of my car and was prepared.

The main reception area for the criminal division was on the sixth floor. The person on the phones was a heavyset black woman in her early twenties.

"Can I help you?" she asked with such warmth that it made me believe she really meant it.

"I'd like to talk to the attorney who worked most closely with Dale Weston when he was here," I said.

"You a lawyer?" she asked.

I shook my head. "No, private investigator." I produced a business card from my coat pocket.

The receptionist examined it briefly. "Mr. Weston's attorney assistant was Ms. Ericson, but she's at lunch now."

"Do you know when she'll be back?"

"She didn't leave but fifteen minutes ago, so I don't imagine she'll— Whoa. Hold on," she said, looking past me. "Speaking of the devil, there she is now."

I turned. Walking across the reception area was a tiny, slender blonde in a raincoat cinched tightly at the waist. It was glistening with raindrops, the hood had been pushed back and off her head. She had a paper sack in one hand, her purse in the other.

"Glenda," the receptionist called in a singsong voice, "you got a visitor, honey."

The woman who'd glanced my way when I'd first turned around, slowed and diverted her course toward the reception desk, her brow furrowing slightly when she realized she didn't know me.

"Ms. Ericson," I said, "my name's Darcy Hunter."

She switched both items she was carrying to the same hand so that she could shake my outstretched hand. "Nice to know you," she replied, still uncertain.

"Here, Glenda." The receptionist handed her my card.

She looked at it. "What can I do for you, Ms. Hunter?"

"I wanted to talk to you about Dale Weston."

She gave me a perplexed look. "What for?"

"It's personal. I'm doing an investigation for his brother, and I have reason to believe Dale's experiences here may have a bearing on the matter."

She thought for a moment. "I think any questions of that nature should be addressed to the personnel department."

"Actually not. It's his work, not personnel status, that's at issue."

"Then you should speak to Dale's boss, the A.G. I was just Dale's assistant. He headed the division, you know."

"Yes, I understand. But I really think you could best help me."

She acted vaguely annoyed. I could tell she was a decent-minded person by the reluctance she showed to simply tell me to get lost. Some people have trouble being brusque when they're treated politely and with respect. "I can't discuss departmental business with you, so I don't see any point in talking."

"Let's just say I'd like an informal chat," I said. "As much as facts, I'd like your impressions. In a work context, didn't you know him better than anybody?"

"I guess you could say that."

"I also have some information about Dale you might find interesting," I added, playing my trump card at the moment that seemed most telling.

"Are you trying to play on my curiosity, Ms. Hunter?"

I nodded. "Yep."

She looked at the clock on the wall. "I went out to grab a sandwich so that I could eat at my desk. I've got an important meeting in twenty-five minutes. I'll give you a few minutes to chat, if you don't mind watching me eat."

"Not at all," I said, feeling the lift of triumph.

She led me back through a maze of offices to a modest space that was large enough for her desk, a guest chair, a worktable and a bookcase, with little room left over to move around. The table was stacked with files and open books. The rest of the room was fairly orderly.

She hung her coat on the hook behind the door and asked for mine. I took it off, but told her I'd fold it over my lap.

She placed her suit jacket on a hanger, slipped it under the coat, and went to the desk. Glenda was now in a white blouse and pencil-thin navy skirt. She seemed even tinier than before, overpowered by the big desk. But she did have a cute figure. She was nicely curvaceous.

Glenda Ericson was pretty in a no-nonsense way. Lightly made up, but very feminine. I wondered if Sally Weston might not have known exactly what she was talking about. I could readily see how a man who spent long hours after work with this woman could develop a desire for her.

Glenda immediately unpacked her sack lunch—a sandwich wrapped in cellophane, an apple and a small bottle of mineral water. She looked up at me. "Care for half a sandwich?"

"No, thanks. I've got a lunch date shortly. But I appreciate the thought."

"You'll excuse me if I eat, then," she said, unwrapping the sandwich.

"Of course."

Glenda picked up half. "So, what are you investigating for Dale's brother?"

Lawyers, I'd found from experience, liked asking questions a lot better than answering them. I told her I was working on the kidnapping, which she said she'd read about. She questioned me some more, which was okay because it was building a sense of obligation. She'd eaten half her sandwich before she was through interrogating me.

"What brings you here to ask about Dale's work, Ms. Hunter?" she asked, yielding the floor.

"It's Darcy," I corrected. "Since I know your time is short, I won't play around. I have reason to believe that Dale Weston was murdered."

Glenda froze, then blanched. She'd stopped chewing and resumed only after a long moment. "Murdered?" she echoed after swallowing.

"Yes."

"What makes you think so?"

"Circumstantial evidence that came to me quite by chance."

"Shouldn't you be talking to the police?"

"I've informed the FBI. Presumably they're talking to the local authorities. I'm not sure in whose jurisdiction the case falls."

Glenda gave me a long pensive look.

"Can I be blunt?" I asked.

"We haven't exactly been coy with each other," she replied. "Go ahead."

"I'm not interested in conducting a murder investigation—the cops will do that—but it would help my other investigation to know who had a motive to kill Dale Weston."

Glenda took a drink of mineral water, then blotted her lips with a napkin. "Two minutes into this conversation and you want me to name a murderer?"

"How about a category of murderers?"

"There are numerous files filled with names of people who didn't care for Dale. That's true of any prosecutor. The longer a person does this kind of work, the longer the list gets, which means Dale's list would have been substantial."

"Is there anyone over the past year or so who made threats against his life? Did Dale ever express a fear that he was being marked for murder?"

"He was as aware as any of us of that danger. But if you're asking if there were specific threats, I'd have to say no. Not to my knowledge."

I ventured a low trump card. "Would Dale have told you, Glenda, if there had been a threat on his life?"

She hesitated only a moment. "You're asking what sort of personal relationship we had, whether Dale confided in me."

I nodded without letting my expression change, though Glenda's nimbleness of mind was truly impressive. Lawyers as a group were pretty sharp, I'd discovered, despite the occasional dolt in their ranks.

"Since we're talking frankly," I said, "what was your relationship with Dale?"

Glenda looked at me directly, and without flinching. "Professional. Entirely professional."

Assessing the situation, I decided I'd either had an entirely honest answer, or a woman who was determined to protect reputations—perhaps his, as well as hers. Something in her body language, though, told me I might have gotten the truth.

I looked back with equal candor. "Again, in the spirit of directness, what sort of man was Dale? Was he a player? Did he have a reputation around the office?"

"You're asking again about Dale and me."

"Well, for instance, why not you?"

"I told you, we had a professional relationship."

"Yes, but was Dale a flirt? Did he make passes at you?"

"Nothing serious. When men and women are around each other, the occasional lilt of an eyebrow or provocative smile is inevitable. But did he touch me or proposition me? No."

"Was there someone else in the office, then? Did he have an affair with anyone?"

"Look, this is all quite salacious and everything, but I don't understand the point. What does Dale's personal life have to do with his brother?"

"I'll change tacks. I know Dale had a mistress. I think she was connected with his work. The only way to verify that is to ask the people who knew him."

"Maybe you should talk to his wife."

"I have, Glenda. I was out at Deerfield Woods an hour ago. I had tea with Sally and listened to little Deirdre practicing scales on her piano. I'm here because Sally said this was where I'd likely find Dale's mistress."

Glenda Ericson's brow rose with indignation. "Did she say it was me?"

"No. She didn't have a name."

Glenda looked at her watch. "I'll make this easy for you, Darcy. So far as I know, Dale didn't fool around with anybody in the office. There was gossip that back in the early days he and Millicent Crosby did some late-night research at her apartment. She was number two and Dale's supervisor then, but I was in grade school at the time and couldn't tell you the accuracy of the story one way or the other. That's the honest truth." She took a bite of the second half of her sandwich.

"Then Dale's mistress was an outsider."

"I don't know."

"But you were aware he was having an affair, weren't you?"

"No, not aware in the sense that I could prove it. Dale never said a word . . . not that I would expect him to. I do know he was having trouble at home. That sort of thing isn't easy to hide when you're around someone a lot. There was gossip that his marriage was on the rocks."

"When was this, Glenda?"

"Oh, I don't know. The last six months or so before he took his sabbatical and went with his family to Europe."

I suspected that what Glenda was telling me was truthful, but, at the same time, something told me she was holding back, guarding her feelings. I wondered if, despite having had a correct relationship with Dale, she might not have had feelings for him that were more than purely professional.

"If I may put you on the spot," I said, "what do you think of Sally?"

"Off the record?"

"Off the record," I agreed.

"I think she's a bitch."

"Any reason in particular?"

"She never did anything to me. I just never liked her. She is a major snob, looking down on women who work...have a career. And she always had a holier-than-thou attitude."

I could see how Glenda might have come to that conclusion, but I didn't comment. I had the feeling I had gotten caught between the professional woman in Dale's life and the wife, neither of whom had much use for the other. What was worse, I wasn't getting anything useful.

Glenda had just about finished her sandwich and I knew my time was almost up. I decided to take a flier. "Ever heard of Camille Parker, aka Camilla Panelli?" I asked.

"Camille Parker? Wasn't she the mother of the baby who was kidnapped from Kyle Weston's farm?"

I nodded. "Yeah. Do you know her from any other context?"

"Like in connection with Dale?"

"For example."

Glenda shook her head. "No, sorry. Never heard the name before."

I shrugged. "I thought maybe he'd mentioned her."

"Is she the one you think was Dale's lover?"

Glenda wasn't going to let me get by with a thing. "I didn't say that."

"You didn't have to," she said with a little smile.

"Lawyers can really be smart-ass," I teased.

"Yes, I know. I'm making the mistake of marrying one. Rich is a lobbyist in Washington."

"Oh, you're engaged?"

She nodded.

"Is this recent?"

"Last summer," she said.

"Congratulations."

"Thanks." Glenda looked at her watch.

"I'd better get out of your hair," I said, beating her to the punch. "I appreciate you shooting the breeze with me."

"That business about Dale's death possibly being murder wasn't B.S., was it?"

"No."

"Then the police will probably come looking for someone with a motive, just like you did."

"It's not a bad bet."

"Well, they'll get the same answers from me."

I stood and put on my trench coat. "That's reassuring." I reached across the desk and shook her hand. "Thanks for your time, Glenda."

"I'm curious," she said. "Why do you think Camille Parker is connected with Dale's murder?"

I gave her an admiring look. "You must be a hell of a prosecutor."

She smiled.

"Nice that these days you don't have to sleep your way up the ladder, huh?"

She nodded and laughed.

"But to answer your question, Glenda, I have reason to believe the same man was in on both crimes."

She picked up her apple and tossed it up and caught it. "Interesting."

"If anything should come to mind, would you give me a call? You've got my card."

"Sure thing."

I smiled and left.

I MADE IT TO HAUSSNER'S at two on the nose. The restaurant was in a commercial district, in a building converted from what had once been three row houses. I parked up the street, walking from there in a light rain.

The restaurant, I discovered, was on three levels. It was very old-world, with dark woods throughout, and the walls were literally covered with paintings, including some by the Masters. Kyle was waiting just inside the door. He must have arrived only minutes earlier; his hair was still wet.

"How'd the piano lesson go?"

He gave me a sardonic smile. "I love my nieces, but a little time with them goes a long way. They're needy now, so I refuse to let something like a lack of musical talent get in the way of my obligation."

"You're a saint, Kyle."

"Was that sarcasm?" he asked, slipping his hand around my waist and giving it a squeeze.

I tried not to notice. "No. I just know I'm not so giving."

"If they'd been Cara's, you would be." The words had slid off his tongue naturally and innocently. It was the first time he'd mentioned my sister since the night of the kidnapping.

An awkward moment passed between us, broken only when the maître d' advised us that our table was ready. He led us to it. On the way Kyle pointed out a Rembrandt and a Van Dyke.

"Originals?" I asked.

"Yes. There are museums that envy this collection."

After we were seated I glanced at surroundings that were not only old-world, but old-money, as well. But I was too preoccupied with Kyle to appreciate the place the way I should have. I was uncomfortable because I sensed this lunch was about us. I wasn't sure I was prepared for that.

"So you've been coming here all your life," I said.

"Dale and I came here with our parents once or twice a month as boys. My father loved it, for the food as well as the art."

I had a mental image of Kyle and his brother as young boys seated at a table with their parents. I imagined Mrs. Weston in a silk dress and pearls, her hair coiffed just so, her doctor husband slightly bored, slightly smug, as he oversaw his family.

I knew that both his parents had been dead for some time, though Cara had met his mother. I recalled my sister telling Mom and me what a wonderful big house they'd had, and how going there she'd felt like Cinderella at the ball.

"It's been a while since I've been here," he remarked, glancing around pleasantly. "It brings back memories."

"I'm sure it does."

The waiter came. I selected a seafood salad. Kyle asked for broiled sole. At his recommendation we each had a cup of lobster bisque. The wine steward brought a white Bordeaux that was one of Kyle's favorites.

"I don't care to drink any wine," I told him. "Not when I'm driving."

"Just have a sip or two for taste," he coaxed.

"It's a shame to waste all that wine just to have a few sips, not to mention the money."

Kyle considered my comment. "You're right." Turning to the wine steward he said, "Scratch the wine. Bring us mineral water instead."

The man left and I suddenly felt terrible. "I'm sorry, Kyle. I shouldn't have interfered. If you wanted wine, you were perfectly entitled to it. I guess abhorring waste was ingrained in me. It's my working-class mentality."

"There's no virtue in being profligate," he said. "You were right."

We exchanged long looks and I knew that everything that had been troubling me was coming to a head. The problem wasn't that I had a blue-collar background and Kyle was rich, or that he was my client and our relationship was supposed to be professional. The problem was Cara.

More than anything, I was angry with myself. I'd let the situation get out of control. And the only way to take control now was to be deadly honest.

"Kyle," I began, "we have to talk. This isn't a business lunch, and it's not really about us, either."

He blinked. "What is it about then, if you don't mind my asking?"

"Cara."

He leaned back in his chair, his expression turning sober.

"I'm sorry to be so blunt about it, but it's been bothering me and I think it's high time we talked about it."

"I'm not sure exactly what it is you're upset about," he said. "Is it something I've done or said—"

"No," I interrupted. "I'm not talking about fault or blame. You've been going through a rough time. It's natural, I suppose, that you'd reach out to someone. But . . ."

"But what?"

I felt a terrible tension. "I'm not Cara!" I blurted. "You've got to understand that."

"What makes you think I don't?"

I took a breath. "When . . . you . . . kissed me," I stammered, "you weren't kissing *me*. You were kissing my sister."

"What makes you so sure?" he shot back.

"Because you don't even know me."

"Darcy, are you telling me that you didn't feel anything, or that I didn't? Because if you're telling me that I don't know what I felt, then you're wrong. Dead wrong!"

I didn't say a word.

"All right." He sighed. "Let me ask a question. Are you trying to tell me that you haven't felt anything for me? Anything at all?"

"I've felt compassion, naturally."

"Is that it?"

My frustration level rose. "Why are you badgering me?"

"I'm not badgering you," he replied. "I'm trying to get you to understand what you're saying."

"I'm simply trying to get this in perspective."

He folded his arms and contemplated me. "What are you afraid of, Darcy?"

"I'm not afraid of anything. I'm being levelheaded."

"Hardheaded is more like it."

"You aren't suggesting we get involved, are you?" I asked with dismay.

"I'm suggesting we let the chips fall where they may. Admittedly, we've got a lot on our plates right now, but is there any harm in keeping an open mind?"

I gave him a sharp look. "I never should have agreed to this lunch."

"You brought it up," he argued.

"If so, I apologize."

An uneasy calm settled over the table. Neither of us spoke for a couple of minutes. All the while Kyle's eyes were on me. I shifted uncomfortably.

"Let's say hypothetically I am attracted to you," Kyle finally said. "Is there anything wrong with that?"

"Yes," I replied, "there is."

"Would you care to elaborate?"

"It's very simple. I'm not interested in having that kind of relationship. True, I'm fond of you. I feel tremendous compassion for you and I want to help you."

"I still say you're afraid."

"I am not!" I snapped. I'd said it a little too loudly and heads turned our way. I lowered my voice. "I don't know why you don't understand. If you want a relationship so badly, why don't you have one with Sally—or someone like her, for heaven's sake."

"Sally?"

"Yes. I was in her house this morning, watching the tea ceremony, saying to myself, 'This is the sort of woman Kyle should be married to.' My God, the woman has more breeding and training for the role than a racehorse has for racing. I'd be willing to bet she'd be receptive."

"Darcy, for God's sake, she's my sister-in-law!"

"That doesn't mean that after a decent interval you couldn't—"

"Listen," he said, cutting me off, "I don't know how you got this bug in your ear, but you can forget it."

"Oh, Kyle," I snapped, getting to my feet and throwing my napkin down on the table, "you don't understand women. Sally would marry you in a minute. Well, no, that's not quite right. It wouldn't look right. In a year."

Kyle shook his head in disbelief. "Where are you going?"

"To the ladies' room," I muttered between my teeth. "Is that all right?"

He laughed. "Be my guest."

I stomped off, noticing I'd gotten the attention of nearby diners. But I didn't care. I was thoroughly annoyed. Kyle had all but propositioned me! The nerve!

By the time I got to the ladies' room, I'd calmed down. I'd overreacted, that was evident. Kyle was still in love with the memory of my sister. Why couldn't the fool see it? Why were men such idiots when it came to relationships?

Sally knew what sort of woman he needed. I could see that, too. Why couldn't *he?* How his brother had let himself get mixed up with a lounge singer was a major mystery. It would have been understandable if he'd at least had the good taste to have gone after Glenda Ericson. It wouldn't have surprised Sally; it wouldn't have surprised Glenda; it wouldn't have surprised me. Men. They were like babes in the woods.

After I'd freshened up and allowed time for the fire to fade from my cheeks, I returned to the dining room, determined to get things onto a less emotional track. I hadn't even told him about my visit to the criminal division of the A.G.'s office, and that was the supposed purpose of the lunch.

I found Kyle staring into space, absently drumming his fingers on the table when I got there. The mineral water had arrived, as well as a basket of German breads. Seeing me approach, Kyle got to his feet. The pleasant expression I affected put him at ease.

"I'm sorry," I began, before he could speak. "I didn't mean to get so emotional. It wasn't very professional of me."

"The hell with professional and unprofessional," he said. "I'm concerned that I offended you."

"No. You didn't. Not really. Maybe we're both a little jumpy. I was hoping to have gotten something at the A.G.'s this afternoon, but I didn't. Maybe that put me in an off mood."

"It didn't go well?"

"It was more or less a bust."

"What happened?" he asked, offering me some bread.

I gave him a summary of my conversation with Glenda Ericson. "Between her and Sally, I'm inclined to believe Glenda, though I think Sally was equally sincere. Camille was apparently Dale's only outside interest, and I believe he was very discreet about the affair and kept his involvement away from people in the office."

"Then there's still no way to connect the kidnapping and Dale's murder—if that's what it turns out to be."

"That's the way it appears at the moment. But I'll be talking to Len Barnes tonight. Maybe he'll have turned up something today."

The lobster bisque arrived and my appetite suddenly sharpened.

"Well," Kyle said, taking his soupspoon, *"bon appétit."*

"Bon appétit," I echoed, feeling a bit the fraud. Families that vacationed in Europe said things like *bon appétit*. Families like mine said "Pass the potatoes."

I tasted the bisque. It was exquisite. I could be a cop's daughter and still know a good soup when I tasted one.

I looked at Kyle. In spite of his calm demeanor, I figured he was still smoldering over our tiff. But that didn't matter so long as my words had opened his eyes. It did annoy me, though, when he'd insisted that I was the one with the problem—that I was afraid. It sounded too much like my mother's drumbeat about me fearing my feelings.

Much as I didn't like to admit it, there was probably some truth to it, but that was a different issue. The important thing was to get this relationship on the proper track.

"How old is Sally?" I asked when Kyle's gaze settled on me.

"Thirty-four."

"She has a lot of social grace."

"Sally was my brother's wife and therefore a part of the family. I love and respect her as such. But Sally, bless her heart, doesn't have a genuine bone in her body."

I spooned more of the bisque. "What did your mother think of her?"

"They got along. Sally's a good politician. She knows when to lick boots and when it's okay to step on toes. After you left she felt out the situation between us. When I told her how attractive I found you, she got very careful."

"You said that to her?" I asked, putting down my soupspoon.

Kyle lifted a cautioning finger. "You brought it up, and I answered your questions honestly. Besides, that was before I got my lecture."

I bit my lip but held my tongue, knowing I deserved it. "Maybe we should discuss our professional relationship," I said calmly. "Do you think there's any point in me continuing?"

"By all means. It's just about a foregone conclusion that the kidnapping was not for the purpose of extortion. I called Len Barnes from Sally's. He's all fired up on the kidnapping-murder connection you've uncovered. He told me there was debris from the explosion of Dale's boat, but not much lab work was performed on it. They're scrutinizing it closely now. He also told me he assigned a couple of men to check out Camille and what she was up to, the past several months. He's thinking along the same lines as you, Darcy. He'd like to connect Camille to someone with a motive to kill Dale."

A thought went through my mind and, even though I didn't articulate it, Kyle caught on immediately.

"Yes, I know," he said, "it might even be Camille. Barnes insists he's a long way from drawing up a suspect list, though."

"There are a lot of unanswered questions."

Our soup plates were cleared. Kyle had another piece of dark bread. He studied me as he chewed.

"Too damned bad it's not baseball season," he said. "Wouldn't a ball game at Camden Yard on a nice July or August evening be great?"

I looked toward the window, now awash with icy rain. "Yeah, in a way that does sound good."

"We've got a date, you know." He pointed at me as if to underscore the message.

The waiter brought the main course.

"How about a movie tonight instead?" he asked. "That way we won't have to wait."

"I don't think you listened to a thing I said."

"Let's make it dinner, then. A working meal."

"We're in the middle of lunch and you're inviting me to dinner?"

"You'll be talking to Len Barnes this evening, won't you? I might as well be in on that, too."

"In the morning Len or I can brief you fully on what's happened."

"I'd rather not wait."

"You rich guys are really pushy, aren't you?"

"Yeah, we get real used to having our way. Besides, I'm much better company at night than in the afternoon."

"Is that a warning?"

"No," Kyle said, picking up his fork. "It's a promise."

10

I DROVE HOME TO Washington in a steady rain, worrying about Kyle Weston. He'd insisted that he was serious about taking me to dinner. He said he had business in town and would be there anyway. I hedged, agreeing that he could swing by and I'd brief him on what Len Barnes and I had come up with.

I'd been a little heavy-handed at lunch, but at least I'd cleared the air, and that was important. If I was going to be working with Kyle, I wanted it comfortable and on friendly terms.

I got home at four. My answering machine was bulging at the seams. There were several routine business calls, an accident-insurance solicitation, an invitation to a Christmas party from one of the women on my softball team and, surprise, surprise, a call from my old paramour, Wade Armstrong. It had been forever since I'd heard his voice—or at least a couple of years. He left a number; I wasn't sure I wanted to return the call. Wade still represented all the reasons I wished to remain single.

I changed into cords and a sweater, figuring I could get in an hour or two of work, and that I might as well be comfortable. By nightfall the rain had picked up and turned halfway to sleet, convincing me it was not fit out for man or beast. I figured Kyle might well head straight home, considering the weather. In a way, I hoped he would. I didn't completely trust him, though I wanted to. And maybe, to be a hundred-percent honest, I didn't fully trust myself.

Around six-thirty, with the storm getting intense, there was a knock at my door. I decided the man must be serious. Peering out the peephole, though, I didn't see Kyle. It was someone really short with a hood protecting him against the rain. A paper boy in this weather?

Opening the door, I saw Glenda Ericson peering at me from under the hood of her raincoat.

"Glenda, what are you doing out in this weather?"

"I'm wondering that myself."

"Come in. Come in."

She stepped inside, dripping wet. Her face and shoes and hose were soaked. She had a briefcase under her arm.

"Take off your coat. I'll get you a towel." I went to the kitchen and brought her a tea towel, which I traded her for her coat. "I'll put this in the kitchen," I told her. When I got back she was dry, smiling slightly, and looking a tad less crisp than she had that afternoon.

"What brings you to Washington on a night like this?" I asked, gesturing for her to come and sit.

She joined me in the sitting area, taking one of the easy chairs. "I was coming down to be with Rich tonight, and decided I'd drop by. It was only a few blocks out of my way. I hope you don't mind."

"No, not at all. To what do I owe this pleasure?"

"After you left, I got to thinking about Camille Parker. I decided that just because I hadn't heard of her, didn't mean she was never involved in a criminal case. So I ran her name through our computer, but came up empty."

"Her real name is Camilla Panelli."

"Yes, I know. I checked that, too. Nothing. Then I talked to one of the old hands around the office, a guy named Sid Wallerman. He worked closely with Dale before I was hired. The long and short of it is, Sid remembered Camilla Panelli. She was a potential witness in a racketeering case that came through the office about six months before I arrived."

"You're kidding."

"No. Sid told me Camille was involved with a Baltimore gangster by the name of Eddie Dee. She was his girlfriend, gun moll, whatever. Dale planned to use her testimony against Dee in exchange for immunity. According to Sid, Dale personally spent a lot of time with her, trying to get her cooperation. He insisted on handling it himself, shutting the other attorneys out. Sid said eventually Camille became a nonissue when the case against Eddie Dee collapsed."

"You mean they didn't prosecute the case?"

"No, it was closed, the indictments squelched. But it didn't matter because the feds were prosecuting a parallel case against Dee for mail fraud, conspiracy and income-tax evasion. They got him. I called to check what happened. Eddie Dee was convicted and got fifteen years."

"So Camille was just a footnote in a case that never went anywhere," I said.

"That's the way it looks. I was curious about what was in the file, though, and checked it out. The surprise was that all the documentation concerning Camille was removed. And as best I could tell, that's all that was missing."

"Very interesting."

"I know you're trying to find that baby," Glenda continued. "And I don't know whether this connection between Dale and Camille is critical to that or not, but if it is, I wanted you to know about it." She fingered her briefcase. "I brought the Eddie Dee file with me. I'm not supposed to take it out of the office except on official business. I can't leave it here, but I thought I'd let you have a peek, in case you can find something interesting that I may have missed."

"Glenda, you're an angel."

The light wasn't very good in the front room and we couldn't both get behind my desk, so we went to the kitchen to study the file. I knew Glenda had more enticing company waiting for her, so I paged through the file as quickly as I could, on the alert for something that might be useful.

Camille's old boyfriend, Eddie Dee, would have made a likely suspect, were he not in prison. The scenario was clear. In the course of making his case, prosecutor gets to know gangster's girlfriend. Gangster gets sent up the river; prosecutor has affair with girlfriend and gets her pregnant.

That could explain why Eddie Dee might want Dale dead, but it didn't explain the kidnapping, nor did it explain the timing. Why wait until now, months after the pregnancy and months after Dale and Camille were history? I knew a well-connected gangster could exact revenge from inside prison walls, but a few things still didn't add up. Why had Camille disappeared? What benefit could be gained by kidnapping the child of a man who was dead?

Contained in the file were summaries of interviews conducted by the police. Organized crime wasn't my thing, but it appeared that the names I was looking at were the who's who of Baltimore gangland. I asked Glenda if she knew about any of the characters in the file, and she told me organized crime wasn't her thing, either, though some of the personalities she was familiar with through office gossip.

I was randomly perusing the bios of the individuals who'd been indicted along with Eddie. Something caught my eye in the piece on Tony Toretti. "This guy is married to Eddie Dee's sister, Anna," I said.

"Wouldn't surprise me. They intermarry like rabbits," Glenda declared. "Easier to trust your wife if she's also your buddy's sister."

"Yeah. I get the point. Do we know what's happened to Tony?" I asked. "It says here he was Eddie's lieutenant."

Glenda looked at the name. "If I'm not mistaken, he also went up with Eddie in the federal case. I think they're both out of action. Sid gave me the entire rundown. Why?"

I shrugged. "I don't know. It occurs to me Anna might be an interesting person to talk to, what with both a husband and a brother in the slammer. Do you suppose this address is still good?"

"Not for Tony," Glenda said with a laugh. "But it might be good for her."

"Mind if I jot the information down?"

"Be my guest. The fact that I'm here with this file at all could cost me my job."

"Sometimes the ends do justify the means."

"Never say that to a lawyer," Glenda warned. "At least, not to an honest one. Don't you know, to us form is as important as substance?"

"For me the issue is that baby," I said.

"Well, I'm a woman, too. And we can be very practical when we have to, right?" She said it with a small smile.

I copied the information I needed and handed the file to her. "Get this back to its home tomorrow first thing," I advised. "The FBI will come around eventually. They'll be more thorough than I, but I find sometimes it works just as well to operate on instinct." I winked at her. "It's also a lot quicker."

Glenda got up and put her raincoat back on. "I hesitate to say give me a call if I can be of help, but I suppose that's the way I feel. I liked and respected Dale even though, like us all, he had his faults."

"Thanks, Glenda."

She was no sooner out the door than I phoned Len Barnes at home. His wife told me he was in the shower and she'd have him return my call shortly.

While I waited I sat in my bay window, listening to the sleet pinging against the glass. The globe on the lamppost up the street shimmered through the sheets of water on the black windowpane. If Kyle was coming, he would be arriving at any time. A stab of disappointment went through me when I considered that he might have decided to flick it in because of the weather. But then I asked myself why I was disappointed, when earlier I'd been hoping he wouldn't show up.

I heard my mother's voice answer the question—"Darcy, you're afraid of your own feelings."

Everyone had their fears—I recognized that—but it bothered me that Kyle had seen mine. I didn't want him to like me for the wrong reasons. And worse, I didn't want to let myself care for him, knowing he was confused. But I was also worried what would happen if it really was me he was reacting to. What if Kyle did care?

I allowed myself to fantasize. I pictured myself in that farmhouse out near Frederick. I saw us taking long walks on summer evenings. I saw us in the box seats at Camden Yard. I saw us sipping sherry by the fire on a winter eve. I saw us decorating our Christmas tree together, and hanging mistletoe.

It all made for a lovely fantasy, yet there was something missing. Something important. It was me; who I was—my work, my career, my identity. Cara, in the thrall of young love, had found ecstasy in the notion of being Mrs. Kyle Weston. Her dream was to live with her prince and have his babies. I wondered if, in some silly, sentimental way, that was still Kyle's dream. How could I be sure he wasn't trying to relive the Cara fantasy, if not find Cara herself?

Out the window I saw a man in a sheepskin jacket at my gate. He dashed up the steps in the pouring rain. I had just enough of a glimpse of him to see that it was Kyle.

I opened the door and found him on the porch, looking pathetic, like a refugee from a hurricane. His hair was soaked and so was his face. I beckoned him in. He was dripping worse than Glenda.

"I wonder if my flood insurance will cover this," I said, glancing at the floor.

"My house is on a hill. You can always come and live with me," he offered.

"The water will have to rise a few more feet before I get that desperate," I chided.

Kyle reached out and pinched my cheek. His fingers were cold as ice.

"How'd you get so cold?"

"I parked six blocks away," he said, taking off his jacket. "The wind ripped my umbrella about halfway here. I barely made it. Only the thought of your lovely face kept me going."

"Watch the smart mouth, Weston, or I'll toss you back out into the deluge."

"Damsels are supposed to appreciate romantic sentiments like that," he teased.

"Not when it's business and the damsel is a detective."

"God, I love the way you say that word."

"What word?"

"Detective."

I gave him a whack and jerked the coat out of his hand. "Stay here so that you don't track water all over my house. I'll bring you a bath towel. Nothing less will do." I noticed that his pant legs were soaked from the middle of his thighs down. The poor man looked miserable. "Be right back."

While I was getting the towel, it occurred to me he'd be a lot more comfortable in dry pants, but I had nothing that would fit. Then I remembered the sweat suit that Wade Armstrong had left behind. He'd kept it, trunks and running shoes at my place so that he could jog in the mornings after he stayed over. When we split and he'd gathered his things, the jogging suit was in the laundry, and had gotten left behind.

Being the frugal type I hadn't thrown it away, but it had also been several months since I'd seen it. I searched through the closet and finally found it at the back of the shelf. I took the suit and towel to Kyle, who was standing where I'd left him.

"Don't ask me where this came from," I said, handing him the suit along with the towel, "but it'll be drier than those pants. If you take them off, I'll iron them dry for you."

Kyle examined the suit. "Where *did* this come from?"

I gave him a stern look. "I should have told you to ask if you wanted to, then you wouldn't have."

"Is it a secret?"

"No, they belonged to an old boyfriend. They were accidentally left behind."

"Did he live here?"

I put my hands on my hips, admonishingly.

"Just curious," he said, poking his tongue in his cheek. "These days it doesn't hurt to know who you're associating with."

"Kyle, you won't be associating with me in a way that it would matter if my closet was chock full of men's underwear—of all different sizes!"

He chuckled. "Is it?"

"No!"

He laughed and I turned red. He was having an awfully good time teasing me and I was reacting with the predictability and savoir faire of a twelve-year-old. I watched him dry his face and hair.

"Feel free to use the bathroom if you want to change," I said. "I'll set up the ironing board. While I'm pressing your pants, I'll tell you the latest news. We have serious business to discuss, lest you forget."

"Care to give me a hint?"

"I think I may have found the connection between the kidnapping and Dale's murder."

Kyle's brows rose. "This I'm eager to hear."

I'd just gotten the ironing board set up in the kitchen when the telephone rang. It was Len Barnes. We'd only been speaking a minute when Kyle returned, filling out the jogging suit rather nicely. I put my hand over the mouthpiece and told him to listen because I was about to tell Barnes the story.

After taking the pants to the kitchen, Kyle came back and dropped into the chair across from me, his leg draped over the arm. He was an arresting sight—the blackened window behind him, the pane shimmering with rain. I stood at my desk as I began to recount what I'd learned. The cord was long enough to allow me to pace, which I did.

I didn't want to implicate Glenda, so I simply told Barnes I'd gotten the information through contacts I had in the A.G.'s office. He listened attentively, as did Kyle.

After I'd finished recounting everything I knew about Eddie Dee, I stopped and asked, "What do you think?"

"I think you either found our man or made a damned good start," Barnes replied.

"There are still a lot of things that don't make sense," I continued. "But you've at least got a reason to pay a visit to Eddie's jail cell, and maybe get some answers."

"I'm going to make a few calls tonight so that all the data we've got on the guy will be ready in the morning," Barnes said.

"What have you boys turned up?" I inquired.

"Nothing so dramatic as what you dug up," he confessed. "But we know Camille was in the Baltimore area the past five or six months, working and looking for work. She had a fairly long gig at a place in Dundalk called The Chesapeake Lounge. Nobody there has seen her or talked to her for the past two months—roughly from the time she and the kid moved into Weston's place. She didn't associate with anybody in particular that we've been able to determine. The latter part of the summer she lived with the baby in a studio apartment in Dundalk. The landlady watched the kid while she was working. My guys talked to the woman. The only visitor Camille had was a woman. No men, no problems."

"Any specifics on the woman?"

"No. Landlady claims she never saw her, just heard voices in the hallway coming and going."

"Hmm," I mused. "This case keeps turning a different way than you expect, doesn't it?"

"Roger. Well," Barnes returned, "let me get off the phone and get to work on Eddie Dee."

"Sure, Len."

"And thanks, once again," he said. "Before this is over I'll owe you dinner or something."

"You'll spoil me," I told him, smiling. "Bye." I hung up and leaned against the desk, folding my arms as I stared across the room at Kyle.

"You're sexy when you do all that detective talk," he remarked, sounding half serious.

I shook my head. "Kyle, why do you persist in personalizing everything? You know I was reluctant for you to come over, unless it was strictly business."

He measured me. "Come here for a second, Ms. Hunter. I think we need to talk."

I strode slowly over to the chair and stood before him. "What?"

He took hold of my hand, toying with my fingers as he gazed up at me. "Your friend Dave, the fellow I met the other night. Do you love him?"

"No."

"Does he love you?"

I gave Kyle an uncertain look, not sure where this was leading. "Dave's fond of me. We're friends."

"He'd like more of a relationship than you're willing to have with him, though. Isn't that a fair statement?"

"I guess so."

"Unless I'm mistaken, Dave is allowed to make himself at home when he comes over. I mean, I did see him in his stocking feet. And I bet you're not averse to a friendly kiss goodbye at the end of a pleasant evening together."

"So?"

"So why not loosen up and extend me the same hand of friendship? I tried to make it clear this afternoon that I enjoy your company. If that makes you uncomfortable, I'm sorry. But I have a hunch—just a hunch—that if you stopped worrying and tried to enjoy yourself, we might actually have a good time."

He still had hold of my fingers. It wasn't affection that I minded. In fact, looking into his eyes, I felt sort of mushy inside. "What you're saying, Kyle, is that I'm a brat."

"What I'm saying is that you need to stop thinking and start feeling. And if it's only friendship and compassion, fine." He gave me a grin. "If it helps to pretend I'm Dave, then be my guest."

I slowly nodded. "Message understood."

"We do have important business to discuss, it's true," he added, "but we're also human beings. We have to eat and we have to kick back and relax occasionally, too."

"We also have to iron your pants," I reminded. "So, come on into the kitchen and keep me company. I'll try not to be defensive, I promise." I pulled him to his feet and he went with me, giving my shoulders a squeeze.

Kyle leaned against the sink as I arranged the trousers on the ironing board. The rain battered the window behind him.

"Quite a storm," he said.

"I'm surprised you didn't head on home and hunker down. It would have been the smart thing to do."

"I was looking forward to taking you out to dinner."

I glanced at him. "It's not a good night for going out."

"That thought occurred to me," he said, his gaze sliding down my body. "It's really a night to sit around the kitchen stove and enjoy some home cooking. But I couldn't very well invite myself."

"People do not consider my cooking a treat, Kyle. I believe I've mentioned my limitations on the domestic front."

"You can iron, I see."

I arched a brow. "One of the torture techniques I learned at the academy was branding with a hot iron. The skill has other applications, as you can see."

He laughed. I continued to press the pants, glancing up at him from time to time. There was an intense silence coming from him—the sign of a man's mind at work. I tried smiling to show that I was friendly. The gesture elicited a bit of a smile in response.

Finally, Kyle stepped over and took my arm, gently turning me toward him. I peered into his eyes, knowing what was coming. I should have realized that once I agreed to end my hostility it would be all over. There's an energy that exists between the right woman and the right man. And Kyle Weston was no fool, even if I was.

He touched my lower lip with his fingertip. We gravitated together and I surrendered. The kiss was sublime. I melted into his embrace, pressing against his hard muscular chest as our mouths met, then opened sensually. Kyle kissed me firmly but with an underlying tenderness.

His arms closed tightly around me and the kiss deepened. I sank my fingers into his damp hair, taking his tongue into my mouth. Our thighs melded. I felt his loins swell. My heart loped, excitement surging through my veins. When I finally pulled my mouth free, I sucked air into my lungs, startled by the suddenness with which I had reacted.

"Does Dave kiss you this way?" he murmured.

"No."

"That's good. I want our friendship to be special."

We hugged. Kyle stroked my head. My brain spun around and around like a top. I didn't know whether to disavow what had just happened or ask for more. My body was inclined to go one way, my mind another. This wasn't quite what I'd had in mind when I'd agreed to friendship, but it was hard to resist.

It's a terrible thing to be so confused about your feelings, your desires. I'd always been skillful at extricating myself from situations where affection was unwelcome. Yet now I found myself wanting to blindly plunge ahead. That was totally out of character, and it unnerved me even more than the affection.

"I hadn't exactly intended this," he said. "I hope you don't get that idea."

I looked into his eyes. "What had you intended?"

"To enjoy your company." He brushed my cheek with his finger. "I guess my instincts took over."

"Is that how you explain it?"

Kyle kissed the corner of my mouth. "Maybe these things aren't explainable."

I took hold of his muscular arms and eased myself away. "This is a rather intense beginning to the evening," I said. "I'm . . . a bit overwhelmed."

"Maybe that's good," he replied.

I felt an urgent need to retreat. "I haven't had time to even offer you a drink or tell you what Len Barnes said."

Kyle held my face in his hands, looking at me with a sweet blend of self-satisfaction and admiration. "Okay, I give in. Let's change the subject. What did Len say?"

I was relieved that he let me off the hook and immediately gave him a summary of my conversation with Len Barnes. Kyle listened thoughtfully. When I'd finished, I asked, "Do you have any idea who Camille's lady friend might have been?"

He shook his head. "She never discussed her personal life with me. I don't know who her friends were or how she spent her time. While she was at the house she generally kept to herself, the exception being when we discussed Andrew or Dale."

"She never had any visitors or talked to anyone on the phone?"

"Not that I'm aware of, Darcy. But then, I'm not always home."

"How about your telephone bill? Have you checked it for strange numbers?"

"No, it never occurred to me." He smiled. "I guess that's why you're a detective and I'm not."

"Let's look into that," I suggested. "If necessary I'll speak with the phone company."

"Presumably you weren't thinking of doing that tonight," he said dryly.

"No, I'll wait until tomorrow, after we've looked over your phone bill."

He rubbed my jaw with his thumb. "Are you always this conscientious?" he asked.

"I tend to get obsessed," I told him.

"As a rule I don't. But I can see how I might learn to be."

I patted his cheek. "Why don't you make yourself useful and fix yourself a drink."

"You having one?"

I hesitated, but decided maybe I could use one. "Yeah, maybe I will."

"What are the choices?"

"I'm afraid they're limited. All I have at the moment is Scotch and some supermarket sherry."

"I drink Scotch and sherry both," he said.

"Then you're in luck."

"Darcy, do you suppose this means we're compatible?"

I chuckled. "It means you're compatible with the men I've dated recently."

"The guys that go with all the men's underwear in your closet?"

I nodded, grinning. "Yeah, same group."

With my directions Kyle found the bottles and glasses. Within moments he'd fixed himself a Scotch and me a sherry. I had his pants pressed, but to get them dry, they needed more time under the hot iron. Kyle installed himself at the table, sipping his drink as he watched me.

"Tell me about the day Camille left," I prompted. "What did she say, exactly?"

"Only that she had to go away for a while. She asked me to take care of Andrew and said she would be in touch."

"Those were her words, but what was her tone, her frame of mind?"

"I think she was afraid. At the time I thought of it as simply the emotion of leaving, of taking a step—and I may be reading into the situation now—but there may have been a sort of desperation."

"You don't know why?"

"No."

"How did she go?"

"She had a used car she'd gotten with the money Dale gave her. She'd bought a few clothes and some things for the baby, too, but she was conservative with her money. Camille didn't want to blow it. She was adamant about securing Andrew's future." Kyle quaffed his Scotch, looking at me.

I hung Kyle's trousers over the back of the chair and told him he could put them on when he wanted to. He thanked me, and while I put away my iron and ironing board, he wandered into the front room. When I'd finished, I carried my sherry in and found him at the bay window, looking out at the storm. Something had turned his mood somber—perhaps my bringing up Camille.

I went over to him, putting a hand on his shoulder. "I think this business with Eddie Dee is a good omen," I said. "Somehow, he's involved. And through him we're going to find Andrew."

Kyle put an arm around my waist and smiled as if to let me know he was okay. "Yeah, I suppose you're right."

The wind blew rain hard against the window. Branches near the lamp up the street bent in the gale. I shivered. Kyle rubbed my back through my sweater.

"Not a very nice night," he said. "Not fit out there for a soul."

"That's true."

He looked down at me and gave my waist a squeeze. "Let's forget the restaurant and pool our cooking talents. What do you say?"

"I think you'd better be good around the stove."

Kyle looked into my eyes. He took my chin again, and I knew he intended to kiss me.

"If we're going to eat, there's only one way it's going to happen." Grabbing his hand, I started for the kitchen, pulling him after me. "One thing at a time, Mr. Weston."

Kyle probably took those words as a promise of things to come. If so, he was probably right. My resistance was at the point of collapse and I knew it.

"Let's see what we've got to work with," I began. "I've got to warn you, though, the selection is very limited."

11

ONE LOOK THROUGH MY cupboards and refrigerator and Kyle shook his head. "There's nothing here but canned goods, microwave stuff and TV dinners."

"I'm a professional woman, not a housewife."

He patted my cheek. "Well, you're cute and, housewife or not, you *can* iron a pair of pants."

"But I don't cook."

"Fortunately, my dear, there's a solution for every problem. Got a phone book?"

"Who are you calling?" I asked.

"Do you like Chinese food?"

"Yes."

"A lot?"

"Yeah, a lot. Why? Plan on ordering some?"

"Unless there's something else you'd prefer," he said.

We compared culinary tastes, realizing that we liked many of the same things. We did part company on sushi—he liked it, I didn't.

"Well, no woman is perfect," he declared, giving me a sly smile.

We ended up where we started—with Chinese food—and Kyle found a place willing to deliver in the rain and sleet and dark of night. We sat in the bay window, having a second drink, while we waited.

Kyle asked where I saw myself in ten years' time. I told him I couldn't see myself anywhere but where I was now.

"I think you're stuck in a rut," he said.

"Where do you see yourself?"

"With someone who cares passionately," he replied.

"About what? You?"

He smiled, shaking his head. "About what I care about and about things she cares about. It's all right if we don't agree on everything. In fact, it's better."

"That's very enlightened," I said, tongue poking my cheek.

"Don't be sarcastic. I'm serious."

"Are you going to ask me how I feel about children?"

"Should I?"

"That seems to be the conversation we're having."

Kyle gave me an appraising look. "Why are you fighting me?"

His question went to the very heart of the matter. My whole being, my very existence, seemed in question. Me, Darcy Hunter, the woman with the 9-mm semiautomatic in her purse, suddenly began to cry. I don't know why, exactly. I just did.

I didn't sob. The tears just silently rolled down my cheeks. I tried wiping them away with my sleeve. They kept coming. Kyle, seeing them, looked stricken.

"God, Darcy, I'm sorry."

"No, no. It's not your fault."

He went to the kitchen and brought me a box of tissues.

"I don't know why that happened," I said.

"Maybe you need to let go a little," he returned softly.

I wiped my nose. "No, it's probably the rain or something."

He reached over and took my hand. "It's not the rain." Then he gave my arm a tug. "Come over and sit with me."

He pulled me onto his lap and held me. The embrace was warm and more than friendly. He gave me a brief, affectionate kiss.

"I think the problem is men," he said. "You've had the wrong kind. Playing softball with them and betting on football games is fine, but it's not enough. You need more."

"Oh, yeah?" I murmured, sniffling.

"Yes," he whispered in my ear. "You need somebody like me."

Kyle was taking things another step, and I knew I should fight him. This was supposed to be a relaxed, friendly evening and he was cheating. But he'd said it so sweetly, and with such caring, that my eyes flooded again.

"I can see it," he said. "I only wish you did, too."

I bit my lip. "Please don't care for me because of Cara. I'm not my sister." Then, unable to help myself, I did begin to sob.

He gave me another hug and then looked directly into my eyes. "Don't think that, Darcy. I'm a man now, not a boy. And Cara was a long, long time ago."

"I know you don't want to think that," I said, still sniffling. "It's just . . . just . . ."

"That you want to be loved for yourself."

I looked at him through my tears. "Why am I so afraid?"

"It's a scary world, Darcy. Even for detectives."

His comment made me smile. He was dabbing my cheeks and we were trading kisses when the doorbell rang.

"That had better be dinner," I said. "I'm not up to a visitor right now."

It was dinner. Kyle admitted a slender Chinese fellow who was wearing a yellow rain slicker. He clutched a soaked paper bag in his arms as he looked at us from under the bill of his rain hat. "What a night, huh?"

Kyle paid for the food, giving the guy a five-dollar tip and sending him on his way. I carried the sack to the kitchen. Kyle followed behind.

"I suddenly have an appetite," I said, trying to make the mood more positive, upbeat. "How about you?" I began unpacking the bag and placing the containers on the table.

"Yeah. Must be the excitement. How often do you talk to someone about the things that matter in life?"

The answer to that was that I never really had. Not with a man. "Maybe not often enough," I answered, a little embarrassed.

While searching my cupboards, Kyle had spotted the box of candles I kept around in the event of a power blackout. He got one out and lit it, while I got us each a glass of water. Then he turned off the overhead light. "Chinese food is so much more romantic by candlelight," he said.

"Do you enjoy romance or just seduction?" I asked.

"I enjoy *you,* Darcy." Then he waved a finger at me. "Don't try to pick a fight just because you're nervous."

I found his insight unsettling. "Are *you* nervous?"

"More beguiled than nervous," he replied.

"I never intended to beguile you. I never even intended to kiss you. And I'd feel better if you were nervous, too."

"All right. I'm nervous."

"Don't say it if you don't mean it," I protested.

Kyle gave me the look of a stern father. "Forget that and pass the fried rice."

He was right. I passed the rice and began serving myself some Mu Chu pork. I inhaled its aroma, but my mind and body were alive with awareness of Kyle. I knew we'd passed some sort of hurdle—I just couldn't say what it was.

We passed the cartons back and forth, then began eating, settling into a companionable mood. Though the sexual tension hadn't abated, my wariness had. I was letting myself relax more than I ever had before. I was glad that we'd talked directly. I liked it that Kyle was both mature and tolerant.

I think he wanted to lower the level of tension as much as I. We chatted about all sorts of things. In the back of my mind I was conscious of the direction things were headed, but I found myself laughing and talking freely anyway.

Toward the end of the meal, Kyle got us each more water, saying that next time he'd bring some beer, a drink that went much better with Chinese food than tap water. I thought about "next time," wondering not only about that, but also about what was yet to come that evening.

After putting my glass down in front of me, Kyle put his hands on my shoulders. Then he leaned over and kissed my temple. He didn't say anything. He just returned to his seat, leaving me with a big lump in my throat.

For a while the only sounds were the click of his chopsticks and the drumming of the rain. The silence became powerful, even eloquent. It spoke of the future; it accentuated my expectation. These minutes, I realized, were a prelude, the slow movement before the presto.

I kept quiet, letting the mood build. My nervousness returned. I don't know how Chinese take-out at a kitchen table could possibly make for an erotic ambience, but it did. My whole body felt alive. I kept looking at Kyle and remembering the feel of his lips, the eagerness of his kiss, his all-but-stated intention to make love with me.

I absently sipped my water. I kept looking at him and he kept looking at me. Kyle put down his chopsticks. "Well," he said, "are you ready for your fortune cookie?"

"Sure, why not?"

He took the small carton in which there were two cookies and held it out for me to pick.

"You first," I told him.

He arched his brow. "Do you prefer others to determine your destiny?"

I shrugged. "This way I can rationalize I might have picked differently."

"Yes," he said, "but the Fates know about second-guessers."

"Shut up and pick a cookie," I replied.

Kyle took one. Breaking it open, he read, "'You will find love.'" For a moment he looked like the cat who swallowed the canary. "That is an excellent fortune," he said. "I like it a lot."

"Don't be too smug, Mr. Weston," I warned. "I might be about to discover I'm going on a long trip—alone."

"Confucius wouldn't be that cruel. But all right, enough delay. Let's find out what your destiny is to be."

My hand trembled as I reached into the carton. I put the cookie down on the table, contemplating it for a moment.

"Parapsychologists claim a ninety-percent accuracy rate on these things, you know," Kyle stated.

I gave him a look and broke the cookie in two. I read the fortune and put it down. Kyle reached over and picked it up.

"'Follow your heart,'" he read. Then he smiled. "I like that one, too."

"Don't get too sure of yourself."

"Your heart, I'm sure, is very wise."

"I think I'd better clean up," I said, getting to my feet.

As I reached for his plate, Kyle took my hand. Then, taking the candle, he led me into the front room where he put the candle on the corner of my desk. "Does that work?" he asked, pointing to the brand-new stereo Arnold Belcher had given me for Christmas.

"Yes."

He went over and glanced at the cassettes stacked on the shelf. "May I play one?"

"Sure."

Moments later my favorite jazz piano tape, Marian McPartland's "Interplay," came on. With the storm raging, the candle flickering and Marian at the keyboard, Kyle took me into his arms and we danced.

My body melted into his and I closed my eyes, surrendering. There was no more considering what was right and what was wrong. I was taking Confucius's advice. I was following my heart.

After a while we stopped moving and kissed. My breast swelled against his chest as Kyle kissed my eyes, my nose, my lips. I trembled. He held me close, his fingers exploring my body through my sweater.

Breaking my mouth free, I mumbled, "You take your fortune cookies seriously, don't you?"

"They're ninety-percent accurate, don't forget," he whispered into my hair.

I clung to him because my knees felt shaky. And my insides were seriously throbbing. It had been a long time since

I'd been all quivery with desire, wanting a man this way. But I searched my heart and knew my feelings were honest—a true reflection of how I really felt about Kyle, not merely a response to the romance of the moment.

As we kissed, our tongues moved back and forth from my mouth to his. I felt my nipples grow hard. My fingers sank into his shoulders as Kyle cupped my buttocks and lifted me hard against him.

My heart was pounding so fast that I was having trouble breathing. He ran his hands up and down my back, then under my sweater, where he unsnapped my bra. As he rubbed his thumbs over my nipples, my head fell back and I moaned. He kissed my neck then, his warm breath searing the skin and making me all liquid. There was no fight in me. If this was a battle, it was already lost.

Kyle took my hand, got the candle, then led me up the dark hall toward my room. In the flickering light he helped me off with my sweater. My nipples tingled in the cool air. He kissed them, taking first one, then the other into his mouth. I moaned again, pressing his face against my breast.

I took a deep breath, knowing that this was what I had wanted for so long—being with Kyle, loving him, letting him love me. I looked down at his head and watched his mouth on my breast. He worked my nipple, rubbing his teeth across it, flicking his tongue over my bud, drawing circles around it before taking me deeply into his mouth once more.

I sighed, wishing I could be like this forever. Before I knew what was happening, Kyle took my hand and drew it to his mouth. He ran his lips over the tips of my fingers. I took in a breath of air, the muscles in my stomach growing tense with this new sensation. Kyle dragged his prickly tongue across my palm and between each finger. I trembled. He did the other hand, making me shiver again, this time more violently.

He helped me out of my cords, then slid his hands over the curves of my hips and along my thighs. He stroked the backs of my legs. He kissed my stomach. The sensation excited me so that I grabbed two handfuls of his hair and crushed his head against me. I was craving his body, wanting the connection, the intimacy. But even as I did, I held back just a little, making him take the initiative.

He didn't hesitate. He painted my skin with his tongue and peeled my panties off, leaving me completely naked. The air was cool on my skin, especially the wet places on my stomach, but my blood was running hot. It got hotter still when he touched me, running his fingers all over me, molding my flesh, bringing it to life with his touch.

I was caressing the back of his neck, my breathing growing staccato as my excitement rose. My teeth clenched. I purred, watching our shadows on the wall. What I saw was removed from all sensation, yet it drew me. It was like watching someone else. The shadow head moved toward the breast. I saw the tongue flick out at the same time my nipple felt its caress. I threw back my head and groaned, wishing he had two tongues, two mouths.

My vagina pulsed, running with hot liquid. My knees felt shaky. I could barely stand. I felt hot and cold at the same time.

"I think we're really on to something," he said, breathing hard himself.

I could only nod.

"So many lost years," he murmured.

He pulled away from me then and undressed. I watched, but I also took the opportunity to scramble under the covers. When he removed his shorts I was able to see his penis rising from the dark tangle.

Kyle was soon beside me. We lay facing each other. We touched. I ran my hand over his chest, liking the fever in his skin, the silky mat of hair under my palm. He gave me a long, sensual kiss, then told me I was beautiful.

We held each other, reveling in the sensation. Kyle closed his eyes and so did I. After a minute he began caressing my arm and back. He nudged me and I turned over. He began kissing my back then, flicking his tongue over my skin, running it along the depression of my spine. I pressed my legs together tightly, knowing that I'd come soon if he kept this up. Never before had a man done such a thing to me. Kyle was making love to my back, and I loved it. I couldn't get enough of the sensation.

I experienced a flicker of fear. The first time with a man was always full of uncertainty. But I wanted Kyle so badly. I'd wanted him my whole life.

I'd wanted him at thirteen. I'd wanted him when all I had was my fantasies. I'd wanted him over the long years when his face and name never came to mind. I'd wanted him, even, when I was with someone else. I guess I'd wanted him without knowing it.

Those were safe ways to desire someone. This, I understood, was real and it wasn't so safe. Not emotionally. And yet, I was unable to stop, unable to turn off the road we'd taken.

Kyle inhaled the scent of my skin, savoring it. I found that really arousing. When he touched my shoulder I turned over again. He immediately kissed my chin and the soft place under it. His hand moved between my legs. Then his finger slid between the folds and entered me.

I was instantly on fire. I hadn't realized how ready I was until he touched me there. I rocked against his hand, parting my legs ever wider as he caressed me expertly. Preorgasmic ripples went through me. But I didn't want to come that way. I wanted him in me.

I began exploring his body the way he had mine. I could feel his throbbing penis against me, and I took it, stroking it, wanting it. But Kyle couldn't wait. He moved on top of me, then scooted down far enough to nip each nipple with his teeth. I groaned.

"Oh, God," I whispered, "do it more, please. Harder."

He did and I gushed with readiness. When he finally pressed his penis against my opening, I easily took him in. A rumble of pleasure emanated from his throat. "Darcy," he murmured. "Oh, jeez, do I want you."

I wrapped my legs around him and he slowly began undulating. The orgasm that had been building in me moved right to the verge. I started rocking hard against him, making each thrust deeper and harder than the last.

This was what I had longed for—giving and taking, using his body and letting him use mine. We pleasured and taunted each other, going faster for a time, then backing off, going slower in order to prolong the ecstasy. Finally, I couldn't take it any longer.

"Oh, now!" I cried.

My body surrendered to wave after wave of pleasure until I lay exhausted. I assumed that Kyle came, but I didn't know because I was only barely aware of him. Never had I given myself up to pleasure that way. Was it him?

"God, Darcy," he groaned softly into my ear as his weight settled on me. "You're fantastic," he said. "Fabulous."

Was I really? I wondered. Others had liked my body. And I'd been satisfied before, but never like this. Kyle was right. *Fabulous* was the word.

I stroked his head and held it against mine. I felt euphoria, fulfillment, but also fear. It wasn't mistrust; it was broader than that—an uncertainty about what was to come next.

The telephone rang and I jumped.

"If that's the FBI," Kyle moaned, "tell them to go to hell."

I patted his cheek. "I have to answer it, Kyle. You know that."

He nodded, picked up the receiver, and handed it to me.

"Darcy?" The man's voice was familiar, but I couldn't quite place it.

"Yes?"

"Wade Armstrong."

Good heavens, I thought. Talk about a voice from the past. And what timing. "Wade, what a surprise." I sensed an alertness enter Kyle's body.

"I know it's a little late," Wade apologized, "but I tried earlier and didn't catch you in."

"Yes, I got your message," I replied. "Sorry, I had a guest over. I didn't have a chance to call."

"I'll get right to the point," he said. "I'm unattached and I've thought a lot about you recently. I figured I'd give you a call and see what's happening in your life."

"I'm afraid I'm involved with someone," I told him.

"Oh? Seriously involved?"

I glanced at Kyle, who was watching me with shining eyes. He drew his finger across my jaw. "Yes, Wade. It's serious."

My old boyfriend fumbled a bit, which was all he could do. Then he laughed and wished me well. I said goodbye and hung up the phone.

"Wade started thinking about what he'd given up, I take it," Kyle observed.

"Something like that."

He gave me a faint, slightly self-satisfied smile. "I liked what I heard."

"What did you hear?"

"That you're involved."

"You didn't expect me to say I was right in the middle of a one-night stand, did you?"

He took my jaw in his hand and kissed my lips. "Darcy, you're involved. *Very* involved. Believe me."

"If you say so."

"I do."

I couldn't begin to understand what that meant. It was far better not to think beyond this moment. So I snuggled against him, resting my head against his shoulder. I could hear the rain beating against the window. The tape in the front room had long since stopped. The candle had nearly burned down to a stub. I put my arm around Kyle's warm body. I asked myself if this was what my heart had commanded, and realized that it was. I also knew that Kyle was right. For better or worse, right or wrong, we were *very* involved.

THE PHONE RANG AROUND eight the next morning, awakening me from a sound sleep. I was shocked to see Kyle's face on the pillow next to me. Then I remembered.

He groaned at the sound of the telephone. I reached over and took the receiver, pulling the sheet over my naked breasts. "Hello?"

"Darcy, it's Tom Edleson."

It was the second stiff dose of reality in as many seconds. Camille, Eddie Dee, Dale, Sally, Glenda—it all seemed like something from a movie I'd seen before. But Edleson's voice reminded me it wasn't. "Hello, Tom." I tried to sound wide-awake.

"Sorry to call so early. Hope I didn't wake you."

"No, no. I was just . . . lying in bed. When you write your own paychecks you can do that every once in a while."

"Well, I wanted you to be the first to know. Eddie Dee was released from prison three weeks ago."

"What?"

"His conviction got overturned on appeal."

"My God."

"We've got a bulletin out on him. We want to talk to him, as you might imagine."

My brain, still halfway stuck in dreamland, started clicking like a freshly tuned engine. "He's got to be right in the middle of this," I said.

"That's our thought, too," Edleson agreed.

"It also explains the timing of events."

"Yeah."

"Mind telling me what you're planning?"

"We'll be talking to his old buddies around town, for starters."

I thought of Eddie's sister, Anna Toretti, and almost suggested to Tom that he put her on their list of people to talk to. But then it occurred to me they'd have a lot to do, and if I were to take a crack at her first, I might be able to catch her off guard. They could always question her later.

"Good luck," I said. "I appreciate you keeping me informed."

"While we're talking, you don't know where I might be able to reach Weston, do you? The night shift out at the farm said he didn't come home last night."

I glanced at the man lying next to me. "He didn't?"

"Nope."

"I'm scheduled to meet him for breakfast later," I said. "Maybe he got stuck in town because of the storm."

"Yeah, maybe. When you see him, tell him to give us a call, will you?"

"Sure, Tom. Any developments?"

"Not other than what I just told you. I wanted him to be aware."

"I can tell him, if you like."

"Yeah, that would be good. If he has any questions, he can always call."

"Right."

I hung up. Kyle was grinning like a Cheshire cat.

"What's so funny?" I asked.

"I thought you FBI types never lied."

"I'm private now. Besides, I didn't lie. I just omitted information. I *am* having breakfast with you, aren't I?"

He started chuckling.

"Why are you laughing?"

"It was amusing watching you play detective while completely nude."

"It was your fault," I retorted.

"Do you do it often?"

"Only when sleeping with a client, smart guy. There is serious news, though." I told him about Eddie Dee.

Kyle nodded. "I gathered it was something like that."

"We're making progress," I said.

He sighed heavily. "Yeah."

"You should be happy."

Kyle took me into his arms. "After last night, Darcy Hunter, nothing could make me unhappy. I'm awfully glad you're on my team. I like your style a lot."

"We're on the same team, now? Is that what last night was about?"

"Last night was about today and tomorrow and the day after that and the day after that . . . for as long as we want."

"I'm not so sure, Kyle."

"You evidently weren't as impressed as I."

His voice had been even, measured, but I could tell he was hurt by my words. "No," I said quickly, wanting to explain myself. "That isn't what I meant at all. It's just that we've come so far, so fast."

"Maybe I'm still a bit more comfortable with my feelings than you are with yours," he returned.

I wanted to think he was right. I really did. If the previous night had proved anything, it had shown me how truly vulnerable I was. But where did that leave me?

I could hardly say our lovemaking didn't mean anything, yet at the same time I wasn't ready to make the kind of big jump Kyle was evidently prepared to take. In that sense, we clearly were in different places.

He caressed my face. "Talk to me, Darcy. Tell me what you think."

I didn't want to commit to anything right then. Fortunately I had a good excuse. Mother Nature was sending me a signal. Heeding her message, I jumped out of bed.

"Hey, where're you going?" Kyle demanded.

"To the bathroom. It's my house. I get to go first."

"I've heard of competitive feeding," he said, "but this is ridiculous."

Blushing, I grabbed a pillow, whacked him with it and ran off to the bath.

"Anybody ever tell you you've got a great ass?" he called after me.

I opened the bathroom door and stuck my head out. "Wade used to tell me that."

"Too bad for Wade. You're involved now, remember?"

"Did that call really happen? Funny, I thought that was a dream." I laughed and closed the door.

"Might as well have your shower and get dressed," he called through the door. "We'll have to go out for breakfast. I refuse to eat frozen scrambled eggs."

"What are you thinking?" I called back to him. "Chinese?"

"No, sushi!"

12

ANNA TORETTI LIVED in Guilford, an area in North Baltimore made up of fine old homes dating back to times when there were only rich and poor in the city—mansions with sweeping lawns for the industrialists and bankers, tenements and row houses for everybody else. I glanced at the homes as I drove. Dr. Weston and his wife might well have raised their sons in one of them, even though most were large enough to house a fraternity, or all the residents of Colton Street, where I grew up.

I passed a boy on his bicycle, imagining how thirty years earlier he might have been Kyle. It was strange to think that this place, this culture, this rose-colored perspective on the world had spawned him, and that now he was an important player in my life—or at least he had been the night before. Reflecting on what had happened, I wasn't sure what to think. About all I could safely conclude was that we both had succumbed to our desires.

Kyle, who I decided was less of a skeptic than I, had stayed resolutely cheerful until we parted—he to return to the farm, me to drive to Baltimore. He'd asked to come with me, but I'd put my foot down. "I like to think of myself as the Lone Ranger," I'd said. "And, cute as you are, you aren't Tonto. To be blunt, you aren't sidekick material, Kyle."

"Why do you say that?" he demanded.

"Too pretty. Sidekicks are eccentric and subordinate," I teased. "Anyway, you'd be a distraction. I've got to be able to keep my mind on what I'm doing."

He relented, but not happily. He did exact my promise to spend the night at the farm, though. I'd agreed reluctantly, fearing that running headlong into a relationship would only make it more difficult to keep things in perspective. But Kyle, I discovered, could be Pollyanna and Harrison Ford at the same time. The real question, though, was whether or not he was deluding himself. That was what worried me.

His plan was to show off his culinary skills by fixing dinner. I admitted it sounded tempting. Taking advantage of my weakness, Kyle made me pack a small suitcase so that I wouldn't feel the need to hurry back to Washington. I asked if we weren't rushing things a bit.

"It's only rushing if somebody's hurt or not enjoying themselves," he replied. "Do you fit into that category? Or is this one of those pro forma statements that women feel obliged to make?"

"Maybe it's a pro forma statement," I told him, "but women say things like this because they aren't the saps men are. We're skeptical by nature."

"So, I'm a sap?" he asked, pulling me close to nibble my ear.

"Yes, but good in the sack. For that, I make allowances."

This all had transpired during a rather extended goodbye. We'd walked to Wisconsin Avenue for breakfast, then back to my flat so I could pack. We drew out the ritual, like a couple of kids who couldn't say good-night. And like an insecure teenager, I feared that he wasn't seeing me for who I really was. I tried not to be negative, though. I asked how he planned to spend his day. Kyle said he was going to talk to Len Barnes about ending the vigil. It seemed obvious there would be no ransom demands. And if by chance one did come along, he'd handle it himself.

We finally tore ourselves apart. I headed for Baltimore, feeling more lighthearted than was either justified or wise. Despite my misgivings I was happy—happier than I could ever remember feeling before, even if I was a little scared at the same time. I even dared wonder if this was what it was like to be in love.

During the drive I put Kyle out of my mind as best I could and tried, with only partial success, to think about the case. It was beginning to look like Eddie Dee was in the middle of things. He could have had Dale killed out of jealousy or a simple desire for revenge. But why the kidnapping, and why had Camille dropped out of sight? Was it fear? Maybe she'd heard Eddie was about to be released and didn't want to be around for the welcome-home party.

I didn't know if I'd be able to get anything out of Anna Toretti. She wouldn't tell me where Eddie was, obviously, but might she enlighten me on his state of mind? That was what I hoped for.

When I came to her street, I slowed, looking for house numbers. Her place was a few doors from the corner. It was dark-shingled, three stories high and set well back from the street on what appeared to be a couple of acres. The porch spanned the entire front of the house. The front door, to my mild consternation, already sported a large Christmas wreath.

The walk was neatly shoveled—an indication of Anna's community spirit. I climbed the steps to the porch and rang the bell. A black maid in a starched white uniform came to the door. I asked for Anna Toretti and was told she wasn't home.

"When do you expect her back?" I asked.

"She didn't say, ma'am. Could be soon. She's talkin' to the people at her little boy's school."

"Can I wait?"

"I'm not supposed to let nobody in, ma'am, when Mrs. Toretti, she isn't home. You want me to give her a message?"

"No. I'll just wait in my car."

She shrugged and I retreated, wondering if I hadn't been overly optimistic about how easy it might be to get a few words with Anna. I'd just gotten to my car when a Lincoln sedan came up the street and turned into the drive. The woman driver, who appeared to be in her late thirties, gave me a wary look. Odds were it was Anna. I was lucky to catch her in the open, so I walked over to where she'd stopped the car beside the house.

She got out, watching me approach, a vaguely hostile expression on her face. She was dark-haired and heavily made-up. I wouldn't say she was pretty, but she had a certain allure. She cinched the belt on her coat as if girding for a confrontation.

"Mrs. Toretti?"

"Who are you?"

"Name's Darcy Hunter," I said, stopping beside the car.

"So, what you want?"

"I want to talk about your brother, Eddie."

"I'm not talking to nobody about Eddie," she replied in her coarse accent. "I've got nothing to say to you about nothing." She scrutinized me for a second. "What you want to talk about Eddie for, anyway? You a cop?"

"No. I'm trying to find a lady friend of Eddie's."

"So, what you askin' me for? You think I know all Eddie's broads or somethin'?"

"Do you know Camille Parker?"

"Oh, jeez," she said, rolling her eyes. "Her."

"You know her, then?"

"I heard of her. All right? That don't mean nothin' except that I heard her name."

"What's with her and Eddie?" I asked.

"How should I know? What you comin' to me for with these questions?"

"I guess because I don't have anyone else to talk to."

"That ain't my problem. All right? I don't talk with people I don't know. I don't talk about Eddie."

"Do you know why Camille might have disappeared?" I asked.

"I told you, I don't know nothin'." She started walking toward the house. I followed along.

"Was she afraid of Eddie?" I asked.

"How should I know? Talk to her, not me."

"I'd like to, believe me. I'm trying to understand why she disappeared. Do you think she was afraid of Eddie?"

We stopped at the foot of the stairs. Anna faced me.

"How does Eddie feel about Camille?" I asked. "Does he hate her?"

"Do I look like Dear Abby or somethin'?"

"Come on. You must know what your own brother thinks. Camille was his woman before he went to prison. He must have loved her," I said. "Was she afraid because she was messing around with another man? Was she afraid of Eddie's jealousy?"

"What can she expect?" Anna demanded. "No man wants his woman screwing around. This surprises you? I don't think it surprised Camilla."

"Eddie's out of prison now," I said. "What's Camille afraid of—that he's going to kill her?"

"The woman's a slut. Why would he waste his time?"

"Camille must have thought he might. She disappeared."

"So she's a coward and a slut. You want to know the problem? Eddie cares too much. Yeah, I said it. That's right. He ain't trying to kill her. It'd be better if he was. Eddie should forget about Camilla Panelli, let her rot in hell," Anna protested, getting more and more excited. "I told him that. But does he listen? Does he worry about his family, his business, his future? No, he worries about that bitch, Camilla Panelli."

I suspected I was getting the truth, but it wasn't helping me understand the situation. I decided to up the ante. "Okay," I said, "so Eddie loves Camille and wouldn't hurt her. Fine. But what about Camille's baby?"

"What about it?"

"Would he hurt it?"

Anna Toretti's face turned red. "My brother might be stupid about broads, but he don't go around hurtin' babies. What you think? That Eddie's some kind of animal?"

"You know the child's been kidnapped."

She turned and started up the stairs. I went with her.

"Eddie wouldn't hurt the baby, would he? That's all I want to know—if the baby's safe."

She stopped at the top of the stairs and glared at me. "You must think I'm stupid. You accuse Eddie of bein' a kidnapper and you want me to say yes, he is? You're nuts!"

"Anna," I said, "I'm just trying to find out what's happened to Camille and her baby. I want reassurance, that's all."

"You ain't getting nothin' from me except goodbye. I know what you're doin'. So get your ass off my property before I call the cops. Or worse."

I decided to throw caution to the wind. "Just tell me one thing," I urged, as she rummaged through her purse, looking for her keys. "Why was Dale Weston murdered?"

She looked up at me, her face turning scarlet. "You got mush for brains, lady. You call Eddie a murderer to his sister, you're askin' for it. I warned you once to get outta here. Now go!"

I went down the steps and out to my car. By the time I'd slid into the cold vinyl seat, Anna was already inside the house. I glanced at the Christmas wreath on the front door. *Now what?* I asked myself.

I'd satisfied myself on two scores, though I couldn't prove a thing. I was now sure Eddie was involved in the kidnapping, and probably Dale's murder. If he was as crazy about Camille as Anna implied, and she had disappeared to avoid him, as was now looking probable, the kidnapping might have been aimed at Camille. Maybe he thought he'd punish her. Or maybe he planned to use the baby to draw her out.

That meant the look of awareness the kidnapper had given at the mention of Camille's name had been genuine. But the reason he'd been aware of Camille was because she was the target. My theory was pure speculation, but I was willing to go with it. A police detective trying to make a case would look for harder evidence, something that would stand up in court. My objective was simpler: I wanted to find Camille and the baby.

Anna Toretti had told me a lot more than she could possibly have imagined, but the fireworks also had created problems. Len Barnes and Tom Edleson would be livid that I'd alerted the enemy that we were on to them. Worse, I wasn't in the best position to exploit the knowledge I'd gained.

I had a feeling Anna would try to get word to Eddie. It was possible they were in contact, but given the fact that he was on the run, I doubted it. More likely she'd communicate through his associates. At that very moment she might be on the phone.

If she feared wiretaps and electronic surveillance, she might try to contact someone in person. I had some time, so I decided to hang around and find out.

I started the car, made a U-turn. I needed a place to park where I wouldn't be conspicuous, but still be able to see Anna's Lincoln if she left home. Two doors up from the corner there was a house being renovated. There was a big Dumpster unit in the street and construction vehicles were parked everywhere. I slid into the space behind the Dumpster, turned off my engine and waited.

I sat for fifteen minutes. The only movement came from the occasional workman who went out to the disposal unit. One young stud gave me a long look, like he was wondering if I was there to find him. Afraid he might come over and strike up a conversation, I looked away. He went back inside.

I was wearing pants, a white blouse and a blazer, plus gloves, a scarf and my lined trench coat. I was warm everywhere but my feet. Hose and my low-heeled pumps didn't cut it—not sitting in a car with the outside temperature around thirty-five degrees. I decided to give it another fifteen minutes, max.

After half an hour my toes were on the verge of frostbite, and still no sign of Anna. I decided to give up. I started the engine and had put the car in gear when I spotted Anna getting into the Lincoln. The Dumpster was between me and the corner, so I'd have to wait a few seconds to see if she was coming my way or not.

When she didn't pass me, I pulled into the street in time to see her disappearing around the curve half a block ahead of me. Speeding up, I managed to get the Lincoln in sight, but I didn't want to get too close. I doubted Anna was an expert at detecting surveillance, but she wasn't a garden-variety housewife, either.

Several blocks ahead she turned onto a major boulevard and went half a mile to a service station. When I saw her turn in, I pulled up at the curb and stopped, maybe fifty yards away. Anna didn't go to the pumps, though. She stopped at some pay phones to make a call. Smart girl.

Anna talked for thirty seconds and hung up—no doubt I was the subject of the call. When she didn't leave, I figured she was expecting a call back. She paced, but not far from the phone, stopping once to light a cigarette. Judging by the way she was moving back and forth, her feet were as cold as mine.

After another ten minutes of pacing and smoking, Anna got a call. She only talked a few seconds, then got into the car and took off, heading back the way she'd come. I slid down in the seat as she passed. She didn't notice me, but I had to make a difficult U-turn in traffic to follow her.

I drove faster than good judgment and the slushy road dictated, but I managed to catch up with the Lincoln. Anna didn't return home, however. She continued on north. Before long we passed beyond the city limits. I tried to keep a discreet distance, but I had to be careful not to get cut off. To do a tail properly you needed three vehicles. Doing it alone, without drawing attention to yourself, was impossible. Fortunately, Anna was not a pro.

When she entered the beltway and headed east, I figured I was in for a ride. Anna drove ten miles to the I-95 interchange, made a bizarre series of turns and ended up heading right back along the beltway in the direction she'd come. We exited where we'd gotten on in the first place, and returned to the service station where everything had begun.

I'd been tailing her for so long that I knew the chances of her spotting me were getting greater. At a certain point, just about anybody would notice.

Again Anna got on the phone. She talked for a few seconds, looking in my direction. I knew she'd spotted me.

When she got back in her car but stayed there, I realized the jig was up. In all likelihood somebody was coming for her—or more accurately, for me. I figured there'd be three or four of them, and they wouldn't be friendly.

Discretion being the better part of valor, I elected to vacate the area. I started the car and drove down the boulevard, ignoring Anna as I passed the service station. It was hard to know if I'd accomplished anything worthwhile. Sometimes it was enough to draw the bad guys out of their holes, where they could make their mistakes in plain view.

Fascinating as the morning had been, I had a pressing problem—I was starving. I started looking for a fast-food place or a decent-looking service station. Within five blocks I found a McDonald's restaurant. As I signaled to turn into the drive, I glanced into my rearview mirror. Damn if Anna Toretti's Lincoln wasn't right behind me.

I gave an embarrassed laugh as I parked. The hunter had become the hunted. Anna continued slowly up the street. I guess she wasn't a fan of Ronald McDonald.

She'd turned the tables on me, caught me napping. I'd been so cocksure of myself that I hadn't bothered to look behind me. Why had she followed me? I wondered. To make a point?

I looked around. The lot was practically empty. It wasn't yet time for the lunch crowd. I went inside to buy a cup of coffee and an Egg McMuffin sandwich.

While I sat sipping my coffee, I considered my options. The most inviting one was being with Kyle, lying together in front of his fireplace. I finished my coffee and muffin and left the restaurant.

There was a surprise waiting for me outside. I found a man leaning against the fender of my car. He had on a dark topcoat and stocking cap. His arms were folded and he was looking right at me.

There was a large sedan parked haphazardly fifty or sixty feet away with two men inside—one at the wheel, the other in back. I casually checked my purse to make sure my gun was accessible. It was. I started walking toward my car.

Most of the slush had melted, but the pavement was wet. I walked carefully, but with my eyes on the man. He was early thirties, well built, dark. He had the look of a thug with a tenth-grade education. His smile, incongruously, was more condescending than friendly.

"This your rig?" he demanded, as I approached.

"Yeah, it is. Want to buy it?" I was edgy, but tried not to let it show. I kept one eye on the men in the sedan.

"Thanks, but I already got roller skates." He laughed and was disappointed I didn't appreciate his humor.

"Well, you aren't collecting for the United Way. What do you want?"

"You're funny," he said. "That's good."

"I'm not in the mood to entertain you," I retorted. "How'd you like to get your butt off my bumper?"

"Funny *and* bitchy," he replied.

"You have something to say, junior, say it."

He smirked, but was through sparring. "There's a gentleman in the car over there who'd like a word with you," he said. "He asked me to ask you to come over for a chat."

I looked at the car. "I don't talk to gentlemen I don't know."

"It's nothin' shady, he just wants to talk. Five minutes, max."

I was inclined to believe him. If rough stuff was intended, it would have been handled more directly. Still, I wasn't eager to test the courage of my convictions. It was a fair bet these guys were connected with Anna Toretti and the phone calls she'd made. She had to have directed them here.

"Tell you what. Just to show you I'm a sport, I'll talk to the gentleman. But not in his car. In mine. Ask the gentleman if he's man enough to talk on my turf."

"Hey," he said, shaking his hand, "you got balls. Or is it an act?"

"It's an act. But if your friend wants to see the grand finale, he'll have to be quick. Tell him I'm getting in my car. In two minutes I'm driving off. Now get off my bumper."

The thug bowed mockingly and sauntered off. I got in my car, took my 9-mm semiautomatic from my purse and held it in my left hand, down the side of the seat. I removed the safety and glanced over at the sedan.

The messenger boy was leaning over and talking to the guy in back through the half-lowered window. After a brief conversation the door opened and the man emerged. He was in a cashmere topcoat, dark trousers and a black fedora. He wore black gloves and black shoes. He was tall, fairly lean, well built. He strode purposefully to my car, going around to the passenger side. As he approached I could see that his skin wasn't the best, but he was blessed with swarthy good looks.

He opened my passenger door and climbed in. He didn't say anything. He stared ahead, out the windshield, then turned to look at me. His appraisal was more critical than sexual, though there was a definite awareness that I was a woman.

"A brief message, Miss Hunter. Anna Toretti's a nice lady. She don't like to be bothered. May I respectfully request you don't bother her no more?"

The politeness surprised me. "I didn't know I was bothering her."

"You was, believe me. She's very sensitive about her brother. He's sensitive about some things himself. We don't know you here in Baltimore, and it would be better for you if we don't. Does that make sense?"

The voice was vaguely familiar, but I couldn't be sure. "To be honest, Mr.—"

"It don't matter," he said.

"To be honest, Mr. It-Don't-Matter, I don't like being threatened."

He smiled with amusement. "Threats is the best you will ever get, so be glad. Threats don't hurt—not like other things that can happen, if you get my drift."

"What does Eddie want with an innocent baby?" I asked.

The man shook his head. "What is it about you college broads? Ain't English the same in college as in the city streets?"

"In a word, no."

The man's patience began to wear thin. He removed his right glove and started slapping it against his bare palm, I suppose to indicate his irritation. Suddenly I realized what I was seeing—a man wearing a single glove on his left hand.

I couldn't tell whether it was a conscious gesture, or an accidental one. But the familiarity of the voice, the man's size and general description, the glove—it all pointed to the man in the ski mask who'd kidnapped Andrew from under my very nose. Every muscle in my body clenched.

"Where's the baby?" I asked, trying to mask the fear in my voice.

He shook his head with disgust. I tightened the grip on the handle of my gun. "Maybe there's only one way for me to make you understand," he said, as much to himself as to me.

Suddenly, he turned and grabbed my face with his bare hand. He gripped my jaw, shoving my head hard against the headrest. His face was inches from mine. I could smell the tobacco on his breath. "Listen, you arrogant little bitch. If you don't back off, that pretty face of yours is going to end up looking like vegetable soup. Now, you cut the smart-mouth crap or you might end up with no teeth. There ain't nothin' so sad as a pretty girl with false teeth. Do you understand me, or do I have to explain again?" As he said it, he dug his fingers into my flesh.

I'd heard his little speech, I figured it was time for him to hear mine. Before he could move, I jammed my gun into his crotch. He let go of my jaw.

"If you value your private parts, don't move a muscle," I said.

He didn't move.

"Now you listen to me, you son of a bitch," I continued, my voice shaking. "The next time you touch my face, I'm going to blow off your balls. And believe me, there ain't nothin' so sad as a pretty boy with no balls. Do we understand each other?"

"Yeah, but I think you still don't hear so good."

"Well, let's test *your* hearing. I want you to give Eddie a message. Tell him that baby is innocent. Tell him to send it home. And if it's hurt, we're going to nail his ass. Understand?"

"You got the gun. I just come to talk," he said.

"Well, I don't like the way you talk. Before we meet again, maybe you can work on your manners."

He stared out the windshield, his jaw working.

"Now get out of my car. Keep your hands away from your coat. If you reach inside it before you get to your car, I'll blow your goddamn head off. Understand?"

"That it?"

"Go."

He got out of the car. I started my engine and I was headed for the street, my tires screeching and spinning, before he even reached the sedan. I turned onto the boulevard and sped up the street. My heart was doing as many RPMs as the engine of my car and I was shaking all over. I checked my rearview mirror. There was nobody in pursuit. Apparently, Mr. It-Don't-Matter and his friends decided there was no need for further discussion.

I wasn't of the same opinion. I decided the jerk and maybe Anna Toretti, too, needed to talk to Len Barnes and Tom Edleson. The familiarity of Mr. It-Don't-Matter's voice, and even the glove, wouldn't hang him, but it provided reasonable cause for an arrest. I got on my car phone and called their office. Neither agent was in. I left the number of my car phone and asked that one of them give me a call while I was on my way to Kyle Weston's farm.

13

I WAS HALFWAY TO Frederick when Barnes called me on my car phone. "What you got, Hunter?"

"Don't get pissed, Len," I said, "but I've been running ahead of the pack."

I heard him groan. "All right. So tell me."

I recounted the morning's events, my chats with Anna and Mr. It-Don't-Matter. There was a pregnant pause when I finished before he said, "Running ahead of the pack is putting it mildly. You've got to back out, that's all there is to it. I can't have my investigation screwed up."

"Come on Len, I didn't screw it up."

"What evidence do I have that's usable? Nothing. If you'd worked with us on it, you'd have had a wire, surveillance, backup. I don't have to tell you what was wrong."

"I got what I did because it was spontaneous, Len. Anna and the hood got emotional with me, and that's what I wanted."

"Well, I want to be able to make a case," he groused, "not win moral victories."

"Okay, I won't do it again. But tell me. Who was the guy who wanted to play kissy face with me—do you have any idea?"

"Yeah. Tom and I have gotten to know the whole Baltimore crowd like they were family, if you'll pardon the expression. I think the punk you had the conversation with is Joey Angelino. He's Eddie Dee's alter ego."

"You mean he does his murders and kidnappings for him?"

"Basically, yes. Incidentally, the lab turned up traces of a plastic explosive in the debris from Dale Weston's boat. That investigation is progressing."

"This Angelino character, what's with the glove?"

"Tom found something in the file this morning. Joey burned his hand badly in a munitions accident a few years ago."

"His left hand?"

"Roger. The glove business hadn't turned up before now, but Tom speculated that maybe when he's on a job he likes to cover the scars. It fits."

"There's no saying the kidnapper had a scarred hand, but it justifies chatting with him, doesn't it?" I asked.

"Especially in light of your experience this morning," Barnes replied. "Frankly, I'm astonished he confronted you, given the fact you witnessed the kidnapping."

"Joey's the self-confident type. Danger thrills him."

"Maybe we can accommodate him."

"I hope so."

"Listen, Darcy, why don't you take a little vacation and let us handle this from here on out? You and Weston go someplace."

"Have you been eavesdropping on us, Len?" I asked playfully.

"Love may be blind, but I'm not," he said with a laugh.

"Special Agent Barnes, you *do* have a heart."

"I'm ending this conversation, Hunter."

"Good. I'm almost home. And I don't mean Washington."

He hung up, laughing. I felt pretty good myself.

IT WAS EARLY AFTERNOON when I arrived at the gate to Kyle's place. The security guard looked bored. The press had stopped coming around, it seemed. The FBI was dispensing the news on the case—such as it was. I waved at the guard as I drove through. He waved back.

I was eager to see Kyle and drove faster up the drive than I should have. I didn't literally arrive in a cloud of dust, but it felt that way. I got out of the car. The snow had stayed on the ground more than it had in either Washington or Baltimore.

The wind was blustery and cold, making me shiver. I noticed the curl of wood smoke rising from the chimney and imagined again how welcome a fire would be—and, for that matter, Kyle. But then I stopped to think about what was happening. I'd gotten caught up in Kyle's game. I was practically giddy with happiness, without stopping to ask what was true and what was false. Could I be so hungry for love that I was blind to the reality of who we were?

As I was getting my suitcase, Kyle came out the front door. He was in a bulky fisherman's sweater and jeans and—I had to admit—looked wonderful. If he'd gotten the night before into perspective, he certainly didn't let it show. He gave me a hug and a kiss and treated me to his happy smile. Yet there was concern on his face as he took my case.

"I was worried about you," he said, putting his arm around my waist as we walked toward the house. "Barnes called and asked for you. He made it sound pretty important. Did he reach you?"

"Yes, we talked. No problem. Everything's taken care of."

I'd already decided I wasn't going to give Kyle a detailed account of my morning. He wouldn't have liked hearing about the rough stuff, though the barking, as it turned out, had been worse than the biting. We went inside. After closing the door, Kyle took me in his arms again, kissing me tenderly, making me think about last night, despite my many misgivings. He smelled of spicy cologne and had a manly scent I'd already come to identify as uniquely his. "I missed you," he announced.

"Did you?"

He wrapped his arms around me and held me close. "A lot."

I smiled tentatively, wanting to let go and be as uninhibited as Kyle. But I couldn't.

"It's been lonely around here," he said. "No cops, no FBI, not even a housekeeper." Then he smiled devilishly. "Now that you're here, maybe that's not so bad."

I slipped from his arms and he helped me off with my coat. We went into the sitting room. "How'd it go today? Did you talk to the sister?" he asked.

I plopped down on a chair and stared at the flames. "Yes. There weren't any smoking guns, but I'm convinced Eddie is behind the kidnapping."

Kyle sat on the arm of my chair. He toyed with the ends of my hair. "Where do things stand?"

"My guess is Eddie is trying to find Camille and he's using the baby to get to her." I glanced up at Kyle and saw his eyes go cold.

"But Andrew's all right, isn't he?" he asked. "I mean, logic dictates Eddie will be careful with him."

"I imagine so. There's no reason for him to be hurt."

I had no way to be sure that was true. Common sense didn't often count for much in these situations. But I wasn't going to share my misgivings with Kyle. He had enough worries.

"It's funny," I said, "but I think we're right back where we started. Baring Eddie being picked up, the way to find the baby may be to find Camille. If Eddie is as determined as he seems, chances are he's been trying to get to her."

"He might already have found her. We could be too late."

"True, but we've got to keep digging. I just wish we had a trail to follow. Basically we've got nothing except what Barnes turned up about Camille's mysterious lady friend."

"I've got *some* news," Kyle said. "Remember you asked whether Camille had visitors or calls while she was here? Well, this morning I spoke to Mrs. Mitchell and she told me she'd taken phone messages for Camille from someone named Peg. Mrs. Mitchell remembered the name because she has a great niece named Peggy."

"Peg," I pronounced. "Not the most unusual name in the world, nor is it terribly common. Maybe your phone bill will tell us how to get a hold of her."

"I already checked, Darcy. You'd mentioned it last night so I looked at my last bill. Two numbers were unfamiliar. I called them. One was the pediatrician in Baltimore. The other was the Chesapeake Lounge in Dundalk. It was on the bill eight times."

"Hey, good work, Kyle."

He beamed. "You didn't think I'd just sit around, keeping the home fires burning, did you?"

I patted his cheek. "You aren't just another pretty face."

He gave me a pinch.

"It's a good bet Peg is connected with the lounge," I said.

"That's what I figured."

"Did you mention her name when you called?"

"No," he replied. "I figured I'd let you handle it."

"Good. We might want to give some thought to how we approach her. What were the times of the calls, by the way?"

"All afternoons and evenings."

"That fits," I said.

"Do you think this Peg is important?"

"I don't know. The FBI investigated Camille thoroughly but their one blank was the mystery woman who visited her. I'll bet Peg's our girl and we'll find her at the Chesapeake."

"Are you going to tell the FBI about her?"

"I don't know. Let me give it some thought." Barnes had asked me to back off—suggested I take a vacation, as a matter of fact—but like a dog with a bone, I didn't want to walk away. It's a disease detectives get.

Kyle brushed my cheek with his knuckles. "I can tell you're not one to be denied," he said.

"It shows?"

"It shows."

I took his hand and pressed it to my face.

"Well, you're off duty now, Darcy," he said. "I think it's time you relaxed."

He lifted my chin and kissed me. It brought back recollections of the many wonderful sensations of the night before. I could see Kyle wasn't going to be an easy man to be around—not without a constant battle with myself.

"Want some coffee?" he asked. "Something to warm your insides?"

"I wouldn't mind a muffin or something. In all the excitement, I managed to miss lunch."

"Well, we'll have to fix that. Come on." Kyle got up and grabbed my hand.

He led me into the kitchen and I stationed myself at the table while he made lunch. I couldn't say he looked like the most comfortable man on earth in a kitchen, but he wasn't like a fish out of water, either. Within minutes he had a warm bowl of tomato soup and a sandwich in front of me. He'd already eaten, so he had a cup of coffee while I ate.

"I almost forgot," he said. "You'll never guess who I talked to this morning."

"Who?"

"Your mother. She'd tried to reach you and got your 'sassy telephone machine,' as she called it—"

"And took the opportunity to call you, instead?"

"Right. We had a nice talk. You and I have been invited up to Harrisburg for New Year's Day."

"Oh, we have? How did that happen?"

Kyle gave me an ornery grin. "I took the liberty of telling her we'd become good friends. I said I found you one of the most refreshingly unique women I'd met in years. I told her you were bright, independent, compassionate—I didn't say fabulous in bed—and that I was very, very fond of you."

"Lord," I exclaimed, putting my head in my hands.

"Are you upset?"

"No. But tell me, what did Mom say?"

"You really want to know?"

I contemplated him warily. "Is it that bad?"

He laughed. "She said, 'Thank God.'"

I rolled my eyes. "Dear ol' Mom. At least she didn't give you her 'Darcy's going to end up a spinster' speech."

He chuckled. "Actually, I think I got a modified version."

Kyle had my mother thinking we were an item, which I couldn't exactly dispute, considering we'd made love. Even so, I could see this thing was beginning to resemble a runaway freight train.

"Well, it's a long time to New Year's," I said.

"Yes. We have Christmas to contend with first. When do you like to put up a tree? I thought maybe you could help me pick one out and we could decorate it together."

Kyle saw the consternation in my eyes. "You're unhappy," he observed. "Was I out of line, talking to Marjorie like that?"

"I don't want to criticize you, Kyle."

"But you're displeased," he said, growing sober. "What's wrong?"

I looked down at my bowl of soup, trying to find the words. "Do you know what it's like to have a gut instinct about a situation?" I began.

"What's your gut instinct?"

"That we're rushing things a little," I told him.

"You want to skip Christmas? Are you saying we should wait until February and then exchange Valentine's Day cards?"

He hadn't even tried to disguise the hurt in his voice. I felt guilty. "Kyle, please don't be angry with me. I'm just trying to be realistic."

He got up and paced for a good five minutes. The silence stretched until the tension was tremendous. Finally, Kyle leaned against the counter, folding his arms over his chest. He gazed at me sternly. "How do you evaluate what happened last night?"

"Last night was wonderful. It's not that."

"Last night was wonderful, but today it's a different story. That's what you really mean."

"Great sex is not the only consideration," I snapped.

"You don't seem the type of woman who hops into bed for a good time, Darcy."

"I'm not!"

"Then is it unreasonable to conclude you might have found something desirable about me besides my sex appeal?"

"Of course. I never would have slept with you otherwise."

"So what's the problem now?"

"I think we might be jumping to conclusions."

"About what?"

I sighed anxiously.

Kyle gave me a long, critical look. He did not seem at all pleased. "The 'we' you refer to is really the 'me,' isn't it, Darcy? Aren't you saying *I'm* jumping to conclusions?"

I lowered my eyes.

"Let's be honest," he declared. "This is about Cara again."

"She's only one factor."

"Bull! She's not a factor at all. Cara's dead! When are you going to understand that?" He'd raised his voice practically to a shout.

"No, the question is, When are *you* going to understand it?"

He shook his head.

"Kyle, I'm not blaming you. I'm not saying you're wrong. I just don't want you to love me as a substitute for my sister. Isn't that reasonable? Can't you understand why I'd feel that way?"

He returned to his chair. "Of course I understand that. But you're making some assumptions that aren't justified." He reached out and took my hands. "Darcy, don't you see what you're doing? You're thinking of me as the kid who was engaged to your sister. And that's what I was then. A kid. I was young. And so was Cara. Had she lived, we might still be happily married now. I don't know. Nobody knows, including you. The point is, I'm not that same person who was engaged to Cara. I'm grown-up now. I've had a life and it hasn't included her."

"But you still love the memory of her," I protested.

"Of course I do. But I'm not wed to that memory, except in your mind."

Listening, I'd gotten very emotional. I swallowed hard, tears began to threaten. "I didn't want you to care for me for the wrong reason."

He pulled my hands to his lips and kissed them. "This has all happened very quickly, I know. Maybe I've rushed you, and maybe I haven't been as sensitive to your needs as I should have been. But I don't want you ever to think you've been a surrogate for Cara—either in my heart or in my mind."

"But why me?" I demanded, as a tear overflowed my lid and ran down my cheek.

"Because I happen to think you're wonderful, that's why. I've never known a woman quite like you, Darcy. I know it's trite to say I was captivated the moment I saw you, but I was definitely impressed. I mean, I took one look and said to myself, here's a woman with substance, with grit, with character. And that doesn't have anything to do with Cara!"

The tears started flowing and I wiped them away. "I was afraid to believe that," I replied. "I guess I still am."

"Your mother said you wouldn't be an easy nut to crack. She explained about Tauruses, how stubborn you can be. And she told me how you've made a career of running from your own feelings."

"Oh my God," I moaned. "I'll kill her."

I felt myself turning absolutely scarlet. Kyle laughed. He came around the table and pulled me to my feet. He held me in his arms and kissed my tear-streaked face.

"Last night, when you put your mind to it, you managed to relax and stop fighting yourself," he reminded.

"Yes, but today I started worrying again."

"Well, it seems to me I'm going to have to keep loving you until you finally accept the fact that I'm a man who knows his heart and won't give up without a fight."

I laughed and pressed my face against his neck. "I feel so stupid."

"In spite of all your perfection, you do have a couple of tiny flaws," he teased. "But I'm broad-minded. I'll overlook them."

"Damned decent of you, Mr. Weston."

I hadn't yet eaten my lunch, so Kyle warmed up my soup in the microwave, then sat with me while I ate. When I'd finished we cleared the table. Afterward Kyle said, "Well, the afternoon is yours, Darcy. What do you feel like doing?"

"How about lying around by the fire and taking it easy?"

"Sounds good to me."

We had a wonderful, relaxing afternoon. I changed into jeans and a sweater, and we looked through Kyle's CD collection and picked out some music. We lay on the floor by the fire and talked. He held my hand and kissed my fingers.

The afternoon was like a slow dance. We both knew where it was headed, but we were drawing it out, letting the anticipation build. Every time Kyle kissed me, I'd start getting excited, but one or the other of us would back off to let the sexual tension simmer a little longer.

I don't know where Kyle learned to be such a masterful lover, but it was enough that he was. I suspected there'd been plenty of women. How could there not have been? But he made me feel very, very special. And that was all that mattered.

The western sky was an orange glow and the fire blazed brightly, when our passion built to a breaking point. Sweaters and jeans, shoes and socks went flying. In seconds we were locked in a naked embrace, kissing frantically, rolling around like a couple of beasts. And it did get warm. Soon our skin and hair were soaked. We caressed each other breathlessly.

Kyle licked my breasts and I kissed his moist skin. He touched me everywhere, raising the pulsing in my body to a fever pitch. Finally I couldn't wait anymore. I climbed astride him, and guided his penis into me.

He felt so wonderful inside me. The way he groaned told me how much he wanted me. He took my breasts in his hands. He pinched my nipples, making them tingle.

I moaned as sensation spread through my body. But the power of our sex was at the place where we were joined. The storm was building there. I clenched him tightly.

Kyle rocked his hips and I gyrated around them, barely able to control my mounting excitement. He held my hips, guiding my movement up and down his penis. My head fell back. The pulsing built as I writhed astride him.

Then it hit. I cried out, then collapsed, panting breathlessly. Violent tremors shook my body. I whimpered, dizzy and delirious, giddy with sensation.

"My God," I muttered, barely able to speak.

I lay on Kyle's chest. I could feel his heart pounding—or was it mine?

After a couple of minutes, I found the strength to lift myself. I gazed at Kyle. His body was soaked. He looked as exhausted as I felt. He was breathing hard, his chest rising and falling rapidly.

"Did that really happen?" I mumbled.

"I think so," he murmured.

Kyle touched my cheek, slipping his fingers under the damp hair plastered to my skin. His glistened in the firelight. "Maybe we should stay like this forever," he whispered.

"How long before we'd starve to death?" I asked.

"I don't know, but what a way to go."

I smiled and lay on his chest again, reveling in our union. I caressed his shoulder, kissed it and thought of the wonderful afternoons to come. I bowed to the inevitable. Soon we'd be spending one of them decorating our Christmas tree. I couldn't help wondering whether these glorious, miraculous moments were meant only to tantalize, or if they truly were a taste of things to come.

Kyle pulled my face close to his. He nibbled on my ear and asked if I'd like to take a shower with him.

"Yes," I whispered. "But give me five more minutes. I want to savor this."

"It's never been better than right now, Darcy. Ever."

"You're right. It hasn't. Ever."

WE HAD OUR SHOWER. Kyle shampooed my hair and I shampooed his. We dried each other off and afterward we went to his bed, intending to rest. We ended up making love again. This time with a gentle quietness, looking into each other's eyes at the moment we came.

Afterward we hugged for a long time, clinging with awe and wonder. This was beyond anything I could have imagined. What was the catch? I wondered. Wasn't there always one?

Eventually we got up and dressed. Kyle made spaghetti for dinner and his Bolognese sauce wasn't half-bad. Part of it came from a package, but he improvised, adding some wine and cream and his own spices.

"Cooking is like making love," he said, as I stood next to him at the stove, watching. "You have to bring something extra to it, or in time the entire process will become boring."

I couldn't imagine ever tiring of what I'd experienced that evening, but I knew he was right. Successful relationships weren't miracles, handed down by God. They had to be worked at and they required a commitment that went beyond desire.

As we ate I looked into Kyle's eyes, in search of the person. I'd never felt so comfortable with a man before. Examining the insecurities I was feeling, I realized I was already beginning to fear loss. Maybe I didn't deserve this. Maybe it was an illusion.

"Don't overanalyze it," he said. "Just be glad we've got it."

"How did you know what I was thinking?"

"You had an 'Is this too good to be true?' look on your face."

"*Is* it too good to be true?"

He shook his head. "I think we're really on to something, Darcy. Something very important and very special."

"How is it you're not afraid?"

"I believe in focusing on the positives."

"Is that your philosophy of life?" I asked.

"It's part of it."

"Where did you pick it up?"

"In a fortune cookie. Where else?"

After dinner Kyle asked if I liked to play Scrabble. I said I did and he got out the game while I picked out some more CDs. We settled down where it all began, on the living-room floor, in front of the fire, and began to play.

I was not a game fanatic, though I enjoyed them. But as we played, I found my mind turning back to the case. Kyle looked up at me, catching me with what must have been a dazed, far-off look on my face.

"All right," he said. "What are you thinking about?"

"Nothing."

"Tell me," he insisted.

"Peg," I replied.

He gave me a look, sensing, I guess, that the dog was once again obsessed with her bone. "What does that mean?" he asked.

"Nothing. I was just thinking about her."

"Do you want to talk about it?" he asked.

"No, this is our evening. I'll think about her tomorrow."

Kyle refocused his attention on the game, finding a forty-point word. I countered with a fifteen pointer, and managed to do progressively worse with each successive turn. I was having trouble concentrating.

The truth was that Kyle and I had begun what could easily become a wonderful relationship. I was beginning to sense that the possibilities were unlimited. At the same time, though, there was important unfinished business—baby Andrew, Camille, Eddie Dee. Until that had been resolved, our time together would be stolen from a harsher reality that was hanging over our heads.

There was also the fact that I was a Taurus. As my mother had so aptly informed Kyle, I was tenacious. I knew I wouldn't sleep well until Andrew was found.

"Kyle," I said as he studied the board, "do you suppose Eddie Dee and his friends know about Peg?"

He looked up at me. "Is it important one way or the other?"

"It's hard to say without knowing what Peg knows about Camille."

"You mean, like where she is?" he asked.

"For instance."

He studied me. "Where is this leading, Madam Detective?"

"I don't know. But the more I think about it, the more concerned I get."

Kyle took my hands. "What are you really saying?"

"That I should talk to Peg—if I can find her—sooner rather than later."

"In other words, you want to go do the town tonight."

I shrugged. "It's awfully easy for someone to put you off on the phone. And I don't want to forewarn her. It's always best to handle things in person, catch someone unprepared."

"Do I have to put on a tie?" he asked.

I reached over to kiss him. In doing so, I upset the board. I gave him a sheepish grin. "Let's say you'd have won anyway."

"I should hope so. I was sixty points ahead."

"Don't be too sure," I countered. "I tend to finish strong."

Kyle twitched his brow. "Yes, I noticed that earlier."

I gave him a look and jumped to my feet, pulling him up. "Come on lover boy. I'll let you be Tonto tonight. You've earned the opportunity."

14

It was a little after eleven when we got to Dundalk. The Chesapeake Lounge was on Holabird Avenue in a low, free-standing building. The parking lot was only a quarter filled. As Kyle parked and switched off the engine, he turned to me.

"Do we need any special signals or anything?" he asked.

"For what?"

"You know—in case we have to do something, take action . . . whatever."

I laughed. "If we get in a peck of trouble, I'll yell 'Run!' That's the signal to get the hell out of there."

"Very funny," he retorted. "I figured a big-shot detective like you might have something a little more sophisticated."

"Do you know pig Latin?"

Kyle gave me a severe look. "I see the Tontos of the world are meant to endure abuse. Just remember, if it wasn't for Mrs. Mitchell and me, you never would have known about Peg."

"If it wasn't for the two of you, we'd be in bed," I teased.

He shook his finger at me. "Darcy, you really have to learn to be kinder to the help."

"Come on, big boy," I said, "let's get this over with."

As we walked toward the entrance I could hear music. A boozy-smelling couple in their thirties came out the door as we went in. To the right at the back I saw a small stage where a trio played slow music. Half a dozen couples danced on the postage-stamp dance floor. Perhaps ten other tables were occupied. The lights were dim. It was difficult to see faces.

Along the length of the left side of the large, low-ceilinged room was a bar. Seven or eight customers were on stools. There were two bartenders.

"Let's sit at the bar," I suggested.

We took off our coats and sat on barstools, holding our coats on our laps. One of the barkeeps, a ruddy-faced, spongy-looking guy in his mid-forties, sauntered over.

"What'll it be?" He put paper coasters in front of us.

"Soda water," I replied.

Kyle gave me a surprised look, then said, "The same."

The bartender's look was full of sarcasm. "With ice?"

"Please."

The man went away.

Kyle leaned close to me. "We don't exactly blend in if we order soda water," he muttered out of the corner of his mouth.

"I don't drink in bars," I informed him. "Anyway, we're not here to blend in, we're here to ask questions."

I peered around. Besides the barkeeps and the musicians, all male, there were two cocktail waitresses. One was a blonde with enormous breasts, the other a skinny brunette. A couple of months earlier on a Saturday night Camille Parker might have been there under a dusty spot, belting out a song. Being a weeknight, though, it was fairly quiet. I wondered if one of the girls hustling drinks was our Peg.

The bartender returned with our drinks, which he placed on the coasters. "That'll be two bucks," he said.

Kyle reached for his wallet.

"Camille Parker work here anymore?" I asked the bartender.

He gave me a strange look. "Camille Parker?"

"Yeah, she's a singer."

"Oh, you mean the one that was here a couple of months ago." He shook his head. "She's been gone awhile. Married some guy with bucks, I think."

I gave Kyle a sly glance. He rolled his eyes and put a five-dollar bill on the bar. The man picked it up, and went off.

"Funny how stories get exaggerated, isn't it?" Kyle remarked.

"Sure you've been playing it straight with me?" I teased. "You and Camille aren't secretly married, are you?"

Kyle turned red. Before he could say anything the bartender returned, placing three ones in front of Kyle.

"How about her friend Peg?" I questioned. "She around?"

"Peg who?"

"I'm not sure. All I know is she's Camille's friend."

He looked wary. "No offense, but you two smell like cops."

"It's a smell that lingers," I replied. "I used to be one. Now I'm not. This is private. We'd just like to chat with Peg."

"I try not to get myself involved in other people's business," he said. "It's safer."

"What's unsafe?" I asked.

"Look—" he leaned close and lowered his voice "—the FBI was in here asking about the Parker woman. You think I don't know that spells trouble?"

Kyle took a twenty-dollar bill from his wallet and laid it on the three ones. The barman glanced at the bill.

"We just want to know where we can find Peg. Is she one of the cocktail waitresses?"

"No."

"Then who is she?"

"You're looking for Peg Smith," the bartender said, after a moment's hesitation. He slipped the twenty and the ones into his pocket. "She and Camille knew each other real well."

"Does Peg work here?" I asked.

"She tended bar here until a week ago."

"What happened to her?"

"She nearly got killed in an car wreck."

"Do you know where she is now?"

A customer down the bar hollered for a drink. The barkeep went off to take care of him. He sauntered back after a minute.

"Listen, I make a point of knowing as little about this stuff as possible."

"Car accidents?" I probed.

He gave me a smile like I didn't know the half of it, which I was sure I didn't. But his expression changed when Kyle took out another twenty. The man put it in his pocket.

"I'd talk to Lola, the cocktail waitress. She and Peg were close. I think she saw her after the accident."

I turned and looked over my shoulder. "Which one is Lola?"

"The one with the boobs."

"Apt description," I said dryly.

I saw the woman moving among the tables and headed for the other end of the bar. Our man caught her attention and beckoned her over. She came, looking unhappy.

"Yeah, what?"

"These good people have a question for you, honey," the barkeep said. He slapped the bar with his hand as a gesture of farewell. "Have a nice evening, folks." He moved off.

Lola, pudgy but sort of pretty and about my age, looked at me and Kyle in turn. "So, what's the question?"

"Can we talk in private?" I asked.

She shook her head. "I don't have a break for almost thirty minutes." She looked back and forth between us. "Why? What do you want?"

Kyle fanned some bills so she could see. "We could make it worth your while to take a break early," he told her.

"Five minutes of your time," I added.

She gave us an exasperated look. "Let me serve the drinks I got up," she replied. "It'll take a couple of minutes." She left.

I turned to Kyle. "Nice touch. Did you see that trick with the bills in a movie?"

He gave me a self-satisfied grin. "Actually, this is fun."

"Kyle, you sound like a virgin her first time in the back seat of a car. Before her boyfriend really gets rolling."

"Are my cheeks glowing?"

"Drink your soda water."

Lola returned after a few minutes and led us back to the employees' lounge. It contained a vinyl couch, a table, a couple of straight chairs and a metal locker. She took a chair. Kyle and I sat on the couch.

There was a fine patina of perspiration on her upper lip. She wiped it with a tissue. "So, what do you want?"

"Tell us where we can find Peg Smith," I said.

Lola slumped. "Jeez," she muttered, staring down at the floor. Then she looked up at us wearily. "Who are you guys? Cops?"

"No," I said, "I'm a P.I. We're interested in Camille Parker. We want to talk to Peg about her."

"You're wasting your time," Lola declared. "Peg's gone."

"Gone where?"

"Look, folks, you could have saved us both trouble if you'd told me what you wanted. I don't know anything."

Kyle held out a hundred-dollar bill, then put it in Lola's hand. She and I both blinked. It was a twenty-dollar question. I made a mental note to talk to him about that.

"Please, you must know something," I said, confident now that Kyle had bought me lots of airtime. "Peg had an accident?"

"Yeah, right. Some accident."

"Tell us about it."

Lola fingered the bill. "Her face got messed up real good. But not in a car accident. Peg got the crap beat out of her."

"By who?"

"She didn't say. But I know it had to do with Camille. Even the feds have been poking around, asking about her."

"Peg knew Camille well?"

"Yeah, the two of them were real tight."

"Does Peg know where Camille is now?"

"I don't know."

"Come on, Lola. She must. Why else was she beaten up?"

"You could be right," she replied. "But she didn't tell me. I went to see her at the hospital, and she never said one thing about Camille and I never asked her. All I can tell you is she wasn't a happy camper and it wasn't just the breaks and bruises. The lady was scared."

I sensed Lola was being honest, but I wasn't sure she'd told us all she could. "Peg's not at the hospital now?"

"No, she checked out a couple of days ago. I'm not real sure when. The doctors were upset, but she wanted out of there."

"Is she at home?"

Lola fidgeted restlessly. "Give me a break. This isn't my business, or Peg's either. And look what happened to her."

"You know where Peg is, don't you?"

"I don't know anything."

It was obvious she wasn't telling the truth about that. I guess it was obvious to Kyle, too, because he produced another hundred. "Camille's life and her baby's life might be at stake," he said. "We know they're in danger. Peg could help us."

"At least give us a chance to talk to her," I added.

Kyle extended the bill. Lola finally took it, fingering it before placing it in her pocket.

Lola hesitated, then said, "Peg's brother came down from West Virginia to pick her up. I asked how she was going to walk. She said he might have to carry her, but she was getting the hell out of Baltimore. She was going home."

"Where's home?"

The woman agonized. "Somewhere around Tygart Lake. I don't know the address."

"What's her brother's name?"

"Sommerville. Sommerville Smith. That's all I know. Honest." She looked at each of us. "Look, I got to go back to work. The tip was nice, thanks." She said, gave Kyle a smile. "I need this job to feed my kid."

"Okay, Lola. Thanks for your help."

She got up, went to the door and stopped. "Don't tell Peg you talked to me, all right?"

I nodded. "Don't worry."

She left us, the scent of her perfume lingering. Kyle and I exchanged looks. We got up and put on our coats.

"How'd I do?" he asked.

"Your manner was nice and you're cute as hell, but you're a little quick with the lettuce. Overgenerous, too."

"I don't like long negotiations," he explained, opening the door.

"Clients prefer that you spend their money like it was your own," I told him, stepping into the hallway. We headed to the front.

"This client doesn't mind a bit, Darcy. The truth is, he's eager to get home to his nice warm bed."

"Calling it a day, huh?"

"Aren't we through?"

"We've got some thinking to do on the way home."

Kyle grinned. "I was afraid, for a moment, you were going to suggest we go barhopping."

We'd come to the front door. We went out into the cold and made our way to the Mercedes. I got in and he went around to the driver's side. He started the engine and headed for the Tunnel Thruway. Kyle glanced at me after I'd sat in silence for several minutes.

"I'm afraid to ask what's going through your mind," he said.

"You like driving at night?"

"Dare I ask why?"

"I'd like to be at Tygart Lake, West Virginia, by sunrise."

"You think that's a good idea?" he asked.

"Len Barnes recommended we take a trip. Tygart Lake is as good a spot as any."

"This detective business has its drawbacks, doesn't it?" Kyle observed, shaking his head.

"Don't worry, honey," I said. "You'll toughen up. It's a matter of commitment."

"I've got just one question, then. Is this going to be exclusively a working vacation?"

"Did you have something else in mind?" I asked, poking my tongue in my cheek.

"I can think of a couple of other things we might do."

I didn't say so, but there were a couple of things I could thing of, as well.

IT WAS FOUR O'CLOCK in the morning by the time we got to a town named Grafton, just north of Tygart Lake. I'd slept while Kyle drove, then I took the wheel the last hour of the trip. I pulled into the first motel we came to. As Kyle fumbled to get his jacket on, I said I had one requirement—clean sheets.

The Sleepy Oak Motel was clean, although the temperature in our room seemed about one degree above freezing. We stripped and jumped into bed at the same time. I was dead tired, but my teeth were chattering so hard I couldn't have fallen asleep if I'd wanted to. And by the time I warmed up, I really got warmed up. Kyle's embrace was just too inviting.

It started with a kiss, and one thing led to another. We ended up making love until an hour before sunrise, finally falling into an exhausted asleep. Taking pity on Kyle, I set the alarm for seven. But when it went off, he wasn't thrilled.

"Let's call a detective and subcontract the case out," he mumbled. "Tonto wants to hibernate."

"A nice cold shower will bring Tonto to his senses," I advised.

"Make it a co-ed shower and you've got a deal." He grinned.

"Kyle, you're so easy to satisfy."

"Tough duty," he teased.

"Come on." I jumped out of bed, wondering where I'd gotten my marine-corps mentality. Maybe it was my way of dealing with the seeming conflict of being sexual in bed, yet competent and professional on the job. That wasn't easy when you played both roles with the same man.

I was no sooner in a hot shower than Kyle joined me. We started out with every intention of staying warm while getting clean. Things quickly deteriorated, though. He soaped me down and I never regained my equilibrium. We made love standing in the shower. When I came, I almost collapsed. Kyle held me up.

I dug my nails into his flesh. "That was a dirty trick, Weston," I murmured. "You know my Achilles' heel, now. I'll never be safe with you again."

He nibbled the lobe of my ear. "Not in the shower, anyway."

I finally staggered out and tried drying myself. I had to lean against the wall. Kyle looked wobbly himself.

"It's the lack of sleep," he said, toweling his body.

"Oh, that's how you explain it," I retorted.

He cuffed me playfully. I gave him a hug and we shared a naked kiss. Afterward I sighed. "Come on, Kyle," I lamented, "we have to get going. We've got a job to do."

We dried our hair and dressed quickly.

"Do we know where we're going?" he asked, putting his keys and wallet in his pocket.

"Grafton is the county seat. If we talk to the sheriff we're likely to find out where Sommerville Smith's place is. There are only fifteen thousand people in the county, so he's probably known."

"How do you know the population?"

"I studied the map in the car last night."

"Oh." He gave me a grin. "My money bought me a brain as well as a body."

I pointed my finger at him. "Don't get smart, Mr. Weston. There are known antidotes to your cologne."

"Is *that* what it is?" he asked, slipping on his coat as I put on mine. "My cologne?"

"It's not your snoring, I'll tell you that." I pinched his cheek. "Come on, I'll buy breakfast."

We had a hearty country breakfast in a coffee shop up the street that was strewn with Christmas garlands, lights, tinsel and an abundance of fake snow. We drank lots of coffee.

I got directions to the sheriff's office from the cashier. The sheriff wasn't in, but his chief deputy, a wiry man with a narrow face and a crew cut, was in charge. I asked if he could direct us to Sommerville Smith's place, saying we knew it was in the vicinity of Tygart Lake.

"What you be wantin' Sommerville for?" he asked.

The question was to be expected. Small-town peace officers made knowing everybody's business a part of their job description. It could work both for and against a person in my line of work.

"We're actually here to see his sister, Peg," I replied.

He looked us over with a measure of skepticism. "If you was friends you wouldn't be askin' for directions."

When I saw Kyle reaching for his wallet, and I grabbed his arm. "I'm a P.I. out of Washington, investigating a kidnapping, and I think Peg can help me find an important witness."

The deputy scratched his head, then put his hands on his hips. "Well," he said when he was satisfied, "I can tell you how to get there, but it'll take you a month of Sundays to find Som's place. How about if I give you an escort? I was thinkin' on patrollin' out that way anyway."

I beamed at him. "Deputy, we'd be eternally in your debt."

He grinned. "That's a mighty long time, ma'am."

We followed him through a series of back roads that led to an area east of Tygart Lake. We finally stopped at the junction of a dirt road. The deputy got out of his cruiser and came over to the Mercedes.

"Som's place is about a mile and a half up this here road," he said. "The folks out this way ain't so used to outsiders. I'd go in nice and slow."

We thanked him and followed the road up a shallow, heavily wooded valley. We finally came to a farmhouse tucked in a dell. The big shade trees were bare. The place looked desolate. Were it not for half a dozen vehicles in the yard, I'd have thought the farm was deserted. Kyle parked close to the path that led to the front door. We got out.

We were about halfway up the footpath when the door opened and a man in his mid-thirties stepped out. He held a shotgun in his right hand. He had on a Pirates cap, a lined denim jacket, jeans and work boots.

"Can I help you folks?" he said, sounding not too friendly.

About then another man appeared at the corner of the house. He was somewhat younger and was dressed similarly, but without a hat. He, too, was carrying a shotgun.

"Is this in your plan?" Kyle muttered from the corner of his mouth.

"Just remember our secret signal." I chuckled before turning my attention to the man on the porch. "Are you Sommerville Smith?"

"And who might you be, missus?"

"Darcy Hunter. This is Kyle Weston. We're here to see your sister, Peg."

His face registered surprise. "Who told you she was here?"

"A friend. It's very important that I speak with her."

"What's your business?"

"Camille Parker."

Smith lifted his hat and scratched his head. Then he told us to hang on a second. He went into the house. A minute later he came out. "Come on up," he said.

The inside of the farmhouse smelled of cooking. The furniture was old and worn. Paint was peeling from the walls. An old woman with a shawl around her sat in a rocker by a potbellied stove. She put her knitting in her lap as we came in.

"Mornin'," she said, without sounding friendly.

"Good morning."

Sommerville Smith went to a door in the back corner of the room. "Peg's in here," he said.

We walked across the creaky floor and stepped into a small bedroom. There was a double bed, a dresser and a chair. That was it. A woman with a bandaged head and a badly swollen face lay propped up on some pillows. Both eyes were black, her cheeks blue and green. Tufts of reddish hair sprouted from the bandage.

"You're Dale's brother," she said to Kyle, her voice weak.

"Yes," he answered. "We're trying to find Camille. Can you help us?"

"You're too late. She's gone."

"You mean she was here?" I asked.

"Yeah, didn't you know?"

"No, we came to see you."

"Well, she was up here with my family. Has been for weeks. She needed a place to go and I knew she'd be safe with them. She *was* safe, too—until Eddie sent his friends to see me. They beat me until I told them where Camille was."

"Then Eddie's been here?" My heart sank.

"There was no way he could get her, not without a fight. My brothers, Som, Den and Sonny, made sure of that. Eddie couldn't take Camille by force, but he did it with the baby."

I saw Kyle bristle. "What do you mean, 'with the baby'?" I demanded.

"Eddie kidnapped it so he'd have something to hang over her head. He's been up here, threatenin', for a couple days. Eddie claimed he loved Camille, but he was goin' to kill her baby if she didn't go away with him."

"Kill the baby?"

"Yes, ma'am," Sommerville said. "He claimed he'd throw the kid in the river. She didn't believe him none until he put the baby on the phone and made him squawk. I said it might not be her baby, but she said it likely was if he'd gone to the trouble of kidnappin' it."

"She held out at first," Peg continued. "But she couldn't take it no more."

"When did he come and get her?"

"He didn't. She went to Morgantown to meet him."

"When?"

"This mornin'. My brother Den and my sister, Jody, went with her to meet Eddie and get the baby. They're goin' to bring the baby back. The deal was we're supposed to wait until tonight, then call the sheriff. Camille agreed to leave with Eddie."

"Do you know what time they're meeting?"

"At noon. He's goin' to turn the baby over—leastwise, he said he would."

"Where?"

"There's a Christmas fair with little travelin' carnival set up by the livestock auction outside of town. She wanted a public place in a bigger town, and we suggested there. Our sister'll be waitin' in Den's truck to take care of the baby."

I looked at my watch. "We only have a couple of hours. How far is it to Morgantown?"

"An hour from here," Sommerville Smith said. "Den had business in Grafton before they went to Morgantown."

"Then we've got time."

"Camille don't want no cops involved," Smith said. "That was the deal. No cops. Otherwise, Eddie shoots the kid."

"My, God," Kyle said. "The guy's a monster."

"Camille wants the baby safe," Peg explained. "She's resigned. I think you should let her do it her way."

"There's no harm in us being there," I told her. "Eddie's not to be trusted. And you know from experience how unpleasant he can be." I went to the bed and took her hands. "Don't worry. Camille will be fine."

Sommerville Smith gave us a description of his brother's truck and directions to the nearest highway. We took off.

"What now?" Kyle asked, as we sped along the dirt road.

"It would be dangerous to bring in the police," I admitted. "But I'm wondering if Barnes and Edleson could fly up here by one o'clock. If not, they may be able to send some other agents. It's going to be tricky, though."

"You've showed your metal already," Kyle said. "Let's let the FBI handle it from here on out."

"That's not a bad idea, but what do we do if we're the only ones close enough to get there in time?"

15

WE CAME TO THE HIGHWAY in fifteen minutes. There was a small gas station on the corner. I called Len Barnes from the pay phone. He listened soberly, then told me he'd do his best to be there. In any case, he'd have a team on-site. "Don't take any chances," he said. "Just observe whatever transpires."

Kyle and I headed on. At the outskirts of Morgantown we stopped for directions to the livestock auction. It wasn't far. Within a few minutes I was able to see a Ferris wheel rising above the barren trees. Kyle slowed. It was twenty minutes before noon.

Kyle parked in the first spot he could find. He turned off the engine and looked at me. I could tell his adrenaline was pumping. Mine was.

I looked around the nearly full parking lot. "How many old beat-up pickups do you think are here?"

"A bunch."

"We might be able to intercept Camille and the Smiths, if we can spot them arriving. But they might already be inside."

"How about the FBI?"

"If Barnes made it, we're all right. If other agents are here instead, we may be able to identify them, or we might not. I don't want to spook Camille, so you'd better not go in. She won't have any idea who I am and neither will Eddie, so I should be able to get close to them."

"I'm not letting you go in there alone," Kyle insisted.

"Kyle, this is no time to be macho. I'm a trained professional, not your dithering girlfriend." I glanced around.

He touched my face and turned it toward him. "Darcy, I don't care how well trained you are. I love you and I don't want any harm to come to you."

My mouth sort of dropped open, right in the middle of my adrenaline rush.

"I know this has been quick," he said, "but let's be honest. We've known each other for years. And I don't just mean because our paths crossed sixteen or seventeen years ago."

I blinked. It was the first time a man I loved had told me he loved me. I hadn't been quite ready to admit my true feelings for Kyle Weston, though I'd played with the idea in my mind. But I did love him. Trite as it sounded, I'd loved him almost my entire life. Now, though, with it all out in the open, the whole world felt funny. I was at a loss. "Kyle...I..."

He squeezed my hand and gave me an imploring look. "There must be another way. Why don't you stay here and see if Peg's brother gets Andrew out safely? If he does, the FBI can take care of the rest."

"We can't be sure either of those things will happen," I argued. "I'm here and ready. I may as well do what I'm capable of doing. God knows, when they kidnapped Andrew, I failed."

"You didn't fail. Anyway, look who's talking macho now."

"I've got to do it," I said quietly. "Please understand."

He stared at me for a long moment, his eyes shimmering. "How do you expect me to just let go?"

"I'll be back."

"I won't ever let you out of my sight again," he said.

He seemed so earnest, I couldn't help smiling. "Let's not get too melodramatic."

"Darcy, you and I are going to spend serious time together when this is over. No outside interference, no cops-and-robbers stuff. Just you and me." He brushed my cheek with his fingers. "I know. Tahiti. We'll go to Tahiti and sip tropical drinks on the beach by day and make love by night. For days on end."

I smiled. "Are you trying to undermine my resolve?"

"Promise me, you'll go away with me," he insisted.

"Okay, I promise."

He pulled me to him and kissed me tenderly. My heart had two reasons to pound. He sighed, sounding anxious. "If you get shot, I'm really going to be pissed," he warned.

"I will, too." I knew, though, that this wasn't helping. I reached for the door handle. "You keep your eyes open for Barnes and Edleson," I instructed. "And if you see Camille, put your head down."

"All right."

I gave him a quick kiss, climbed out of the car and headed for the entrance. The crowds were bundled against the cold and seemed full of good cheer. Christmas music played over a loudspeaker. "Joy to the World" somehow seemed incongruous with the work I was about to do. There were a lot of small children in the crowd. I understood why the Smiths had chosen this place.

I moved about the booths laden with Christmas decorations. There were wreaths and ornaments, centerpieces, lights, food. I studied the faces, aware that Camille was the only one I'd be able to recognize, and then only from her picture. I started gravitating toward the carnival, wishing I knew exactly where they planned to meet.

I looked at my watch. It was a couple of minutes till noon. I kept my mind busy, trying to figure out if Eddie would play it straight, and what kind of arrangements he'd likely made.

The Christmas music was nearly beyond hearing. I moved among the rides for smaller children. I passed flying elephants and bumper cars. I searched for a woman with Camille's dark hair and the pretty, yet sad face I'd seen in pictures.

I came within sight of a small corral and a sign advertising pony rides. There, sitting on a bench, I saw her. Camille Parker was in a trench coat with a chiffon scarf tied over her head. She had on dressy pants and heels, looking more like she belonged on that stage at the Chesapeake Lounge than at a Christmas fair in Morgantown, West Virginia.

Standing next to her was a young man wearing jeans, boots, a down vest and a baseball cap. He looked enough like Sommerville Smith to be his brother, so I assumed he was. They both seemed nervous.

I wanted to get closer without being conspicuous, so I decided to join Camille on the bench. Having no idea who I was, she hardly paid any attention as I sat down.

I positioned my purse beside me so that I could get to the semiautomatic. My heart was beating heavily, my hand trembling slightly. Eddie Dee was no fool. He'd look over the setup carefully before making his move, and he'd notice me. I wasn't as conspicuous as Camille, but I didn't quite blend in, either. Just by being there, I knew I was taking a chance.

I looked around at the crowd, trying to feign a casual, bored expression. Maybe I was waiting for my husband to bring my kid back from the rest room. Whatever I was doing, I didn't know the woman next to me.

The first sign I had of Eddie's arrival was Camille tensing. I glanced up casually and saw a man carrying a baby wrapped in a blanket. He was less than a hundred feet away and moving toward us. Judging by Camille's reaction, he was my man.

There were people between us. Eddie was a large man with wavy black hair, like the rough-hewn Victor Mature I'd seen in old movies. He was staring at Camille, a crooked smile on his face. She stood and mumbled something to Den Smith.

I scanned the nearby faces, knowing there had to be at least one gun in the crowd. I picked him out. He was tall like Eddie, thinner, well built, in a black topcoat. Then, about the time I noticed the single gloved hand, realization struck. It was Joey Angelino.

I turned away, hoping he wouldn't recognize me. At the same time, I slipped my hand into my purse. Camille and Smith started walking toward the hoods. Eddie gestured in the direction of the corral. The four of them met at the fence.

As I watched, Eddie Dee reached out to Camille and, putting his hand behind her neck, pulled her face to his and kissed her. Her entire body was so stiff that it was obvious his affection wasn't welcome. She immediately took the baby, looking at his face under the blanket. It was the closest I'd seen her come to smiling. My heart went out to her, knowing how relieved she must be to have her baby in her arms at last.

Eddie was preoccupied with Camille, but Joey was looking around, his hand resting at the opening to his coat. He hadn't spotted me.

Camille gave Andrew a kiss and immediately shoved the baby into Den Smith's arms. He seemed surprised when she pointed in the direction of the entrance and gave him a shove. As Smith left with the baby, Eddie took Camille's arm. He gave her another brusque kiss. She tried to pull away.

"You got what you wanted, didn't you?" he shouted angrily, the sound of his voice rising over the noise of the crowd.

Watching them, I'd taken my eyes off Joey. When I looked back at him, he was staring straight at me. He shouted something to Eddie, pointing in my direction.

In the split second that followed, Joey pulled his piece from under his coat. Simultaneously I drew my gun. Camille screamed and Eddie shoved her aside.

By the time Joey pointed his gun at me, I was on one knee. I squeezed off a round. The force of the bullet knocked Joey to the ground. Eddie had drawn his gun, too, but apparently he wasn't interested in shooting it out. Amid the screams of people fleeing the gunfire, Eddie bolted, leaving Camille on her knees and Joey on the ground.

I took off after Eddie. We darted and wove through the crowd. There was too much noise for me to shout at him to stop, and I couldn't risk a shot.

I saw two police officers ahead. Eddie did, too, and dashed in another direction. The merry-go-round was dead ahead.

Eddie leaped on it, turning to see if he was being pursued. The cops ran past me, oblivious.

By the time I got to the other side of the merry-go-round, Eddie had knocked down some temporary fencing to make his escape. But in doing so, he'd caught the eye of several other cops in the parking lot. They converged on him. Eddie ducked behind a car and fired twice. The police returned fire. I saw Eddie go down, and I ran to the fence.

He was fifty feet away or so. I stood there, shaking, feeling sick, remembering the hit I'd taken, the one that had nearly ended my life. The police crept to the spot where he lay. One of them bent down to examine Eddie. "Dead," I heard him say. The word stabbed at my heart. Eddie Dee was dead.

I headed back to the pony rides. By the time I got there, a couple of cops had the crowd under control. I recognized the men in suits. Len Barnes was one.

I pushed my way through the crowd, stopping when I saw that Joey Angelino was still on the ground. A cop was supporting his head and Joey was talking. I was relieved I hadn't killed him. I'd never shot anyone before. And I realized I never wanted to again.

Camille was a short distance away, talking to Tom Edleson. She was wiping her eyes and looked pretty shook-up. I couldn't blame her. I was on the verge of tears myself.

I had no desire to be there, so I pushed my way back through the crowd and numbly headed toward the entrance. Halfway there, I spotted Kyle. He saw me just after I saw him. We hurried toward each other. He threw his arms around me and we embraced.

"Thank God," he muttered as he stroked my head. "Thank God."

My eyes filled with tears and I began to cry silently. Kyle kissed my wet cheeks and held me.

"Andrew's all right," he said. "Peg's sister has him."

I turned and looked back. "Let's tell Camille, Kyle. I think she'd like to know."

WE COULDN'T LEAVE Morgantown immediately, but Len Barnes expedited things as much as possible, saying we'd be able to head home by noon the next day. Kyle checked us into a fancier motel and we spent most of the afternoon giving our statements. Tom Edleson told me that Joey Angelino was doing well, but that Barnes was preparing to slap him with so many charges that he would probably wish he'd never get out of the hospital.

After dinner we went back to the motel and I crashed. Kyle was tired, too, but he wanted to meet with Camille, so he took off. I was asleep when he got back around nine, not awakening until he sat down next to me on the bed.

The room was dark except for a faint glow of light coming from the direction of the window. I lifted my head and saw a miniature Christmas tree complete with tiny lights.

"I saw it in a store window and couldn't resist," Kyle explained.

I sat up and gave him a hug. "You're really a sweet man," I told him.

He gave me a lazy smile, his eyes shining. "I wanted to inspire you to help me decorate my house."

We embraced again. I looked over his shoulder at the little tree. Maybe I'd gone soft and gotten all sentimental, but I felt a tremendous warmth, a true sense of sharing and togetherness. I hadn't felt that before with a man. Ever.

"How did it go with Camille?" I asked.

"The kidnapping opened her eyes. She wants to keep Andrew with her while she decides what to do with her life. I told her I was ready to help in any way I could. She was very grateful. Told me that as far as she was concerned, I was Andrew's only family and that one way or another I'd figure prominently in his life."

He brushed back my hair. "I told her what you'd done to track down Eddie Dee. She asked me to thank you. Said she was very appreciative. And I could tell she felt liberated. It could make all the difference in the way she looks at the future."

"I hope everything works out for her," I said. "She's had a rough few weeks, too."

Kyle sighed wearily, but he looked happy despite his fatigue. "Seems to me like we've done our duty by everybody else. Now I think it's time we concentrate on each other."

Those words sounded awfully good to me. I caressed Kyle's face and we kissed.

He pointed toward the tree. "Maybe we can start by having you open an early Christmas present."

"Christmas present?"

"Yeah, go take a look."

I got up from the bed and went over to the table. There was a motel envelope under the tree with my name written on it. I glanced back at him.

"Open it," he said.

I tore open the envelope. Inside were two open airline tickets to Tahiti, one with my name on it, one with his.

"You really meant it," I said.

"Darcy, Tahiti's only the prelude." He walked over and took me by the shoulders. "The way I see it, we're going down there to be together and get away from all the distractions—the cops-and-robbers business. It'll be just sun, water, a few tropical drinks, and you and me." He took my jaw in his hand. "And maybe along the way you can decide if I'm irresistible enough to make Christmas together a permanent arrangement."

"Kyle..."

"You don't even have to decide while we're there, if you don't want to. Hard as it might be for you to believe, I *am* a patient man."

I shook my head in disbelief. "You're incredible."

He smiled and took me in his arms. "All I know is, I love you and I want to be with you always."

My eyes flooded, and I started to cry.

"You know," he said, brushing my tears away with his thumb, "for a cop you can get awfully sentimental, can't you?"

"You noticed?"

"Honey, I notice everything about you."

I laughed and gave him a big hard squeeze. "You actually asked me to marry you, didn't you?"

"I had to before you sent me your bill."

I wiped away the last of my tears. "You're getting the bill anyway, buster."

"You would charge a husband for your services?"

"You aren't my husband yet."

He tweaked my chin. "Would you charge a lover?"

"It depends on how good he was."

He grinned. "Well?"

I contemplated him. "I'll need to think about it." Giving him a wink, I went over to the bed and pulled back the spread. Then I turned and faced him, settling my hands on my hips. "Well," I said, "are you going to stand there all night, thinking of a good comeback, or are you going to get into bed?"

He slowly walked over to me, took my face in his hands and replied, "This is one time, Ms. Hunter, when actions just might speak louder than words."

DESERT
DESTINY

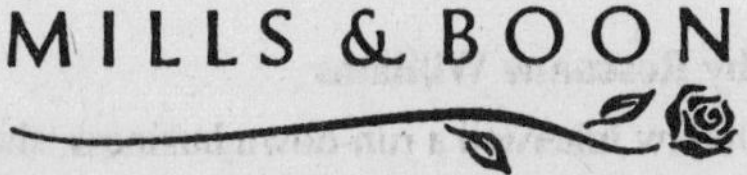

MILLS & BOON

This month's
irresistible novels from

Temptation

NAUGHTY TALK by Tiffany White
Live the fantasy...in Lovers and Legends

Once upon a time a handsome knight errant went searching for the secrets of women's deepest desires—or so the story goes. Nicole Hart wanted revenge on Anthony Gawain. Masquerading as a provocative sex therapist on his TV show presented just the opportunity Nicole needed to teach him a thing or two...

JUST THE WAY YOU ARE by Elise Title

Why had she married uptight Mike Powell? But the minute Lucy had signed the divorce decree she was sorry. Mike had had it with his wife's fiery temper. But now they were parting he remembered just how vivacious and sultry she could be. What lengths would they go to to get back together again?

DECEPTIONS by Janice Kaiser

As a teenager, Darcy Hunter was guiltily infatuated with her older sister's fiancé, Kyle Weston. Following her sister's tragic death, Kyle dropped out of Darcy's life—but not fully out of her heart and fantasies. What would she do now that she was being drawn back into his dangerous circuit?

SEEING RED by Roseanne Williams

When Larinda Outlaw inherited a run-down business, she thought her dreams had come true. Now she could get hold of some cold, hard cash. Instead she got hot, sexy Cash Bowman who stood in the way of her plans to sell.

Spoil yourself next month
with these four novels from

Temptation

THE OTHER WOMAN by Candace Schuler
This is the first in a blockbusting **Hollywood Dynasty** trilogy.

The newspapers were full of gossip about Tara Channing—TV's sexiest seductress and star of the new movie *The Promise*—and her surprising relationship with Gage Kingston whose family was a legend in Hollywood. He had sworn never to fall for another actress, and Tara had had her own share of heartache, too. Would their love survive all the media attention?

YOU GO TO MY HEAD by Bobby Hutchinson

With her company on the verge of bankruptcy, the only person who could save Annabelle Murdoch's dream was Ben Baxter. But, sexy, laid-back Ben wasn't interested in business. He was interested only in awakening her to the pleasure of life and love...

LOVESTORM by JoAnn Ross

Saxon Carstairs was a loner, but his isolation was shattered when gorgeous Madeline washed up half-dead on his beach. Helpless and unable to remember anything beyond her name, Madeline aroused all Sax's instincts—protective, heroic *and* carnal.

THE MISSING HEIR by Leandra Logan

Responsible for locating Douglas Ramsey's missing heir, Caron Carlisle was shocked when the person who said he could solve the mystery turned out to be Rick Wyatt—the man who had broken Caron's heart years before.

A Tempting FREE Offer from Mills & Boon

We'd love you to become a regular reader of Temptations and discover the modern sensuous love stories that have made this such a very popular series. To welcome you we'd like you to have 4 TEMPTATION books, a CUDDLY TEDDY and a MYSTERY GIFT absolutely FREE.

Then, every month you could look forward to receiving 4 brand new Temptations delivered to your door for just £1.95 each, postage and packing FREE. Plus our FREE Newsletter filled with of author news, competitions, special offers and much more.

It's easy. Send no money now.
Simply fill in the coupon below and send it to-
Reader Service, FREEPOST, PO Box 236, Croydon, Surrey CR9 9EL.

Free Books Coupon

Yes! Please rush me 4 FREE Temptations and 2 FREE gifts! Please also reserve me a Reader Service subscription. If I decide to subscribe I can look forward to receiving 4 Temptations for just £7.80 each month, postage and packing FREE. If I decide not to subscribe I shall write to you within 10 days. I can keep the free books and gifts whatever I choose. I may cancel or suspend my subscription at any time. I am over 18 years of age.

Ms/Mrs/Miss/Mr ______________________ EP73 T

Address ______________________

____

Postcode ______________ Signature ______________

Offer closes 31st October 1994. The right is reserved to refuse an application and change the terms of this offer. This offer does not apply to subscribers already receiving Temptations. One application per household. Offer not valid for current subscribers to Mills & Boon Temptations. Offer only valid in the UK and Eire. Overseas readers please write for details. Southern Africa write to IBS Private Bag X3010, Randburg 2125. You may be mailed with offers from other reputable companies as a result of this application. Please tick box if you would prefer not to receive such offers ☐